A Husband for Adva

The backstory of the Samaritan woman at Jacob's well.

Daughter of Samaria Series – Book 1

Jeanette Brewer

Editor: Annah MacKenzie

Cover Design: H-Izz Design and

iStock.com/Selimaksan

Published by Author Academy Elite
PO Box 43, Powell, OH 43065
www.AuthorAcademyElite.com

This is a work of fiction. All of the characters, organizations, and events portrayed in this novel are either products of the author's imagination or are used fictitiously.

Library of Congress Control Number: 2023903112
Paperback ISBN: 979-8-88583-186-4
Hardback ISBN: 979-8-88583-187-1
E-book ISBN: 979-8-88583-188-8

Available in paperback, hardback, and e-book.

Dedications

To the Triune God
Father, Son, and Holy Spirit—for illuminating the story of this unnamed Samaritan woman at Jacob's Well and helping me to write down the details.

To my parents
who followed this book's journey for years. To my mom who passed away before the book was completed and gave me a fresh understanding of grief. To my dad who never lost enthusiasm for it to be finished and published.

To my adult children
Erin and Nathan, and their children who gave up birthday visits so I could write. I believe that the Lord will restore to you the years that the locusts have eaten (Joel 2:25).

Contents

1
The God Who Sees Me

Eleazar filled the trough with water and the manger with grain. Shem, the donkey, swatted flies with his tail as he walked to the other side of his stall to eat his banquet. Pausing briefly to look at the tall, gnarly oak trees at the back of his property, Eleazar closed the barn's back door and latched it closed for the night. In the quietness of the barn, the words of his father's deathbed blessing from ten years past came rushing into his memory: "Eleazar, when Abraham traveled to the land which *Elohim*[1] had promised to him," the voice intoned, "he came first to Shechem and rested at the oak tree. There, Abraham worshipped *Elohim*, the all-powerful and all-knowing Creator.[2] My son, you are a child of Abraham's promise. This is your heritage! Read from the Law of Moses[3] to your family and you will be blessed."

The years had weathered Eleazar, making him appear older than his thirty-seven years. His wife Tirzah had blessed him with four daughters, and she was expecting another child. Eleazar filled his lungs with the aroma of

---

1 *Elohim* is the Hebrew word for God the Creator, mentioned in Genesis 1:1.

2 Genesis 12:6-8. NET.

3 The Law of Moses—also called the Torah, the Pentateuch, and Book of Moses—refers to the first five books of the Bible: Genesis, Exodus, Leviticus, Numbers, and Deuteronomy.

dirt, straw, and manure as he shut the other barn door for the night. "Yes, I am a blessed man," he said aloud, as if his father were there with him.

Eleazar followed the limestone path across the courtyard to the one-room clay house where his wife Tirzah had laid out his banquet for the night. She and his daughters were waiting quietly for him to wash his hands and to join them at the table for their evening meal.

After the blessing Tirzah served Eleazar first, then she and the daughters would have their portion. In the middle of the table was a tall stack of flatbread cakes which the family used to spoon the beans and other vegetables into their mouths. When the meal was finished and the table cleared, Eleazar washed his hands again before gathering the scroll from its place on the shelf behind the door. Tirzah lit an oil lamp and placed it on the lampstand for Eleazar as he read from the Torah to his four daughters.

"Papa, tell us more about Father Abraham," said Tamar, who was eight years old and very inquisitive. Eleazar beckoned Adva, Tamar, Ziva, and Havilah to come to his place at the table. He rolled open the scroll and pulled his *tallith*[4] up and over the heads of the girls like a tent.

"Daughters, remember that this section is about Abram before Elohim changes his name to Abraham."

"And Sarai before Elohim changed her name to Sarah," interrupted Adva, the eldest daughter at ten years of age.

"That is correct, Adva," said Eleazar as he began to read aloud in Hebrew:[5]

---

4 A *tallith* is a prayer shawl to be worn over the head of a Samaritan or Jewish worshiper during scripture reading, worship, or festivals.

5 From this point forward in the text, scripture taken directly from the Bible will be indicated by italics.

Now Sarai, Abram's wife, had not given birth to any children, but she had an Egyptian servant named Hagar. So Sarai said to Abram, "Since the Lord *has prevented me from having children, please sleep with my servant. Perhaps I can have a family by her." Abram did what Sarai told him.*

So after Abram had lived in Canaan for ten years, Sarai, Abram's wife, gave Hagar, her Egyptian servant, to her husband to be his wife. He slept with Hagar, and she became pregnant. Once Hagar realized she was pregnant, she despised Sarai. Then Sarai said to Abram, "You have brought this wrong on me! I gave my servant into your embrace, but when she realized that she was pregnant, she despised me. May the Lord *judge between you and me!"*

Abram said to Sarai, "Since your servant is under your authority, do to her whatever you think best." Then Sarai treated Hagar harshly, so she ran away from Sarai.

The angel of the Lord *found Hagar near a spring of water in the wilderness—the spring that is along the road to Shur. He said, "Hagar, servant of Sarai, where have you come from, and where are you going?" She replied, "I'm running away from my mistress, Sarai.*

Then the angel of the Lord *said to her, "Return to your mistress and submit to her authority. I will greatly multiply your descendants," the angel of the* Lord *added, "so that they will be too numerous*

> *to count." Then the angel of the* LORD *said to her, "You are now pregnant and are about to give birth to a son. You are to name him Ishmael, for the* LORD *has heard your painful groans. He will be a wild donkey of a man."*[6]

The girls giggled and covered their mouths with their hands. "What would a wild donkey-man look like Papa?" Tamar asked.

"It refers to the boy's character more than his looks. Let us see what else the Angel says," Eleazar replied. "*He will be hostile to everyone, and everyone will be hostile to him. He will live away from his brothers.*"[7]

He paused for a moment before continuing, "Well, think of our donkey, Shem."

Tamar and Ziva nodded enthusiastically.

"There are times when Shem refuses to plow or carry. He kicks, brays, and sometimes he sits down. Can you recall a time like this?" asked Eleazar.

"Yes, Papa," replied Adva, peeking around Ziva's head.

"What do we do when our donkey behaves this way?" continued Eleazar.

"We get a stick and whack his bottom," said Ziva, who was seven.

"Does this sound like what the Angel is saying about Ishmael? Let's read it again."

> *He will be a wild donkey of a man. He will be hostile to everyone, and everyone will be hostile to him. He will live away from his brothers. So Hagar named the* LORD *who spoke to her, "You are the God who sees me," for she said, "Here I have seen*

---

6 Genesis 16:1-12. NET.

7 Genesis 16:12. NET.

> *one who sees me!" That is why the well was called* Beer Lahai Roi. *(It is located between Kadesh and Bered). So Hagar gave birth to Abram's son, whom Abram named Ishmael. (Now Abram was 86 years old when Hagar gave birth to Ishmael.)*[8]

With those words, Eleazar rolled up the scroll. "Goodnight my little princesses. May the Lord's angels watch over you as you sleep."

"Papa, why was Hagar told to go back to someone who mistreated her?" asked Adva.

"Adva, we will look at that more closely tomorrow during your reading lesson."

"Yes, Papa."

The girls obediently scurried, kissing their father's cheek and hugging their mother with her rounded belly. "Goodnight, Baby!" said Havilah, who was the youngest and had just turned four.

"Goodnight, Mother," Adva said, as she grabbed Havilah's hand and led her off to bed. Adva noticed that Mother looked more tired tonight. "I will put everyone to bed," she said. Tirzah smiled in thanks. Adva pulled their mats from the corner of the room and unrolled their beds. The girls snuggled in for the night with the youngest in the middle of the nest.

Morning came quickly. Adva began her chores and urged Tamar, Ziva, and Havilah to get dressed. When she finished, she presented the girls dressed and ready for the day. Mother sighed. Tirzah would give birth to number five soon, and she found comfort in knowing that Adva could run for the midwife when it was time and manage the household while Tirzah nursed the baby.

---

[8] Genesis 16:12-15. NET.

With all her chores completed, Adva asked, "Mother, may I go find Father for my reading lesson?"

"Yes, Adva. He is in the barn."

Adva ran across the courtyard. Inside the barn, the air was heavy with the earthy smell of the new barley that had been harvested a few days past. Today, as it threatened to rain, the scent of barley tickled her nose. "Papa, I am ready for my lessons," she declared eagerly.

In the middle of the barn's breezeway, Eleazar sat at the grinding stone where he was sharpening the tools used to harvest the barley. As he pumped the pedal with his foot to control the wheel's speed, he dropped olive oil on the stone to give the lubrication needed. Adva watched his skill intently.

Adva, the first-born, had learned to read and write under her father's tutelage, much like any boy her age. Few girls learned to read or had any formal education in Samaria. However, Eleazar had decided that God gave him a first-born girl for a reason. If the next child was a boy, his son would take the place of Adva in the studies when he came of age. Eleazar admired Adva's hunger for learning. The questions she asked were both thoughtful and vexing. While most parents would not have tolerated her persistent questioning, he tried to nurture her curiosity but prayed it would not cause strife with her future spouse. Many of his kinsmen warned him of his folly, but Adva satisfied his yearning to share knowledge with a child he did not yet have. Perhaps number five will be a boy.

"Grab a stool and come close, Adva," directed Eleazar. Adva got the three-legged milking stool from the corner by the door and brought it close to Eleazar. "Adva, do you remember how angry you got at your knife last week when we were harvesting the barley?"

"Yes, Papa. I was angry because it would not cut," she replied.

"Was this the one you were using?" Adva looked closely. She felt the handle in her grip.

"It seems like the one I used. Oh yes, here is the spot on the handle that kept giving me splinters."

"Let me see." Eleazar ran his fingers over the rough wood. He found the spot just as a splinter pierced his skin. "Yes, I see what you mean," he said, picking the splinter from his thumb. "I will fix this for you. But first, let me sharpen the blade. I need you to promise that you will be careful. When this is sharp you will be in danger if you snag your finger or leg. That is why I have kept it dull while you were learning to use it. Do you understand?" asked Eleazar.

"Yes, Papa," she said as she stared into his warm, brown eyes.

Eleazar shuddered from the trust in her gaze. He put some oil on the grinding stone and began pumping the pedal again. But after a moment, he abruptly stopped. "Adva," he said, "touch the stone and tell me what you feel."

"The stone is hard and rough, but the oil makes it feel smooth. My fingers glide over the stone," she replied.

Once her hand had moved away, Eleazar resumed by placing the knife so that it just barely touched the spinning stone, moving the blade from one end to the other in a smooth motion. He took his foot from the pedal and waited again for the stone to stop spinning. "Hand me that cloth by the door," directed Eleazar. He put some drops of oil on the blade then wiped it with the cloth Adva had given him. The blade looked smooth and shiny in the part that had touched the stone. Eleazar handed the cloth back to her. "Here Adva," he said, "now pull the cloth tight between your two hands."

She did as her father asked, and with one quick motion he sliced through the cloth. Adva, now holding two pieces, marveled at the swift cut of the cloth and the new sharpness of her blade. "I will be careful with that blade or I may only be able to count to three," she laughed.

Eleazar chuckled at Adva's quick understanding. "After we hang these tools on the wall, we can go inside and re-read the story of Hagar."

Upon entering the house, Eleazar and Adva washed their hands using a pitcher and basin. Tirzah and the other girls were spinning and carding wool in the opposite corner of the room. Tirzah had a few skeins of yarn already and the girls would help with a few more before the day was over. There would be yarn for weaving this winter. Mother told the girls to be quiet and listen while Adva had her lesson.

Eleazar picked up the *tallith*, placed it over his head, and opened his arms wide for Adva to come close. He enveloped her under his canopy and unrolled the scroll, laying it gently on the table. Adva read aloud the same verses that had been read the night before.

"*Sarai, Abram's wife, gave Hagar, her . . .*"[9]

"Papa, what is this word?" Adva asked.

"Egyptian. It means that Hagar was born in Egypt," Eleazar replied.

Adva began to read again from the beginning.

"*Sarai, Abram's wife, gave Hagar, her Egyptian servant, to her husband to be his wife. He slept with Hagar, and she became pregnant. Once Hagar realized she was pregnant, she despised Sarai.*"[10]

"Adva, stop. What did you read?" Eleazar asked.

"I read that Abram's wife, Sarai, gave him her maid to have a baby."

---

9 Genesis 16:3. NET.

10 Genesis 16:3-4. NET.

"That's right. What else?"

"Hagar conceived."

"What does that mean?"

"She was going to have a baby, just like Mother."

"Yes, that's right," Eleazar said as he looked over at Tirzah and smiled, "What else?"

"Hagar was happy that she could have a baby and Sarai could not. She despised her mistress."

"Yes, that sounds like pride. Do you act respectfully when you are proud?" asked Eleazar. Adva shook her head. "Do you think she made fun of Sarai? Do you think that Sarai treated her well when Hagar made fun of her?"

"No. But at least she did not get leprosy like Miriam,"[11] replied Adva.

Eleazar chuckled, "Yes, she did not get leprosy. But what did her pride cause her to do?"

"She ran away."

"Yes. Read here what the angel says to her," directed Eleazar.

"The angel of the LORD found Hagar near a spring of water in the wilderness—the spring that is along the road to Shur. He said, 'Hagar, servant of Sarai, where have you come from, and where are you going?' She replied, 'I'm running away from my mistress, Sarai.' Then the angel of the LORD said to her, 'Return to your mistress and submit to her authority.'"[12]

"What did the Angel say to her?"

"Return to Sarai and submit to her authority."

"Who had to change her attitude?"

"Hagar." Adva paused to think before she asked, ". . . even when Sarai mistreated her?"

"Why did Sarai mistreat her?" asked her father.

---

[11] Numbers 12:1-15. NET.

[12] Genesis 16:7-9. NET.

"Because Hagar criticized her."

"Is that respectful?" asked Eleazar.

"No," answered Adva.

"Who has authority over you?" Eleazar asked, directing her to acknowledge the hierarchy of authority in their family.

"You and mother."

"Yes. Who has authority over your mother?"

"You."

"Who has authority over me?"

"*Adonai*."[13]

"Yes. That is correct. Do you think it is difficult to submit to authority?" Eleazar asked, continuing to direct the conversation using questions.

"Yes," Adva said, thinking about yet another question. "Why did Hagar think she was better than Sarai?"

Eleazar smiled at her curiosity. "Children are of great value to families. They carry on the family's wealth, name, and traditions. I could not run this farm without your help. Mother is going to need your help when the next child is born in a few weeks, and you will be your mother's greatest helper. Hagar thought that she had more value to Abraham because she was going to have his child. But Sarai was his first love and that had not changed."

"But Sarai did not like Hagar after she was going to have Abram's baby."

"Sarai also wondered if Abram would continue to love her even though she was not able to give him a child. She heard Hagar's words and it disturbed her. Sarai feared that she was not as valuable to Abram as Hagar. But God made a covenant with Abram and Sarai, and she was going to have her own child. We will read about that soon."

---

13 *Adonai* is the Hebrew word for Lord and Master, mentioned first in Genesis 15:2.

Eleazar began to roll up the scroll and placed it in its cloth bag. He returned the bag to its place of honor on the shelf and removed the *tallith.*

"Papa, was there a time when you had to submit to authority like that?"

"Yes," he replied. "The High Priest selects men for special tasks in the synagogue. Although I was prepared for the duty, I was not selected. Even though I thought I was a better choice, I had to submit to the man that was chosen. It was very difficult, but your mother helped me see the value of submitting to his authority. She is a wise woman."

"You love Mother, don't you, Papa?" asked Adva with admiration.

"I love her dearly," said Eleazar, glancing tenderly in Tirzah's direction as she continued to work with the other daughters. "Adva, do you remember when we were sharpening the knife this morning?" Adva nodded. "Your knife was dull and not very useful to you by the end of the harvest," he recalled.

"Yes, I could not cut anything by the end of the day," replied Adva.

"The grinding stone is hard and it spins fast. Adding the oil to the stone helps the blade to glide across it. The blade gently touches the spinning stone, causing some of the metal to fall away and leaving a smooth and shiny point. It is sharp and useful now. But it is also dangerous. Submitting to authority is like the grinding stone. It sharpens us and makes us useful. We may not like touching the grinding stone, being sharpened. But if *Adonai* is holding us in His hands, we will not be burdened with more than we can endure. But some earthly authorities can be dangerous, and we must be able to discern whom to submit to by prayer. Our prayer is like the oil, and it will keep us close to *Adonai* and He will protect us."

Eleazar paused to swat at a fly that was buzzing around their heads. When the fly persisted, Eleazar sighed and continued to test Adva's understanding. "Adva, what else do we know about Hagar?"

"She was an Egyptian servant."

"Yes," Eleazar continued. "You remember that our forefathers came from Egypt too. Joseph married an Egyptian woman and fathered Ephraim and Manasseh. We descend from the tribe of Ephraim. Jacob adopted both boys into the family of Israel with a blessing. This line has had many kings and princesses, like yourself."

Adva stood and bowed low to the ground to her father, the King. Eleazar laughed and bowed back. "Do you know that Egyptians worship other gods instead of *Elohim*?" asked Eleazar.

Her brow furrowed in bewilderment. "There are other gods?" Adva asked.

"In our Samaritan tradition, there is only one God and that is *Elohim*. But other people in other places worship false gods. In Egypt, the people worship many gods. The god of the sun and seasons is called Ra. The god of the moon and sky is Horus. They are both depicted with the symbol of an eye, and it is said that they watch over Egypt. It was important to Hagar to know that Abram's God, *Elohim*, was the God who watched over her. Knowing this made it easier to submit to Sarai."

"Papa, what was the name Hagar gave to *Elohim*?" wondered Adva.

"In our ancient Hebrew, the words are *Il Raa'ee*[14]—the God Who Sees Me."

"I believe that *Elohim* sees me," Adva said boldly.

---

14 *Il Raa'ee* is the ancient Hebrew word meaning "The God Who Sees Me," as mentioned in Genesis 16:13.

"He does, Adva," Eleazar said just as he noticed a light coming in through the door. "Now then, it is getting late and you need to fetch water for your mother."

"Papa, may I take Shem with me? I will be able to carry more water as Mother wants to wash today." Adva grabbed her scarf from the doorpost and tied it swiftly about her head.

"Yes, you go and come right back. No time to stay and talk with the women of Sychar. I need Shem this afternoon."

"Papa, I like going to the well later in the day because there are not so many women talking. I can sing and talk with *Elohim*. Today, I will call Him *Il Raa'ee* as I talk to Him." Adva shut the door of the house and ran to the barn to find Shem restless in the far corner of his stall. He stomped his forefoot and brayed at her presence.

"I am sorry I startled you, Shem. You and I get to go to Jacob's well. We will drink from the same waters as Rebekah and Jacob. I will sing to you and you will gladly carry the water that Mother needs." Shem brayed loudly as if in protest. Adva laughed. "Poor Shem. I don't know if you are protesting the water or my singing."

"I love your singing," bellowed a husky male voice from the shadows of the barn.

Adva shrieked and turned in the direction of the voice, clasping her hands to her chest as she recognized the man. "Oh, Master Malachi! I did not see you. I will tell Papa you are here," Adva said as she turned to run back to the house, but his large frame now blocked her path.

Malachi reached for Adva's arm and held it tightly, drawing her close to his side. "I came to see you, dear Adva, and of course, your father. You get more beautiful every day." He pulled the scarf from her head and grabbed a handful of hair in his other hand, inhaling deeply. "You smell like myrrh and sage," he uttered. "I came to ask your father's permission to marry you."

"But I am only ten years old. My father will not permit my marriage until I am older," Adva choked.

Master Malachi was dirty, his tunic threadbare in many places, and he smelled of sheep. As a shepherd, he would wander for months in the pastures of Mt. Ebal and Eleazar would often invite him to stay with the family when it was time to shear his sheep. Just as Malachi's herd began to bleat from the pen at the back of the barn, the figure of Eleazar cast a long shadow across the barn's floor, which caused Malachi to loosen his hold on Adva.

"Malachi, I would appreciate it if you would not hinder Adva further, she is getting a late start today," Eleazar asserted. "Adva, be on your way."

Adva took her scarf from Malachi's hand and quickly retied it around her head. Her hands shook as she gathered the harness for Shem and the saddle for the water pots from the back wall. Adva was using the special saddle that she had made for Shem to carry multiple water pots. She was struggling to get the buckles to latch. Eleazar, seeing her struggle, came over to give her a hand.

"*Il Raa'ee*," Eleazar whispered in her ear, "*Il Raa'ee*." Her father's voice helped Adva to stop shaking. Eleazar turned to his guest, assessed him from head to toe, and then embraced his old friend. "Malachi, what brings you to town? Is it time to shear those sheep?"

"Yes, Eleazar, it is time," replied Malachi jovially. The two men walked out the back of the barn towards the sheep.

Tirzah stood in the doorway of the house as Adva passed with Shem. "Hurry back, Adva. The day is passing us quickly."

"Yes, Mother," responded Adva. Shem brayed in protest. "Oh please, do not be like Ishmael today, Shem. Be a good donkey for me."

When Adva returned, Tirzah met her and took a jar without saying hello. Adva entered with another jar and placed it on the table. As she turned towards the doorway to fetch the last two, there stood Malachi with the remaining jars in his hands.

"Where would you like these, Mother Tirzah?" asked Malachi.

"Outside by the doorway will be fine, thank you. Adva, please wipe down Shem and take him to Papa. He is waiting for you at the woodshed."

"Yes, Mother," Adva said as she bowed in respect to Master Malachi while skirting any closeness to him.

"Mother Tirzah," asked Malachi, "when you are finished with your wash water would you please save it for me? I will carry it to the barn so that I might bathe before dinner." He placed the water pots by the doorway, turned, and walked toward Adva and the barn.

Instead of entering the dark barn, Adva chose to remain in the sunlit courtyard. She removed Shem's water saddle and set it on the bench to the left of the barn door. She gave Shem a carrot and wiped him down with a cloth.

The other girls saw Adva and came running, but when they noticed Master Malachi they slowed to a walk. When Adva finished, she grabbed Shem's harness and led him, Malachi, and the girls to the woodshed. Nothing was said in the short trip to the woodshed. As Havilah inspected Master Malachi, Ziva nudged her with her elbow, silently imploring her not stare at their guest.

Eleazar was half inside and half outside the woodshed. "Malachi, would you give me a hand with this door? I believe the hinge broke. Thank you, Adva. Now you and the girls go help your mother with the washing."

"Malachi, did you get your knives sharpened for the shearing?" Eleazar asked, wiping sweat from his brow.

"Yes, Master Eleazar. Your grinding stone is a wonder. I cut my finger on the first test, but after that I used something else to test the blades. You are a blessed man," he said as he watched the girls return to the house.

"*Adonai* has been good to me," stated Eleazar proudly. "Can you put that nail in the hinge when I lift the door?" The two men toiled and groaned for a short time but finally got the door to swing and close properly.

Eleazar showed Malachi the new crib that he had made for Tirzah and the new baby. The crib was made from cedar and had a beautiful rose brown color. Eleazar had oiled it until it shined and the wood was smooth.

"You have done an excellent job on this. It is lovely; such workmanship." Malachi paused before his next question, "Does Tirzah still use wool and flax to weave cloth?"

"Yes, she uses both. But we will not be growing flax this year. Hopefully, we will get a new crop next year. We could use some of your wool. Do you need a new blanket?" asked Eleazar.

"I would love a new blanket."

"I do not know if Tirzah has one set aside. I know that she is not able to weave right now. It will not be long before the baby arrives."

"I'm sorry that I have come at an inconvenient time. I will shear the sheep and leave again soon. I am grateful to you and your family. With my family so far away, yours is like my home. You have been very gracious to me," Malachi stated as he hung his head and shuffled his feet back and forth like a young boy. "I behaved very badly when I arrived and I am ashamed. Will you forgive me, my friend? Adva is so beautiful. She will make any man a good wife. I came to persuade you to allow her to be my wife."

Eleazar scratched his head and tugged at his beard. "Yes, she will be a good wife when it is time. But I believe she is too young yet to be betrothed. Besides, she is a great helper to me and her mother and we cannot do without her while the others are so young."

"I will try to be patient," Malachi said, "but I wish to make my intentions known. I want to join our families and I have found no other woman that stirs my soul as Adva does."

After a time of work in the fields with Shem, the two men walked back toward the barn as Tirzah was wringing the last tunic from her tub in the yard. "Malachi, you may have this wash water and the last stall on the right in the barn. The girls laid some fresh straw in the stall, which you can use as your bed during your stay. You will also find there the gift of a fresh blanket. Blessings to you," said Tirzah as she stretched her back and breathed in the hot air of the late afternoon. She hung the garment over the fencing and waddled away to the house.

Eleazar and Malachi carried the wooden washtub by its two leather handles out to the barn. By the time they got to the stall, their clothes were wet from the sloshing water. The girls had placed two towels on the stall rails for the men to use to wash. And just as Tirzah promised, there was a fresh pile of straw for a bed with a new blanket folded and resting on the three-legged stool. There was a bar of soap on the blanket, a clay jar of scented olive oil, and a carved wooden comb for grooming his hair and beard.

With a sense of pride, Eleazar stated, "Tirzah has taught the girls to show hospitality for our guests. Adva helped make the soap last year, and she worked hard to find just the right mix of ingredients. The soap is scented with sage and mint. I do not think the women want us to smell like sweat and sheep."

Eleazar laughed as he dipped his towel into the wash water and then entered Shem's stall. Shem stomped his hind foot and brayed at the intrusion, then shook off a few flies. Eleazar pulled off his tunic and wiped the sweat from his face and chest.

"Oh my," cried Malachi from the other stall. "Your lovely wife has given me a new linen tunic. I am so blessed by your hospitality. I will repay you with the best wool from my sheep."

Eleazar called back to Malachi from across the barn, "You are a blessing to us too. I have no sons, and you always come at a time when I need another male to get a job completed. Bless you and please come to eat as soon as you are finished here." He pulled the sweat-soaked tunic back over his head and walked to the house. Hearing the girls' squeals and giggles, he sighed contentedly and opened the door.

"Papa!" cried the three girls, running toward him.

Eleazar held up his hand to stop them, "Do not hug me yet, I must change my clothes." The girls giggled and turned back to setting the table. Adva stirred the soup as her mother sat on a stool fanning herself. Eleazar looked at her with concern and she waved him off with a flick of her wrist.

When Eleazar returned to sit at the table, he smelled of sage and mint. His beard was oiled and combed, and his hair was soft to the touch. With open arms, he beamed, "Now I am ready for family hugs."

The girls squealed and ran to their father's arms in delight. He hugged and kissed them all. The oil from his beard left their faces shiny. "Come, Mother. Join us," begged Ziva.

Tirzah rose from her stool with effort. She lost her footing a bit and stumbled. Eleazar rose quickly to grab her before she fell. With a smile, he held her close and planted a kiss on her forehead. "My poor blessed wife. The child you bear is making you sway. It will not be long before he arrives."

Adva ladled the soup into seven wooden bowls. The bread was in the center of the long table along with a bowl of seasoned olive oil and a large bowl of fresh blackberries. Wine or goat's milk was poured for each setting.

"Blackberries!" Eleazar cried with delight. "We should have guests more often."

"Adva has been hard at work today. She will sleep well tonight," said Tirzah.

"She is not the only one who will sleep well tonight," Eleazar said, rubbing his calloused hands.

At that moment, the door swung open and Malachi stood in the doorway. With the sun glowing low in the sky behind him, he appeared like a large dark shadow and the girls gasped. As he stepped through and shut the door, he wore the new tunic that Tirzah had made. It was handsome, with fine embroidery around the neckline and down the chest. The garment had been made for Eleazar, but Tirzah offered it to Malachi when she saw that his own tunic was thin and tattered, barely covering his body. If he was to be around Tirzah's daughters, he needed better clothing.

To avoid delaying their meal, Malachi had rushed his grooming. His black curly hair was still dripping with oil. Every time a drop ran down his face, he would quickly wipe it away, hoping that no one had noticed. He had tried to comb his beard but the comb only went so far until what was left was an unruly tangle. The beard must either be cut or combed more later. The tangle bobbed in front of his chin whenever he talked or chewed, and each time Malachi would quickly grab it with his fist and become quiet. Adva felt sorry for him and wanted to ease his distress but dared not suggest that he let her untangle it. Malachi was a large muscular man, with hands larger than Eleazar's. His thick fingers did not make it easy for him to pick up small things, and he seemed clumsy with the meal.

"It has been a while since I've eaten with a family," Malachi stated as a blackberry fell from his fingers and rolled across the table. "I'm a bit out of practice."

Eleazar poured more wine into Malachi's cup. "Drink, my friend, we are blessed with your presence at our table. You look very fine in your new tunic. Tirzah, your work is beautiful."

"I believe this tunic was meant for you, Eleazar," said Malachi, fingering the embroidery work.

"Yes, that seems to be true. But your need was greater than mine today," confessed Eleazar graciously. "I think your old tunic would have disappeared entirely with the next washing."

Tirzah smiled knowing that Eleazar understood why she had given the tunic to their guest. She had wrestled with the thought of giving away the tunic for most of the day. She would begin to work on another one as soon as the cloth was woven. Perhaps Adva could help.

2
Birth of a Son

Sometime well before dawn, Eleazar woke Adva from a sound sleep. "Adva, wake up. I need you to go for the midwife. Your mother is in labor. Get dressed quickly, Malachi has offered to escort you. You must hurry, your mother travails more with this child than any other."

Adva heard panting from the other side of the curtain. She pulled a tunic over her head, put on her scarf, and met Malachi at the door. He held a lantern and had harnessed Shem for her to ride.

"No, Shem will slow us down more than help us," Adva said. "Put him back in his stall and I will meet you here in a moment. She went off in the dark toward the woodshed. She broke off a twig from a small bush, bit into it, and it tasted right to her.

Holding the lantern, Malachi looked about for Adva as she returned from the woodshed. "You must have the eyes of an owl," he said.

Adva entered the house and gave the twig to her father, explaining that he should boil it in water and give it to Mother as a tea to ease her pain. Eleazar did not question his daughter, who seemed to remember everything when it was needed.

The sun was just coming up as Malachi, Adva, and the midwife returned. The midwife rushed into the house and found Eleazar with Tirzah. "The child wants to come feet first and seems to be in a hurry to come. Get some fresh water and clean cloths!" barked the midwife.

"Adva will have to go to the well for more water. All we have is this jar and our rainwater," replied Eleazar, signaling to Adva.

"Get a fire going outside," the midwife said to Malachi. "I must try to turn the baby."

"Yes, I will build a fire in the courtyard."

The other girls were up and in the way. "Tamar, get your sisters dressed and give them some milk from the goat. And stay in the barn away from the house until I tell you otherwise," spoke Eleazar in a stern voice.

Adva harnessed Shem for another trip to the well. She hoped that he would move quickly and she prayed as she walked. But today she did not know what to pray for. She just knew she must hurry, and she grabbed a carrot to use if Shem became difficult.

"*Il Raa'ee*, watch over Mother and the new baby."

When Adva returned, Eleazar was pacing in the yard and tugging at his beard. He helped to remove the water jugs and took one inside. Adva was about to follow with another jug.

"Leave the jug there. Do not come inside until I tell you to come." Eleazar shut the door.

Malachi kept water boiling on the fire outside. At the sixth hour, as the sun was straight up in the sky, he told Adva to go to the well for more water. Tamar and Adva had been rinsing bloody cloths all morning. The girls were tired and hungry. Adva gave each of the girls an apple before tossing the last one to Malachi with a faint smile. She forgot to get an apple for herself. She did not think about that as she quickly harnessed Shem and returned to the well.

The walk was hot and dusty, but Adva was glad she had something else to do. With every bucket of bloody cloths that came through the door, she feared her mother's life was ebbing away. On this journey, Adva did not sing. Instead, she repeated to herself the silent prayer that only her spirit could voice: *Il Raa'ee, please take care of Mother and the new baby.*

When she arrived at the well, there was only one woman and she asked about Tirzah. Adva relayed that her mother was in labor and that she was not progressing well. She also told her that the midwife, Zipporah, had been there since daybreak. The woman offered to send help from town, and Adva thanked her as she dropped her bucket into the water. After she had given Shem water at the trough, Adva loaded him with the water jars. As she walked, a cart of people from Sychar came upon her. They gathered her water and headed to her home to help with what they could. Adva had to walk the rest of the way with Shem because he could not keep up with the cart. With the water secured and the cart quickly rolling toward her home, Adva stopped to rest under a tree and share a carrot with Shem. With this, he brayed happily.

Adva was tired and thirsty. She had not eaten today nor did she drink any of the water at the well. Her carrot tasted bitter and she gave the rest to Shem. As she rose from her spot under the tree, her legs felt heavy and she could barely move. She knew she needed water to make it back home. She could not decide whether to go back to the well or continue the rest of the way. She decided that home was closer.

When the townspeople arrived at the home of Eleazar and Tirzah, Malachi asked one of the women to watch the little ones. He was going to go after Adva. He took a skin of water with him because the air was now extremely hot.

When Malachi saw her, Adva was staggering from side to side. There were no trees under which to rest. When Malachi reached her, he gave her some water. She drank it too quickly, then vomited. Malachi knew of heat stroke and could tell by Adva's reddened face and dry skin that she was in trouble. He removed her scarf and soaked it in water. He then washed her face and tied the wet scarf back on her head. He had her drink again, and this time it stayed down.

"Adva, are you able to hold on and ride Shem?" Malachi asked.

"I think so," she answered weakly.

Malachi hoisted Adva easily onto Shem's back.

"My word, I have sheep that weigh more than you do. You grab his mane, and I will hold the harness. Did you give Shem water at the well?"

"Yes, of course," Adva replied brusquely.

"Well, did you drink some yourself?" Malachi asked with the same edge to his voice.

"No, I was in too much of a hurry to return," Adva confessed. "I am glad the townsfolk came by to get the water for Mother. Is she okay?"

"No one has said. We will be back home soon. Can you drink more water?" he asked.

"Yes, please."

Adva drank a few gulps. She returned the skin to Malachi who also drank some more and wiped the sweat from his brow. The three walked toward home as fast as Shem could go. As they came into the yard, someone came for the cloths that had been washed and set to dry in the sun. Malachi lifted Adva down from the donkey and made sure that she could stand on her own. She wobbled a bit but stepped away from Shem as Malachi led him to the barn.

"Tamar, get Adva a cup of goat's milk from the bucket in the barn," Malachi commanded. Adva sat on the bench in the shade of the barn.

"What's wrong with you?" asked Tamar, as she gave Adva the milk.

"I have heat, I believe. I did not drink enough water today. How is Mother?" Adva asked as she drank all the milk from the cup.

"No one is saying anything. Everyone is sad and quiet. I do not think things are going well," said Ziva, joining the conversation.

At that moment, the midwife came out the door and yelled for Adva. "I am here," Adva replied.

"Do you know where the yarrow plants are in your field?" asked Zipporah.

"Yes, I know where they are. Do you need the leaves, flowers, or the root?" Adva asked as adrenaline filled her veins.

"I need the leaves at the base of the plant. You must take three leaves from three different plants and then make your mother a tea to stop the bleeding," Zipporah instructed before turning to go back inside the house.

"I will get it right away. Yarrow grows close to the woodshed. Master Malachi, can you come with me and get more wood from the shed while I get the yarrow," requested Adva feebly. She did not think it wise to go by herself.

Adva and her mother had a small garden of flowers and herbs that they used to treat various maladies that would befall the household. Her mother had taught Adva what to grow and which parts of the plant were useful. There were also many dried plants in their home, some of which she used for her soap recipes. Havilah was beginning to love the garden too. Adva quickly picked the yarrow leaves.

Master Malachi loaded up his arms with wood from the shed and walked with Adva back towards the house. Adva put another pot on the coals and added the leaves to the water as it started to boil. She took the small pot of steaming tea to the house and knocked on the door. A woman she did not know answered the door, took her pot, and closed the door again.

"Adva, is there another pot we can use to cook dinner for the crowd?" Malachi asked. He was trying to find ways to be helpful. He, too, felt powerless with all that was happening inside the house.

"Yes, in the barn. There is a big copper pot I use for making soap," replied Adva.

"That should work. I will butcher a lamb and you and your sisters can get vegetables from the root cellar."

Suddenly, the front door flung open. Eleazar emerged from the house and began weeping. He passed Adva and her sisters without acknowledging them as he walked through the barn and into the field looking toward Mt. Gerizim.

"Adva, do not panic," said Malachi as he watched her grow pale. "Continue to pray as you prepare this meal. I will tend to your father."

"Yes, Master Malachi," Adva replied in obedience, but tears streamed down her face. "*Il Raa'ee*, watch over Father, Mother, and the baby," she said aloud.

Eleazar began to wail with grief upon reaching the field. When he could go no further, he knelt in the dirt under a large oak tree, grabbing fistfuls of dirt and hurling it at his blood-covered chest. He prostrated himself before the Lord and cried out in sorrow. When Malachi caught up to him, he knelt beside his friend, still not knowing who had died. Feeling Malachi's hand on his shoulder, Eleazar sat up.

"*Elohim* has taken my son from me. I have waited so long for a son. He is gone. My hope for an heir to continue the line of Joachim . . . my first-born son has died," cried Eleazar, rocking on his knees.

"As you live and breathe, there is still hope for a son to be born," comforted Malachi.

"The midwife has declared that Tirzah will never bear another child. Although Tirzah lives now, she has lost a lot of blood and needs time to heal. Oh, what am I to do? *Elohim*! Have mercy on me!" Eleazar lamented, pounding his fist against his chest. After a few moments, Eleazar abruptly paused and looked skyward, as though he was beginning to question the divine order of things. "I am a cursed man," he went on. "Have I been wrong to treat Adva as a first-born son? Perhaps *Adonai* cannot give me what I perceive I already have. Oh, woe is me."

"What do you mean you treat Adva as a son?" asked Malachi.

"I have taught Adva to read. She reads well. She can write. She knows and memorizes the Torah. She possesses great wisdom, and I have taught her as I would have instructed a first-born son. I once believed there was a divine reason *Adonai* had granted her this thirst for learning and that he had bestowed her upon me as a blessing. Now I am not certain. Perhaps it is her unlawful position that has cost me my son. *Adonai* is punishing me for teaching her," wept Eleazar. "My son did not even breathe his first breath. He looked like a field burnt by the sun. I am a cursed man."

"Eleazar, you are not cursed. You have been blessed with a beautiful and faithful wife. She has given you beautiful daughters. Adva is a blessing to your family. She knew which herbs to give Tirzah to assist with the birth and she is always quick to help. Her knowledge has served you well this day."

"But it did not save my son. What good is it?" spat Eleazar.

Malachi grabbed Eleazar's shoulders and spoke harshly, "But it may save your wife!"

There was a silence between the two men. Malachi released Eleazar from his grip and Eleazar arose from the ground and began to pace the field. Malachi searched for words of comfort and finally spoke quietly as if in prayer: "*Elohim is a merciful God, he will not let you down or destroy you, for he cannot forget the covenant with your ancestors that he confirmed by oath to them.*[15] These are the only words of Moses that I remember from childhood. I repeat them to myself when I am in need of comfort. I said these words at my mother's burial."

The words Malachi spoke helped to slow Eleazar's pacing and soften his sobbing. After another pause, Malachi stated matter-of-factly, "We should return to the house. We must bury your child before the sun sets." Gently, he placed his hand on Eleazar's shoulder. "You must be strong for those who remain with the living." Eleazar cried a moment longer then cleared his throat and walked silently with Malachi back to the barn.

Baby Aaron ben Eleazar was buried in the cave at the feet of Eleazar's father, Joachim. The infant was wrapped in a small blanket that Tirzah had made for her newborn son, which would now cradle him for eternity.

At Eleazar's request, Malachi sold the cedar crib in the marketplace for a nice sum, which paid for the beef, vegetables, and herbs that Tirzah needed to heal and regain her strength. Tirzah was deemed unclean for forty-one days after the birth of a son and had to remain separated from the family.[16] During this time, she rested in the curtained bed-

---

15 Deuteronomy 4:30-31. NET.

16 According to the Samaritan religion, after giving birth to a son, the mother was required to separate from others and avoid all touch for forty-one

room where she had labored. Although they were forbidden from touching her, her family could sit with her if they brought their own stool, and the girls made sure that she had food and water. But for the most part Tirzah grieved alone during her time away. Eleazar made his bed on the roof at night, heartbroken that he could neither physically comfort his wife nor be comforted by her.

Master Malachi had stayed with the family during the forty-one days of Tirzah's rest. He helped to plow under the field of barley stubble and reseed the field with flax. He also used this time to slaughter, salt, and smoke two sheep, and he was able to tan the skins and make leather. Adva sewed the leather together to make two skins: one to carry water and one to carry wine. The sheep had been sheared and the wool was sold, and today Malachi was leaving for the pastures of Mt. Ebal.

As Tirzah and the girls were packing provisions of smoked mutton, goat cheese, apples, and yams, the yard was full of noise. The sheep were bleating anxiously.

Malachi had recently purchased a goat in Sebaste to carry his supplies. The goat, which he named Jaspar, had followed Havilah around all week. Havilah loved the goat and was having a hard time parting with him. "Master Malachi, please take good care of Jaspar. He is the best goat alive," Havilah said, giving the goat one last hug. Jaspar bleated loudly.

"Havilah, will you put these in his saddlebags? Let me remind you that he has a job to do," said Malachi. He took the pouch of food that Tirzah offered him and hung it around his neck. "Thank you for your kindness and hospitality,

---

days (forty days for the mother and one day for the son). After the birth of a daughter, the requirements were eighty days (forty days for each female). Specific cleaning procedures were required for the mother and everything that she touched.

Tirzah." He bowed and kissed her hand. Then, turning to Adva, he cupped her face gently, "Goodbye, Adva. I will see you next spring when it is shearing time again."

Eleazar, Malachi, and his flock walked to the far edge of the flax field which was now standing a foot tall. "This will be a good crop. Next month, the stalks will be drying in the sun on the roof of the house. Thank you, my friend," said Eleazar.

The two men embraced and Eleazar wept again for his losses; he was truly sorry to see Malachi go. But Malachi was beginning to get restless and knew it was time. His herd now had thirty adults and eighteen new lambs. He had to slow his pace a bit to allow the little ones to keep up with him. He was already missing his place in the barn. He had left three sheep in the pen to be slaughtered for food. This was his family and he wanted to care for them as they had cared for him, and Malachi hoped it would help to win the favor of both Eleazar and Adva.

After stopping by the woodshed, Eleazar returned to the barn and found the sheep that Malachi left behind. He fed them and put them in the fenced pasture. Havilah, hearing the bleating, came running.

"Sheep! Father, we have sheep!" cried Havilah with excitement.

"Yes, Havilah. You may help care for them, but don't get too attached. They will one day be your dinner."

"Yes, Papa," she replied, kicking at the dirt.

As Adva pulled Shem from the barn to go to the well, Tirzah spoke, "Adva, please take your sisters with you today."

Adva looked at her mother with surprise but saw the lingering weariness in her face. "Yes, Mother. You know that it will take me longer if I take my sisters with me, but it is good for us to go together. They need to learn the way."

"Tamar, you hold on to Shem's harness. We will let Havilah and Ziva ride part of the way," Adva said as she fastened the girth tight. She got the four water jars that fit in the saddle. Everything was in place, but she decided at the last minute to get a few more things. "Wait here. I will get us some apples and cheese to eat on the way back."

Adva, stepping into the root cellar, got two apples and a wedge of cheese which she tucked into the pouch around her neck. After closing the root cellar, she stepped to the back wall to retrieve her knife with its sheath and put it into her pouch. Adva overheard her mother speaking to her father just outside the barn, near the sheep's pen. In the darkness of the barn, she watched and listened unobserved.

"It has been over fifty days since we buried Aaron. Do you think we can try again? Adva is taking her sisters with her to the well and we have a little time to ourselves," Tirzah said tenderly to her husband.

"Do you think you have healed?" Eleazar asked. "You mean more to me than bearing children. You are the delight of my eyes and I could not bear to lose you."

Tirzah stepped closer and wrapped her arms around his waist. "Eleazar, I need you," she whispered. Eleazar's hands cradled her face and he kissed her mouth softly. With the kiss, the two lovers felt a powerful surge of both lust and grief.

Although Adva wanted to watch a while longer, she knew she was witnessing a sacred time between a husband and wife. She looked away out of respect for their privacy, but in her heart, she wished for such a marriage for herself and her sisters. She wanted to love someone so much that it hurt to be without them.

Shem was braying while Ziva danced, her scarf spread over her head like butterfly wings. While sitting upon Shem's back, Havilah was giggling at Ziva and Shem.

Everyone seemed ready to go. Adva hesitated as she peered over her shoulder to see Malachi and his sheep in the distance. If she listened intently, she could hear the bell on Jaspar's collar. Shem brayed again as if to say, "Let's go!"

"Okay, Shem. I'm coming. So much drama this morning."

Adva and her sisters enjoyed their time away from the farm. Adva taught Ziva a new song and showed Havilah a new plant. They walked home singing and skipping after having a nice snack in the shade of a sycamore tree. Adva got her sisters to come into the barn with her when they arrived back home. After placing the water by the door of the house, she showed them how to unharness Shem and asked them to help brush him and to give him a carrot for his good behavior.

Eleazar came out of the house and walked to the barn. He listened and smiled as Adva showed the other girls how to care for Shem. "And what else did you learn on your trip to the well?"

"Papa, I learned a new song," said Ziva. "Do you want to hear it?"

"Yes, but at dinner tonight. You can practice it until then," answered Eleazar.

"Papa, I'm sleepy," said Havilah as she yawned.

"Mother has some things for all of you in the house," stated their father.

"Oh!" said the younger ones as they scurried into the house, leaving Adva with Eleazar.

"Adva, thank you for taking your sisters to the well. Did you have any trouble?" he asked.

"There were some men watering their sheep, goats, and camels. We had to wait a while before we could get our water, but we had apples and cheese while we waited and the men gave us no trouble."

"You must start going earlier in the day. The women from town will help protect you from strangers. Strangers have no reason not to take what they want from you," said Eleazar, staring into her beautiful face. "Adva, you are turning into a woman right before my eyes."

"Father, that cannot be true. I am only ten."

"You will be eleven next month. There are men who are watching you blossom and asking me to betroth you to them. Malachi was not the first."

Adva threw her arms around her father's waist and pleaded, "Papa, I am not ready to marry."

"You are right, Adva," said her father, placing both hands on her shoulders and pushing her away. Eleazar placed his finger under her chin and lifted her face to him. "Your mother and I spoke today. We agreed that you will no longer study with me but will learn how to be a wife with your mother."

"Papa, I love our time of reading. There is so much more I want to learn."

"I know, I have fed your love of learning but it is not good for a woman to know more than her future husband will."

"Who told you that? Malachi?" Adva asked, putting her hands on her hips.

"No, Adva. The truth is in our traditions and in the Torah. I have treated you more like a son than a daughter. I was wrong to do so, and I am sorry."

"Oh Papa, do not be sorry. I will obey. But please, do not be sorry," she pleaded sadly.

"So be it, Adva. I do treasure our time, but I will not continue to feed your thirst for knowledge. Nor will I teach your sisters to read and write. Nor will I allow you to teach them more than what a woman should know. Do you understand? Perhaps, if we follow *Adonai's* laws better,

He will bless us with another son. *All these blessings will come to you in abundance if you . . . ?"*

"*Obey the Lord your God*," replied Adva.

Together they recited the other blessings that were written by Moses for the people of Israel so long ago. "*You will be blessed in the city and blessed in the field. Your children will be blessed, as well as the produce of your soil, the offspring of your livestock, the calves of your herds, and the lambs of your flocks. Your basket and your mixing bowl will be blessed. You will be blessed when you come in and blessed when you go out.*"[17]

"Yes, Papa, it is good to know the words of Moses and to obey *Adonai*," Adva answered in respect. "Papa, when the *Taheb*[18] comes, will he allow women to know him and read the Torah?"

"I do not know. *Elohim* loves his daughters and his sons but they have distinct roles to fulfill. You, my daughter, have a purpose to fulfill as a woman. *Adonai* does not make mistakes."

Adva, heartbroken that she would no longer study with her father, wiped a tear from her cheek. "Papa, I trust you to choose a husband for me, but don't do it any time soon." She turned and walked to the house. She stopped at the door as the sadness overtook her, and she raced to the herb garden to have a moment to herself.

Eleazar watched Adva from the barn, but he was certain he was doing the right thing. He turned around and began to clear the straw from Malachi's stall to return things to normal.

---

17 Deuteronomy 28:2-6. NET.

18 *Taheb* is the Hebrew word for the Restorer Prophet, like Moses, who will come and restore worship to Mt. Gerizim. He is the Messiah figure mentioned in Deuteronomy 18:18.

As Adva entered the house, Tamar and Ziva were carding some of the wool from Malachi's sheep. Havilah was curled up on her blanket in the corner sleeping, and Mother was spinning the carded wool into yarn cords. Adva blinked her eyes, which were red and swollen. The room seemed dark as she shut the door.

"The girls told me about the men at the well today," said Tirzah. "Did you know them?"

"No, they spoke a different dialect. It was not Greek or Aramaic. But they were respectful," Adva answered.

"That is not what Ziva said. She said you had the girls sit down, and you pulled out your knife to show them you had a weapon."

"Mother, I pulled out my knife to cut our apples. We ate our fruit while we waited for them to finish watering their herds. I just made sure that they saw me cut our apples," Adva said with a faint smile of satisfaction.

"Adva, you must start going earlier in the day so that the other women are at the well with you. There is safety in numbers."

"Yes, I understand. I will do so beginning tomorrow." Adva took off her scarf and hung it by the door. She ran her fingers through her hair and rolled her eyes as her fingers could not detangle the hair. "Mother, is there another way to wear my hair? It always seems to be in my way and it takes too much time to comb and keep tame."

"You have beautiful curly hair. It will bring your husband great delight," said Tirzah.

Adva sighed, "But until I have a husband, is there another way to wear my hair?"

"You may want to braid it tight to your head. Grab all your hair and divide it into three groups. Then cross group one over group two and under group three. Here, practice with Tamar. I will show you. Tamar, come sit in front of your sister for a moment. Bring your carding with you," said Tirzah.

Adva gathered all of Tamar's hair behind her head and began to cross and weave it into a braid. She tried it several ways. Tamar grew tired of being her model and went to do something else.

"There is another way to do a braid. Here, sit on the floor in front of me and I will show you how it's done," said Tirzah. She began to braid and add more hair with each twist. "It seems your hair may need some oil to keep from tangling so much. Go bring me the lamp oil and your comb." Tirzah began again with the hair at the back of her neck and went around the side, to the front, and then back again where she braided the rest of her hair down her back. Adva liked the tight weave of hair to her scalp. She undid Tirzah's work and tried to do it herself. She worked at it until she had a braid that was close to her scalp and could not be grabbed by anyone again.

The next morning Adva was the first to rise. She took the time to braid her hair and wrapped a scarf around her head. She went to the barn and milked Cleo the goat. When she returned to the house, Tirzah was busy at the firepit. Adva sat the milk bucket down on the table and Tirzah handed her some rewarmed bread from last night's meal. She took a bite, put the other bread into her pouch, and placed the strap over her head. Then she gathered two empty water jugs, her leather bucket, rope, and a shoulder yoke, which was a light piece of cedar that rested easily upon her shoulders. The water jars rested in slings of leather straps at each end of the yoke. The rope and leather bucket fit into the pouch that she had around her neck.

The walk was cool and the ground was wet with dew. The road to Sychar was not as dusty as it often was later in the day. The birds sang and Adva hummed a tune. She missed having Shem with her but knew he was needed at home. When she arrived at the well, there were five older women and two young girls around her age present. Each one took their turn. She recognized Mother Rachel and politely said good morning to the women. They all asked about her mother and expressed their condolences. They talked about people in town: Master Japheth's wife had a new servant; the miller was charging more to grind their wheat; Mira had received purple cloth from a certain Roman centurion. The younger girls asked Adva about Master Malachi.

"What is Master Malachi like?" they inquired.

"Master Malachi is a large, hairy man who smells like sheep."

The girls giggled. To Adva, the chatter seemed like noise. She did not enjoy her time at the well. When it was finally her turn to fill her jars, there were two other women waiting for her to finish. The water jugs seemed heavier on her way home today.

When she finally got home, Tamar asked who she saw at the well today. She asked about some people by name. "Tamar, I did not see any of those people, but I will ask if you can come with me tomorrow," Adva answered, annoyed by the barrage of questions.

After the evening meal, Eleazar gathered the family together for the reading from the Torah. Adva sat by her mother and did not sit with her sisters on her father's lap.

Eleazar looked over at Adva who was looking at her feet. He did not say anything to her because she was obeying his request, but in his heart, he missed having her close during this time. "We are continuing to read about Abraham and Sarah. Girls, you remember that *Elohim* has changed the name of Abram to Abraham and Sarai to Sarah. Tonight, we have another event with Hagar the Egyptian handmaid."

Adva perked up and leaned a little closer to the reading from her place at the table.

> *But Sarah noticed the son of Hagar the Egyptian—the son whom Hagar had borne to Abraham—mocking. So she said to Abraham, "Banish that slave woman and her son, for the son of that slave woman will not be an heir along with my son Isaac!" Sarah's demand displeased Abraham greatly because Ishmael was his son. But God said to Abraham, "Do not be upset about the boy or your slave wife. Do all that Sarah is telling you because through Isaac your descendants will be counted. But I will also make the son of the slave wife into a great nation, for he is your descendant too." Early in the morning Abraham took some food and a skin of water and gave them to Hagar. He put them on her shoulders, gave her the child, and sent her away. So she went wandering aimlessly through the wilderness of Beer Sheba.*[19]

"Papa, how far is Beersheba?" Tamar asked.

"Beersheba is about a four-day walk from our home."

"Is that close to Egypt?" asked Ziva.

"No, it is still far away from Egypt. Yes, Hagar is a long way from her home."

"It seems like a mean thing to do, to just let her go to wander," Tamar declared.

"Well, let's see what else is written,"

> *When the water in the skin was gone, she shoved the child under one of the shrubs. Then she went and*

[19] Genesis 21:9-14. NET.

sat down by herself across from him at quite a distance, about a bowshot, away; for she thought, "I refuse to watch the child die." So she sat across from him and wept uncontrollably.

But God heard the boy's voice. The angel of God called to Hagar from heaven and asked her, "What is the matter, Hagar? Don't be afraid, for God has heard the boy's voice right where he is crying. Get up! Help the boy up and hold him by the hand, for I will make him into a great nation." Then God enabled Hagar to see a well of water. She went over and filled the skin with water, and then gave the boy a drink.

God was with the boy as he grew. He lived in the wilderness and became an archer. He lived in the wilderness of Paran. His mother found a wife for him from the land of Egypt.[20]

"It was not a cruel thing," Eleazar explained. "Ishmael had to be separated from Isaac, the child of the promise. But God took care of Ishmael. He had promises of his own."

"But they almost died," said Ziva, in her theatrical way.

"It seemed that way. But Ishmael is not a small child here. He is sixteen years old, a young man. He had to cry out for God to forgive his sin of mocking Isaac. Remember, he is a wild donkey of a man."

Havilah giggled.

"Sometimes God doesn't make sense," Tamar said.

"Yes, sometimes God doesn't seem to make sense, but we have to trust that He has our best interest in mind,"

---

[20] Genesis 21:15-21. NET.

Eleazar said and looked at Tirzah. "Now, time for bed little ones."

"Goodnight, Papa," the girls chimed in unison.

Adva kissed her mother and father and went to help her younger sisters unroll their beds and snuggle in for the night. But Adva's heart was restless and she could not fall asleep. Long after the lamps were out and she could hear that her parents were asleep, Adva took a blanket and went up onto the roof.

The sky was full of stars. Adva remembered the promise that *Adonai* made to Abram: *Gaze into the sky and count the stars—if you are able to count them! . . . So will your descendants be.*[21]

Adva spoke aloud, "*Elohim*, although I am a daughter of Sarah, your princess, why do I feel like Hagar the servant? Because You made me a woman, I can no longer read the Law of Moses. I can no longer read or study with Papa. I do not want to be like the women of Sychar, who wag their tongues endlessly and say nothing of importance. The young girls come to the well to watch for men and boys who water their sheep. They giggle like Havilah as they bat their eyes and flaunt their breasts like they are choice melons for sale. Please *Elohim*, spare me from this by having Father choose my husband wisely. Until then, I will tie my hair and bind my breasts to keep them to myself."

A cool breeze kissed her cheek, and she pulled the blanket about her shoulders and soon fell asleep.

---

[21] Genesis 15:5. NET.

3
Birthday Surprise

More than a year passed and Eleazar's family had grown to include another daughter. When Adva and Shem returned from the well this morning with water for the family, the courtyard was noticeably quiet. Concerned, Adva hurried into the house thinking something was terribly wrong.

"Surprise!" said Father, Mother, Tamar, Ziva, and Havilah. Abigail, the newborn, startled in her basket but went right back to sleep.

"Happy birthday, Adva," said Father. He gave her a kiss on the forehead as he removed the water jar from her hands. "I will get the other water jars."

"They are outside by the door," said Adva.

"Come rest yourself here," said mother pulling a stool close to her. "We have a gift for you that we can no longer hide."

Ziva's blanket functioned as a curtain on the back wall of the room. When Eleazar had put the last water jar on the table, Ziva pulled back her blanket to reveal a medium-sized loom with weights and beams. To the right was a small stool with a basket full of spindles, cards, and other necessary tools for linen and wool.

Adva covered her face with her hands and gasped; never had she seen so great a treasure. She could tell it had been hand-crafted by her father and mother.

Gathering herself, she rose and went to inspect it all. The wood was polished smooth to the touch, and even the carding paddles shone with a glossy luster.

"Is this mine?" asked Adva.

"Your father has been working on this for a while. The girls and I helped when we could," answered Tirzah.

"Oh my, it is so beautiful! Is this oak or cedar?"

"Remember that big oak tree that fell two years ago? This is part of that tree," answered Eleazar proudly.

"I am without words. Thank you all for a lovely birthday surprise."

Adva continued to look over everything in detail. She was taking a mental inventory of all the things she could make. She imagined the threads in her hands as she fingered the carding paddles and the wooden needles. She knew her family took a lot of time to put together this generous gift.

"Mother, you were not making new ceramic weights for your loom, were you? You are so clever," Adva spoke as she touched the ceramic weights that she helped to make herself last summer.

"Adva, I used a new oil on the wood. The carpenters in Sebaste say the Egyptians use flax oil to give it this shine. They call it linseed oil. I was able to purchase some and try it on the loom. I want to try and harvest a crop this next season. I have asked at the market, and I believe I know what we must do to be successful," stated Eleazar.

Ziva came close to inspect the loom. "You will need a good loom when you marry Malachi the shepherd," she said. "He will give you lots of wool. You will make beautiful blankets, and you will sell them in the market and become rich!" With this, Ziva did a little twirl with her blanket.

With this, Adva's countenance had turned very dark. "Who says I am to marry Malachi?" she barked.

"Everyone knows you will marry Malachi," replied Ziva, oblivious to her sister's anger.

"I know no such thing," replied Adva, turning to her parents. "Father, is there something I need to know?" she asked.

"No, I have not yet given my consent to the man you will marry. I'm still praying there is a worthy man to marry such a beautiful woman," said Eleazar, hoping to lighten the mood that had soured so quickly.

Adva smiled weakly at her father's kind words. "Benjamin will be by again today to sharpen his father's knives. I guess a butcher needs very sharp knives," she said coyly. Adva knew she had piqued Tamar's and Ziva's attention with those words.

"I think Benjamin finds an excuse to visit my daughters," said Eleazar. "Tirzah, you had better fix another plate for our midday meal. He will want to stay for Adva's birthday celebration."

"Benjamin said he would be here at noon and would have to return home in the afternoon," stated Adva.

"I like Benjamin," Tamar replied. "He is strong and has curly hair like Adva. I wonder if his beard will be curly too . . . when he is old enough to grow one."

"Tamar, don't speak of such things," Adva said, her cheeks reddening at the thought of Benjamin's face with a beard.

"Oh, look at Adva's face. Father, I think Adva likes Benjamin more than we know."

"I see that," teased Eleazar.

Adva had had enough of all this talk about marriage and boys with beards. She felt smothered by the conversation and needed air.

Exasperated, Adva grabbed her scarf from the hook. "I'm going to the barn," she declared. But when she pulled the door open, she ran smack into Malachi, knocking her to the floor with a thud.

Ziva, Havilah, and Tamar all giggled.

"Adva, are you in a hurry to go somewhere?" asked Malachi. His large frame filled the doorway and blocked the sunlight as he offered her a hand up off the floor.

"I'm sorry. Yes, I must go to the barn. Are you staying to shear your sheep? I will fix your stall while I am there."

"Yes. But I have a gift for your birthday."

"How did you know it was my birthday?" she asked with both curiosity and disgust.

"I have known your birthday for at least four years. Twelve is a magical year when boys turn to men and girls turn to women. I am hoping that your father consents today to have us wed."

With hands on her hips, "What is wrong with everyone? I do not want to get married yet. Not to Malachi or Benjamin or anyone else!" Adva stomped off to the barn. The slam of the door awakened baby Abigail.

Malachi's eyes got big and angry. "Who is Benjamin?" he asked, turning to Adva's father. "Eleazar, we have an agreement!"

"Malachi, I have promised Adva to no one and I will not do so today. You wait here for my return and we will discuss this further. Girls, listen to your mother and do anything she needs you to do. I am going to try and redeem this special day for Adva."

The sun was bright and there was a cool breeze. Eleazar took a deep breath and said a prayer before walking to the barn, where he could hear Adva forking straw from the loft with force. He was half afraid she would break his pitchfork. He could hear her mumbling to herself: "I am not a cow to be sold to the highest bidder. I am a woman. I am like Rebekah. I can choose to marry Isaac or not. There is so much more to life than marrying and having babies. I want to know things. I want to travel. And I do *not* want to marry a man that smells like sheep."

With that Eleazar laughed, "Oh Adva, you sound as dramatic as Ziva. Come down here and talk to me."

"Yes, Papa," she replied, slightly embarrassed that he had heard her ranting. Adva climbed down the ladder with ease. She still had the pitchfork in her hand.

"I'll take that," said Eleazar, taking the fork from her grasp. "I do not want you to use it against me." He placed the fork on the wall opposite the ladder and motioned for Adva to sit on the bench against the wall of Shem's stall. The sunlight was beginning to cast shadows inside the barn.

"Adva, why don't you want to marry like the other girls, uh, *women*, your age?"

"Father, there is so much more to life than farming, toting water, and birthing babies. There is more that I yearn for. There is a restless spirit within me."

"Hmmm." Eleazar thought for a moment. He continued with a lesson to share with Adva. "Do you remember the story of *Elohim's* creation?"

Adva nodded her head, "In the beginning, *Elohim* created the Heavens and the Earth."

"Very good. And on the sixth day, *Adonai* caused Adam to fall asleep and he formed Eve from Adam's rib. He took Eve from Adam's side, not from his arm or little finger or foot. She was formed from a bone near his heart. And what does Adam say to *Adonai* when he meets Eve for the first time?"

Adva closed her eyes, reached within her memory, and found the words that Eleazar was asking of her. "Adonai brought her to the man," she recalled. "Then the man said, *This one at last is bone of my bones and flesh of my flesh; this one will be called* woman, *for she was taken out of man.*"[22]

"Very good, Adva," replied Eleazar. "*And* Adonai *saw all that He had made and it was good.*"[23] Not just good, Adva, but perfect. God planted a garden for them, and it was filled with every tree that is pleasing to the eye and good for food; the tree of life and the tree of the knowledge of good and evil. Then we learn that the serpent tempted Eve. How did the serpent tempt Eve?"

"He tempted her to eat the fruit of the tree of good and evil."

"Yes, but how?"

"The serpent asked Eve, 'Is it really true that *Elohim* said you must not eat from any tree of the orchard?' And Eve tells the serpent that this is so, and that she must not eat from the tree of good and evil or she will die."[24]

"Yes, that is true. But then the serpent tells the woman that she will *not* die if she eats from this tree. Instead, she will become like *Elohim*, knowing good and evil. And when the woman learned that the beautiful fruit would make her wise, she took a bite and gave it to her husband, who also ate. What happened next?"

"They were ashamed of their nakedness and so they made clothes to hide from each other and from *Adonai*."[25]

"You speak the truth. I hear that you, Adva, are dissatisfied with the way that *Adonai* has made things and you want more. Be careful that your thirst for knowledge and new things does not get you into trouble, like it did for Eve," Eleazar stated before pausing to allow Adva to absorb the

---

22 Genesis 2:22-23. NET.

23 Genesis 1:31. NET.

24 Genesis 3:1. NET.

25 Genesis 3:7. NET.

lesson. "Do you understand, Adva?" Adva nodded slowly as it began to make sense to her.

Eleazar continued, "I want a husband for you that will delight in you for your beauty and your mind. Just like Abram treasured Sarai as the princess she was. This is what I want for all my daughters."

"Papa, I am sorry for my foolishness. I will pray that *Elohim* rids me of my desire for more so that I can be satisfied with what He has given me. But there is this deep thirst within me that cannot be quenched. I keep coming back to the well of ordinary life, but I continue to leave thirsty."

Eleazar rubbed his beard in contemplation. He took a deep breath and continued, "Adva, when you were born, I had a prophetic dream. I dreamed that you, as a grown woman, met a man at Jacob's well. This man would satisfy you and bring you peace, true *Shalom*. He would change your life. Your mother and I believe that *Elohim* has spoken great things over your life. You are named 'rippling waters' because you shall be as a single drop that causes ripples to spread across the water's surface. In the same way, you will influence many. *El Ruach*[26] will ripple through you to others."

"Papa, how can this be true? How will I influence many if I never leave Sychar?"

"I do not yet know. But be careful that you do not try to be more than what *Adonai* has planned for you. *Adonai* can bring great things for you right here in Sychar. If you leave Sychar before you meet this man, you will miss all that God has for you. Moses spoke blessings from Mt. Gerizim right here. Those blessings are for you and your future generations if you follow *Adonai* and his laws."

There was another pause as Adva contemplated her father's prophecy.

---

26 *El Ruach* is the Hebrew word for the Spirit of God, mentioned first in Genesis 1:2.

"Papa, in your dream, did I *meet* this man at the well like Zipporah met Moses or was I *with* the man at the well?" Adva asked.

Eleazar pursed his lips in deep thought and answered, "I believe that you meet a man like Zipporah and Rachel."

"Well then, this man is neither Benjamin nor Malachi," stated Adva. The two of them laughed.

"We will wait for *Adonai*. I think we must return to the house. We left in anger and we have some fences to mend," spoke Eleazar as he stood and offered his daughter a hand up from their bench. They embraced and walked arm in arm toward the house.

Unbeknownst to them, Benjamin had been crouching at the doorway listening, waiting to sharpen his knives. Hearing their footsteps, he jumped to attention.

"Hello," said Benjamin, his face red with embarrassment.

"Hello, Benjamin. Have you been listening long?" asked Eleazar.

"I just heard something about Adva's name, rippling waters, and a dream you had." Benjamin's voice cracked as he confessed, wanting desperately to be the man of Eleazar's premonition. "Adva," he offered timidly, "*we* met at the well."

"Yes, but we met the first time at the market in your father's shop. I was buying beef for my mother," stated Adva.

"Oh yes, of course, you are correct," he conceded without argument, almost cowering.

Eleazar made note of this interaction, placed his hand on Benjamin's shoulder and asked, "Are you hungry? We are about to celebrate Adva's birthday with a special dinner."

"Yes, I'm always hungry."

"Good! Come, we will feast. Adva, you go apologize to Mother and Malachi. I will be inside in a moment after we leave Benjamin's knives out here to be sharpened after our meal." As Adva walked toward the house, Eleazar took Benjamin into the barn. "You could buy a grinding stone, sharpen your father's knives, and have a business of your own," Eleazar said.

"Would you show me how to sharpen the knives, Master Eleazar?" asked Benjamin.

"After the celebration," replied Eleazar.

When Adva entered the house, Malachi was pacing the floor. Adva could feel the tension in the room. As Tirzah was nursing Abigail in the corner, she waved for Adva to talk to Malachi. Adva obeyed and as she approached Malachi, she placed his large hands in hers. She could feel the callouses on his palms and fingertips. She knew this was a hardworking man, not like the boy-man that was in the barn with her father.

"Master Malachi, I am sorry I treated you unkindly. It was not my intention to hurt you. I was angry before I saw you and you received the anger that was never meant for you. I am sorry. Will you forgive me?" she asked in earnest. Her large brown eyes pooled with tears as she truly meant every word she had spoken.

"Adva, I want you to know that no wife of mine will ever speak to me that way," Malachi spoke irritably, yanking his hands from hers. "Even though my wife may show tears of remorse, I will not play her foolish games."

"Perhaps this is why we are not betrothed, Master Malachi," Adva replied, turning her back to him.

Malachi, having been bested again, stomped to the door and slammed it closed as he proceeded to the barn. Baby Abigail started crying again and could not be consoled. "Oh Mother, I am so sorry. What can I do to make this day better?" asked Adva.

"Here, take Abigail and go up to the roof. Girls, why don't you join Adva on the roof for a bit? I will tell you when it is safe to come back down to our meal," said Tirzah.

The girls climbed the stairs to the roof. Adva sat in the corner rocking Abigail, who enjoyed the warmth of the sunlight and fell asleep. Ziva crouched down to eavesdrop on the activities taking place in the barn. Malachi was ranting, she reported. Havilah, hearing the sheep bleating, asked if she could go see Jaspar the goat.

"Havilah, can you go to the herb garden and get some chamomile for tea? Then you can take a turnip to Jaspar by the back gate. Here, take my pouch for the chamomile," Adva said, pulling the pouch from her neck. "Ziva, what is going on down there?"

"Malachi has scared Benjamin so much that he is going home and will come back tomorrow for the knives," Ziva whispered. With this, Tamar got up and raced down the steps to say hello and goodbye. Now that Abigail was sleeping, the two other sisters could share secrets. Ziva came and sat beside Adva. "Your birthday sure has livened things up around here," she said with a twinkle in her eye.

"Oh Ziva, may your twelfth birthday give you all the drama that you can stand. But I would like my birthday to calm down," confessed Adva.

"Did Malachi frighten you?" Ziva asked.

"No, not really. His words may have frightened me had I been married to him. But I am not," declared Adva.

"But you may be."

"No, I trust that Papa has a better man for me."

"Do you think it is Benjamin?" asked Ziva quietly.

"I do not know. Benjamin is not yet a man. His voice still squeaks." Both girls giggled, and when the laughter subsided a peacefulness returned to the air.

"Girls, you can come down from the roof," called Mother.

Tamar and Havilah followed Father and Malachi in through the front door. Ziva walked down the stairs from the roof like a princess and Adva carried Abigail over to her basket. The table was prepared and set. After everyone was seated around the table, Eleazar suggested that they hold hands and speak Aaron's blessing over the meal. Malachi looked uncomfortable because he was not sure what the words were. However, once the others had started, he chimed in with a deep voice that echoed throughout the house: "*The Lord bless you and protect you; The Lord make his face to shine upon you, and be gracious to you; The Lord lift up his countenance upon you and give you peace.*"[27]

The next morning Tirzah, who was nursing Abigail in the corner of the room, said to Adva, "Will you please make the breakfast this morning? You will have to milk Cleo first thing as we have no more milk in the pitcher."

Adva rushed to the barn, forgetting that Malachi was in there. When she saw that Malachi was relieving himself at the rear doorway, she turned her back to the barn quickly. She waited a moment and made some noise with her bucket before entering the barn. "Master Malachi, I have come to milk our goat. Is it proper for me to do so?"

Seeing her fine shape in the doorway, he said, "Yes, you may enter."

"I am sorry to disturb you so early," said Adva courteously.

"Seeing you this early is good for my soul, sweet Adva. You are the morning light," replied Malachi. Adva smiled at the idea that he thought such things about her.

---

[27] Numbers 6:24-26. NET.

Adva had to squat to milk Cleo because the milking stool was in Malachi's stall. Malachi watched her from the pen's gate. When she had finished, Malachi carried the milk to the house and opened the door for her. "Thank you, Master Malachi. Please put the bucket by the table."

Before doing so, Malachi hovered over her, pressing very close to her ear. "Adva," he whispered, touching her hair as if it were delicate fabric, "I am not a bad man. I desire you as my wife and I will never give up on having you as my own." Adva shivered at the words he spoke. They were both a promise and a curse. Within them was a power that did not feel like adoration. It did not make her feel safe or loved.

"Good morning, Malachi," said Eleazar. "Do not delay Adva from making our breakfast. Tirzah is having sickness from our sixth child."

"Congratulations, Eleazar!" Malachi said, stepping away from Adva. "You are a blessed man. Your quiver is full." Adva turned away quickly. She felt shamed by Malachi's words but she kept silent.

Adva poured the milk from the bucket into the clay pitcher on the table. Then, as she went to place the empty bucket by the door, Malachi covered her hand with his own on the bucket's rope handle. She could not withdraw her hand because his hand held hers to the rope. "I will take that to the barn with me when I go," he said. Together they placed the bucket by the door, then Adva quickly recoiled.

Eleazar watched this from a distance. "Adva, did you hear?" he asked, trying to distill the tension. "You will soon have another sibling."

"I am happy for you and mother. I will fix something good for breakfast. Can Tamar go to the well for me this morning?"

"Yes, I think that may be wise. In fact, I think that chore should become Tamar and Ziva's. You will need to do more things for your mother and Abigail. I have started a fire for cooking. Can you fix a tea for your mother from your garden to help her stomach?"

"Yes, that is a great idea. I will go at once."

"I can help you," replied Malachi.

"No, that is not necessary," she retorted quickly. "You have much to discuss with father. I will be back soon." She tied her scarf about her hair, draped a shawl around her shoulders, and was quickly out the door.

"Eleazar, if you let me marry Adva, our children could grow up together," stated Malachi.

"Malachi, you frighten my daughter," said Eleazar.

"I do not mean to scare her. I just want her to know that I desire to have her as my wife. She is a beautiful woman. I do not know how much longer I can wait," said Malachi, confessing his impatient urges as if to a friend and not to a potential father-in-law.

"Malachi, I'm not sure this discussion is fitting for my wife and daughters to hear."

"I'm sorry, Mother Tirzah," Malachi confessed, looking down in remorse. "There is no hiding that I desire your daughter."

"Perhaps we should take a walk to the barn." Eleazar herded Malachi toward the barn. "Did you sleep well?" he inquired, changing the subject.

When the door closed behind them, the other girls gathered around their mother. "Do I get to go to the well by myself?" asked Tamar.

"No, you and Ziva go together, please. You may take Shem with you. We are going to need lots of water today. Please load Shem and you each can carry a jar as well."

"We will take Adva's yoke and take turns carrying it," suggested Ziva.

"That is wise," replied Tirzah.

"I wonder if we will see Benjamin at the well today?" Tamar mused. "We must eat quickly if we want to arrive when everyone else is there. Ziva come help me pick out a scarf to wear."

"Yes. Help me too," said Ziva.

Adva entered the house and looked around to see who was in the room. "The room is clear of men," said Tirzah, consoling her eldest daughter. "This would be easier for you if you had an older brother. You would understand how men are. I had three brothers. I understood how they behaved before I married. They are a little rough around the edges. A wife must soften them up after marriage."

"I do not like feeling like something to be bought and owned," she confessed as she began to make the tea for Tirzah. She put the washed leaves into the bowl and poured hot water over them. She added honey to the mix.

"Yes, I believe our shepherd will need much more honey to take away the bitterness I feel from him. Perhaps we can soften him a bit before marriage, but we must also soften your quick words that light the fire within him."

"Mother, please help me to understand all of this. I do not feel that Malachi is the husband for me. I feel like a prized animal that is being hunted. I will be pursued until the arrow pierces my heart and all my lifeblood is drained. And then the hunter will brag of his conquest."

Mother Tirzah shuddered with the intensity of her daughter's words and she prayed it would not be so. "Come, let us make hot cakes. I have some cooked apples with honey for the family. When we get everyone out of the house, then we can talk and make some decisions."

4
Goats

Tamar and Ziva left for the well. They were nervous and excited all at once. When they arrived, there were only two women ahead of them, the last of the town's women. Everyone else had headed home. However, a herdsman was waiting his turn, after the women finished, to water his goats. Tamar and Ziva sat under a tree to get out of the sun.

As they waited in the shade, the sisters watched the herdsman and his herd of goats. He was a few years older than they were, average height, with short curly brown hair. He seemed unusually clean for a herdsman. As he wiped sweat from his forehead, the sisters invited the stranger to join them in the shade. The other women carefully surveyed the scene between Tamar, Ziva, and the herdsman so that they could share the gossip tomorrow. But in seeing the comfort and ease with which the shepherd and the girls spoke to one another, the townswomen assumed they were kinfolk and left them alone at the well.

"Hello, my name is Levi. I am traveling to Sebaste," said the goat herder.

"Hello," the girls said together.

"My name is Tamar. This is Ziva, my younger sister." Levi smiled and gave a bow. Ziva stared at him, taking in every detail.

"How many goats do you have?" asked Tamar.

"Thirty-five today, but the does will give birth soon. I hope I can get them to Sebaste before they give birth."

"Do you ever run into any shepherds in your travels?" asked Tamar, sitting with her arms crossed over her knees.

"Yes, I know a few."

"Do you know a shepherd by the name of Malachi?" Ziva asked, scratching her head and swatting a fly.

"Yes, I know him. How do you know him?" Levi asked.

"He shears his sheep at our father's farm. He is there now," replied Ziva.

Levi smiled, "Malachi bought a pack goat from me last year."

"That would be Jaspar. My sister, Havilah, loves that goat," stated Tamar.

"How many sisters do you have?"

"I have one older sister, Adva. Then me, then Ziva," she said, pointing to her sister who bowed on cue. "Then there is Havilah and the youngest, Abigail, who is three months old. Now Mother is expecting another baby. We do not know if it will be a girl, of course."

"So many girls in one house. You have no brothers?"

"No," Ziva said with a sigh. "Oh look, it is your turn, Levi." The two girls continued to sit under the oak tree because watering thirty-five goats would surely take a while. However, they did not mind watching Levi draw water. He was strong and moved quickly to water all his goats. He looked over his herd.

"One of my does is panting quite heavily," Levi said. "It appears that she is in labor. She will not make it far before she gives birth." He paused while he thought of a solution.

"Our farm is not far from here. We have another pen that the goats could rest in," offered Tamar.

At that Shem let out a big noise, "Eey Howee!"

"See our donkey agrees with us," said Ziva.

"Do you think your father will mind?" Levi considered. "I will come."

"We need to fill our jars then we will head for home," said Tamar.

"It will go faster if I haul your water," Levi offered. Ziva got the two jars from the yoke and Tamar removed two jars from Shem's saddle.

"That is a useful saddle for carrying water. Who created that?" asked Levi.

"That would be our resourceful sister, Adva," said Ziva.

Tamar went back to the donkey for the other two jars. "Adva had to haul the water by herself when we were too young to come to the well. She created the saddle to allow her to make one trip instead of two."

"I would like to have one for my pack goat to carry," requested Levi.

Ziva answered proudly, "Adva made one for Malachi. She could make one for you too."

Levi gave Ziva a full jar and another to Tamar to put back on Shem, who had made his way to the drinking trough and was enjoying the last of the water from the goats.

"Oh, I'm sorry Shem. I forgot you need water too," Tamar said as she dumped her jar of water into the trough.

Tamar returned to give the empty jar to Levi. When their hands touched, there was a spark of warmth between the two of them and Levi looked into her eyes. "Well, we can't forget about Shem," he spoke with a gentle smile.

When Levi smiled, Tamar stepped backward, tripped over a rock, and started to fall but Levi caught her arm with his other hand.

"Are you okay?" he asked. "Ziva, give your sister some of your water while I fill the next jar. Ziva, you should have some water too."

Levi filled six jars of water for the two sisters. Shem was watered and packed to head for home. Tamar tried to carry the yoke of water first, but it was more than she could carry by herself. Seeing her struggle, Levi found a way for a pack goat to carry the jars of water and the yoke.

"Well, I guess our sister Adva is stronger than I thought," said Tamar, a little embarrassed that she could not carry the yoke.

"Levi, I am glad you were at the well today. We would not have made it home without your help," said Ziva.

They started off toward their home, chattering all the way. Shem saw Adva in the yard from quite a distance and started running for home. Ziva started running after him for fear that he would break one of the jars in his saddle. Adva stepped from the barn just as Shem arrived.

"Eey-Howee!" brayed Shem.

"Ah, so you want your carrot. Well, let me get this water to Mother. Wait a minute, where are Tamar and Ziva?" asked Adva. She looked and saw Ziva running. Off in the distance, she could see Tamar and a herd of goats heading to the farm. "Father! We have company!" Malachi and Eleazar came from the barn to see Ziva run into the yard. Tamar and Levi and the goats would take a while to arrive.

"Shem . . . took off running . . . when he saw home," said Ziva, huffing and out of breath.

"Who is your sister bringing home?" asked Eleazar.

"His name is Levi. He has a herd of goats. One of the does is in labor and needs a place to give birth. Tamar suggested that he come here and use the old pen. Master Malachi, you bought Jaspar from him last year. Do you remember him?"

"Yes, he is a good lad about sixteen years old if I remember correctly," said Malachi, "His father is a good man. My father knows him well."

"Adva, Levi loves the harness you made for Shem. He wants to buy one for his pack goat," babbled Ziva.

"Malachi, let us go out to meet the herd while Ziva and Adva unload Shem," said Eleazar. "The old pen may collapse if any of those goats lean on it. But maybe the does could use the pen to birth and the rest of the herd can feed on the weeds in the eastern field." Eleazar sighed and began to walk to the herd of goats moving this way.

"Did we do something wrong?" Ziva asked Adva.

"Animals require feed, straw, fencing, and water. Perhaps there is not enough for Malachi's sheep and the goats. Goats can be unruly and get into things very quickly. Plus, Mother is not feeling well," replied Adva.

"Oh yes, I forgot all of that," said Ziva. "But just wait until you meet Levi. You are going to like him. Tamar is smitten with him. He will not stay long. He is headed to Sebaste. He is the eldest of three brothers and he has one older sister. He took his goats to market in Jerusalem. He now has a herd of thirty-five."

"Eey-how!" brayed Shem.

"We must get this water to Mother, Shem needs his carrot, and his rub down. I will take the water. You get the carrot. Can you rub him down and take off his saddle? Mother needs my help in the house."

"Yes, of course. You go and prepare her for extra guests," added Ziva.

Adva sighed loudly and grabbed a jar to take to the house, "Grab some extra potatoes and carrots from the root cellar and bring them to the house. I will fix more stew for our meal."

Adva got to work preparing the stew, using the beef Benjamin had traded for the knife sharpening. It was rare to have meat in their house. It was a wonderful smell, but it seemed to make Tirzah feel worse. Adva's tea had not eased the sickness that plagued her mother. She prepared a different tea for their meal. Adva wondered whether water or goat's milk might be better for her mother.

"Adva, can you open the door to let in some fresh air?" asked Tirzah.

"I will do that. It is getting warm in here," replied Adva. When she opened the door, there was a young man in the doorway preparing to knock, causing Adva to gasp.

"Oh, I am sorry to startle you. My name is Levi," he said with a broad smile and a bow. Levi stood in the doorway as Adva stared at him. He was about the same height as Malachi but much thinner. He had short curly hair much like Adva's. His beard was sparse and did not hide his dimples, while his eyes were bright green. Adva had never seen green eyes on a man.

Levi also studied the eldest daughter with delight. He noticed her curly hair peaking under her head scarf. He noticed the spoon in her hand and the smell of the stew. Levi asked, "Are you cooking with rosemary and cardamon?"

Adva swallowed. "Yes, do you like it?"

"Oh yes, my mother makes it that way. She loves spices."

"I'm sorry, I was opening the door to give my mother some air. Do you need something?" asked Adva.

"Yes, your father sent me to ask if you have some hemp or flax twine. We are repairing the pen for my goats. Your sisters are watching over the goats and I have does birthing kids in another pen. I am sorry that I am so much trouble," apologized Levi.

"Adva, who is at the door?" asked Tirzah.

"I am sorry, please come in while I find the twine. Mother Tirzah, we have another guest. This is Levi, a goat herder. Tamar and Ziva brought him home from the well today." Adva walked across the floor to the loom at the back wall.

"Good morning, Mother Tirzah," he said, bowing low to the floor. Raising his head his caught sight of the loom. "What a beautiful loom! Who is the craftsman?" Levi asked.

"My father made the loom and mother made the tools," Adva stated with pride. She found a large spool of twine that she wanted to help string her first project. "Ah, here is the twine Father wants you to use."

"I must speak to him about his carpentry. I would love to learn the craft from him. I do not wish to herd goats for the rest of my life," confessed Levi.

"I am sure that father would like an apprentice. Perhaps you could arrange that with him. Will you be joining us for our midday meal?"

"I do not think I will be able to join you. Even if the pen is repaired, I cannot leave my goats. Now that my first doe is in labor, I have four others that will closely follow. Six must give birth before I can continue to travel to Sebaste."

"Please tell my father and Master Malachi that dinner will be ready at the seventh hour if they can come," stated Adva.

"I'm sorry to put you out, but may I ask if you have an extra blanket to keep the sun's heat off the newborns?"

"Yes, have Tamar come and get that for you. Havilah will be a good help for your goats. She is quite good with animals, but I am not sure if Tamar will make it through the first delivery."

"Yes, I agree. Tamar is watching the other goats so I can help your father and Master Malachi with the repairs. I should go back," he said with some reluctance in his voice. "Adva . . . living water. You must tell me the story behind your name." With that said, he turned and raced across the courtyard. At the barn, he peered back to see her still standing in the doorway. "Thank you for the twine," he called out, rushing through the barn. The commotion caused Shem to bray loudly.

Adva returned to her stew and put another log on the fire, humming a soft tune. She added more water to the pot. Across the room, her mother was smiling after witnessing the encounter between Adva and Levi. She would talk to Eleazar about the young man. "Praise *Adonai*," she whispered to herself.

Eleazar and Malachi returned from the fields at the seventh hour. Levi could not come to the meal because of the birthings. Two kids were nursing as the two men walked past the pen. Havilah begged to help, and Father reluctantly agreed that she could return after the meal to give Levi a chance to eat. It was as if Levi, a stranger just this morning, had already been adopted into the family.

It was only yesterday that Tirzah had asked *Adonai* for more men in the family. She hoped that a boy child would come in nine months. But if Levi could apprentice with Eleazar this winter, he could bring some much-needed help to the family. Tirzah also sensed that he would be good for the girls.

After the family had eaten their fill, Adva took a bowl of hot stew to Levi to see if there had been any progress. Malachi wanted to follow Adva, but Eleazar distracted him with a question and requested his help in the fruit groves.

"Malachi, we will shear the sheep in the morning. We have three men to help us get them all done," Eleazar announced. "With Tirzah not feeling well, it is important to clear the house of all the guests so that she can rest."

"I was hoping to visit a while this year," Malachi responded, "but I understand."

Adva sat on a large rock and watched as Levi devoured the stew she had prepared. "That is the best meal I have had since leaving home over a month ago. I hope the other does complete their birthing tonight, as I do not wish to worry my father. I asked Tamar for some herbs to help the new mothers, but I believe that you are the herb gardener in the family," confessed Levi.

"No, my mother is the best herb gardener. I have learned from her how to identify the plants as well as their medicinal purpose," said Adva humbly.

Levi asked, "Do you grow any shepherd's purse?"

"Yes, I think we have some of that. Let me bring you some from our garden." Adva scooted off to the herb garden and quickly returned with some leaves and stems. She handed the plants to Levi then sat and crossed her arms over her knees to watch as he mixed the herbs in his bowl with some olive oil. He put a small amount in his hand and fed the mix to his does, both those waiting to give birth and those that had newborns already. The goats gladly received the treat from their shepherd. Agnes bleated her thanks and he rubbed her head.

"You have a few more hours before dark. Will you have to sleep in the pen with the new mothers?" asked Adva.

"Yes, if they have not been successful, I will have to continue to care for them throughout the night." Adva smiled at his attentiveness to his flock. Havilah pointed at a doe that was panting.

"Yes, she will be next it appears," said Levi. "I should get back to work. Havilah you have been helpful, but if you have other chores to do, I will be fine. You can come back later."

"Thank you. Although I prefer working with animals, it is my night to clean the kitchen and put away the dishes." So Havilah picked up his bowl and left the pen. Adva also started to go.

Levi asked, "Would you like to meet the does?"

"I really should be getting back to the house," Adva said with reluctance.

"Oh, I will not keep you long. This one is Keturah. This one is Ziva. Your sister wasn't sure she liked that the goat had her name, but she is just as dramatic as your sister." They both laughed. "This one is Agnes. She is the matriarch of my herd. She is wise and looks after the other younger mothers. She will be the last to birth as always. This one is Sharon and the one in the corner with her kids is Goshen. She was the first to go into labor at the well. She was happy to have a lovely place with tall grass and straw in which to rest. I am grateful to you and your family for letting us pasture here. I hope I will not be too much trouble."

"I will get you another blanket and some straw to bed on tonight."

"None are in active labor. Please just show me your loft and I will get some straw for myself."

They walked to the barn talking about the farm and what they grow. Eleazar and Malachi could see them from a distance, and Malachi's jealousy burned within him. Eleazar tried to calm his temper. "Adva is showing him the barn. We will meet them there and you will have no reason for alarm." The men quickened their pace and walked in one door as Adva and Levi walked in through the other.

"Master Malachi is our guest in this stall. This ladder leads to our stored straw if you need any for your bed. Hello Father, Master Malachi. Did you see that the apple trees are about to blossom?"

"Yes, Adva. Thank you for letting me know. It looks like a good year for apples," replied her father.

"Father and Master Malachi can assist you with anything else you may need and I will get another blanket for you." Adva walked quickly to the house because she could feel the anger radiating from Malachi and no longer wanted to be in his presence.

"Your daughters have been a blessing to me and my goats today. Thank you for your kindness," Levi said.

"You just stay away from my Adva," said Malachi, with clenched fists by his side.

"I am sorry. I did not know that Adva was betrothed," replied Levi, innocently scratching his head.

Eleazar quickly stated, "She is not betrothed to anyone. Malachi believes he is first in line, but *Adonai* has not yet told me who will get that honor."

"You are a wise man, Master Eleazar," Levi said, before quickly changing the subject. "I was admiring the loom that you made for Adva. She says you are a master craftsman. I would love to learn from you as an apprentice. I do wood carvings while I am pasturing the goats, but I would like to learn more. Would you consider teaching me, as your apprentice?"

"I will discuss it with Tirzah, and we can talk further in the morning," said Eleazar.

"I will be sleeping in the pen tonight with the does. There are three more that need to give birth before we can travel on to Sebaste. I will get some straw and get out of your way," said Levi.

Eleazar replied, "My daughter will be back soon with your blanket. Ah, she has sent Havilah with the blanket."

"Has Sharon given birth yet?" asked Havilah.

"No, I think Ziva will be next." Seeing the expression on Eleazar's face, Levi answered, "Yes, one of my goats is named Ziva." They all laughed and it broke the tension in the air.

"Papa, may I stay and help with the goats?" begged Havilah.

"No, Havilah," Eleazar answered, shaking his head. "It is not proper. Go help your mother and your sisters. You may help in the daylight tomorrow." Havilah scampered to return to the house.

Holding the blanket to his chest, Levi begged to leave and return to the birthing, "Thank you for the blanket. I will gather some straw and return to the pen."

"You are a welcomed guest in our home, Levi," he said. "Come, Malachi, I want to show you something." The two men walked around to the front of the house where two hibiscus trees stood in full bloom. "Aren't these lovely?" Eleazar beamed. "Adva planted them last year. She was hoping to make a dye from the blossoms, but instead she uses them to make a sweet, flavored tea." Eleazar grabbed a blossom in his hand and twirled it between his fingers as he spoke. "Malachi, Adva is as fragile as these blossoms, and she is easily crushed." Malachi watched as Eleazar pinched the delicate flower between his thumb and forefinger. "But unlike the hibiscus bloom," Eleazar continued, "when Adva is crushed, she will become bitter. And you, my friend, frighten her. I will not betroth her to a man who frightens her. You must find a way to win her heart if you want my blessing."

"I understand." Master Malachi stepped back and inhaled a deep breath of perfumed air. "I need to shear the sheep and get back to the foothills of Mt. Ebal. If we shear the sheep tomorrow, I will be able to market the wool the next day in Sychar and leave on the third or fourth day. Perhaps I can be at my uncle's home in a month's time."

"How is your Uncle Kenan?"

"Kenan and his wife, Rue, are doing well. They have an olive farm that does quite well. My Uncle Eliab has a market in Aenon. If I do not sell all my wool in Sychar, I will sell the rest in Aenon. I also plan to butcher some of the flock there. Uncle Eliab buys and sells with the merchants from the East. Lots of spices."

"Spices. Now that is a subject that might get Adva's attention. Talk to her about herbs and spices. She may give you a list of spices to buy for her, which would require that you return. You may want to tell her about your home in Damascus. She likes to hear about other places."

"I will try that tomorrow. I am tired, my friend, and I will need to get up early for the shearing. I am going to sharpen my tools tonight if I may use your grinding stone."

"Yes, of course. Let me show you where the oil is. I also have a lamp and lampstand that will be of good use."

At dawn the next morning, it was dark and cool, but Adva could hear men talking at the table. She arose quietly so she would not disturb her sisters. She dressed in a corner of the room and sat on the stairs to the roof to brush and braid her hair.

"Good morning, Papa," Adva said as she entered the kitchen. "Good morning, Master Malachi."

"Did we wake you?" asked Eleazar.

"Yes, but I will get your breakfast quickly so that you can begin to shear the sheep before it gets too hot."

"Thank you, Adva. Your mother is still resting. This baby is requiring all her energy. It must be a boy," Eleazar chuckled.

"It is difficult to nurse one baby and create another one. This will be a long nine months for Mother. Did Abigail sleep through the night?"

"No, she awoke about an hour ago and has just gone back to sleep."

"Father, Master Malachi, may I make a request?"

"What is it, Adva?" her father replied.

"I would like to choose the wool of two rams. I want to purchase the wool for my weaving. I would like you to shear them first and I will collect their wool."

Malachi responded, "You may buy the wool from any of my sheep. But why must I do those first?"

"I want to keep the wool pure from the other sheep. I already know which rams I want."

"You may come and point them out to me when we begin," replied Malachi.

"Thank you. I have the money from my soap sales to pay you," Adva stated.

"I have never done business with a woman before. Is this proper, Eleazar?"

Eleazar answered proudly, "Yes, my daughter is quite skilled in the business of the marketplace. She goes often for our family."

Adva smiled at her father's kind words. "Let me get your breakfast. Thank you for starting the fire for me, Papa."

"I started it for your mother, to break the chill in the house. It will need to be rekindled," he said quietly.

Adva began to mix barley flour into cakes. In another pot, she combined cinnamon, honey, lemon, apples, and nuts and placed it on the hot coals. The cakes baked near the flames on hot stones. As they finished baking, she put them in a bowl and ladled the honey sauce over the cake. She placed a tray of goat cheese on the table to counter the sweetness. She filled two cups with water and served it all within a short time.

The sun was just coming up, turning the sky a rosy peach color. The men ate quickly and left for the barn. Adva quickly ran after them to remind them about the wool she needed. She was able to point out which rams would provide her prized wool, one black and one white.

She placed a rope around the necks of the sheep to set them apart from the others.

"When you have sheared the one, I will gather the wool up into a sack. After you shear the next one, I will gather that wool for another sack. I do not want to mix the two together," explained Adva. "Thank you."

Levi heard the chatter and came to say hello. He reported that two does were slow to give birth. "Perhaps they do not want to be watched," he offered.

"Levi, will you come to the house and have breakfast with my sisters?" asked Adva.

"Is that allowed?" he asked, looking to Eleazar.

"Mother is with us," Adva said to Father.

"Breakfast is made and waiting for you. Havilah will want to help with your goats," stated Eleazar.

"I will be there soon. I would like to help you both with the shearing. Maybe Havilah will watch the goats so that I may check on the herd in the field," replied Levi. Malachi grunted under his breath at the idea, but the only one who heard him was Eleazar.

Levi and the sisters ate quickly. Levi returned to the goats with Havilah and he gave her precise instructions. He then checked on his other goats and returned to help with the shearing.

Tamar and Ziva were readying Shem to go to the well. They were eager to be early enough to get the choicest gossip today.

Adva checked on her mother, bringing her some breakfast. Tirzah chose to eat the goat cheese and leave the sweet bread. She also gave her mother some goat's milk and a steaming cup of mint tea. Abigail was still sleeping.

"Mother, I will be at the shearing of two sheep, and I plan to wash that wool today. Do you need anything?" asked Adva.

"No, I am fine. Where will you wash the wool? Do you have rainwater to use?" inquired Tirzah.

"I will be by the firepit near the spice garden. Yes, I have saved enough rainwater to wash my wool. I have chosen an all-white ram and an all-black ram for their wool."

"I will not be able to call you if I need you from the spice garden. Perhaps you can wait until Tamar and Ziva return to begin your washing."

"I can do that, Mother. You rest while you can. The house will be quiet for a while. I'll be back soon."

Adva watched the men from a distance. They sheared the black one first. As Adva gathered her wool, the men stepped back to drink from the pitcher that she had brought out to them. The three men talked about their techniques of shearing and what worked best for them. On the next ram, they each demonstrated a better way to shear and each man believed his way was the best. As soon as the men finished shearing the ram, Adva eagerly gathered her next bag of white wool. When she left the shearing area, the men were each going to get their own ewe to see which man could get her sheared in the fastest time. Adva thought they were being silly but it seemed to make them happy and excited.

Havilah had just watched a doe give birth to two kids and she was giddy with wonder. She ran to tell Levi, which slowed him down and prevented the youngest from winning the contest. Malachi and Eleazar were tied until Malachi noticed a spot that Eleazar forgot to shear. Malachi announced himself the winner, and the shouts were heard inside the house. Tirzah smiled.

"What are they doing?" asked Tirzah as she stood in the doorway looking toward the barn. Adva dragged a sack of wool and leaned it against the side of the house.

"They are competing to see whose shearing technique is best," said Adva with a chuckle. "Such silliness."

"That is where you are wrong, Adva. Men are conquerors. They compete. It is woven into the fibers of their being at creation. You must learn to welcome this behavior and use it to get things done. They will finish faster by competing. Whoever loses this race will challenge the others to a rematch. It will make their work fun, and it will rejuvenate them. They will come in at midday bragging of their skills. You must listen and offer praise."

Adva regarded her mother's understanding of men and tucked it away into her memory for future use. She would also watch her mother at their midday meal and learn from her. "What should I begin to cook for our midday meal?" Adva asked.

"We can wash and chop the vegetables. Tamar and Ziva can cook while you wash your wool," Tirzah replied.

When Tamar and Ziva returned, Adva helped the girls put away the water and took care of Shem. Shem nuzzled Adva as she brushed his coat. She made a mental note to plant more carrots this year. She also wanted to check on the apple grove, so she walked Shem out to the pasture, which was now filled with goats. The donkey brayed loudly at the intruders, but Adva laughed, "You can share like the rest of us, Shem."

The goats were playing with a pile of rocks and grabbing at low-hanging tree branches. "It's a good thing they are not near the apple trees," Adva said aloud to herself. The goats had cleared the brush and weeds from the large field. Some had eaten their fill and were lying quietly in the sunshine. The does, who had given birth yesterday, and their new kids had been introduced to the herd and they were off in a corner nursing. As Adva shut the gate to the pasture, she closed her eyes and took a deep breath, savoring the scent of apple blossom. She quickly sensed that she was no longer alone. Still, she was reluctant to open her eyes; she wanted to savor the moment of quiet. As Shem brayed again, Adva shook her head and opened her eyes. There was Levi, quietly staring at Adva as if he were trying to memorize every detail of her face. Adva flushed with embarrassment, and the intensity of his gaze caused her to step back.

"Goats are curious creatures," she said, changing the mood. "We have not had a whole herd of them in a while, not since I was a little girl."

"Yes, they certainly are. Would you like to meet the rest of the herd?" asked Levi.

"No, I do not want to get attached to them, and I have work that is waiting for me," confessed Adva reluctantly.

"Oh, stay a moment more. At least let me introduce you to the new mothers. You can help me name the kids. Havilah named the ones at the barn." Levi stepped to the corner of the pasture and enthusiastically beckoned Adva to join him. She smiled and walked his way. "This nanny is Goshen. Her ram was Bethel. These two are her kids, tell me their names. This one is male. The one with the black spots is a female."

"How about Sinai and Midian?"

"I see you went with place names too. It is settled, then. His name will be Sinai and hers will be Midian. This doe is Gilgal . . ." Levi and Adva finished naming the kids and returned to the barn. The conversation was easy between them, and it seemed as if they were old friends. Both Eleazar and Malachi noticed their comradery. It made Eleazar happy. But it made Malachi jealous and angry.

"The kids have been named in the pasture. Adva knows her geography," said Levi. "And Havilah named the ones in the barn. Master Eleazar, you have been kind to me and my herd. I'd like to give you a pair of goats to help feed your growing family."

"I do not want to start herding goats. But my milking goat, Cleo, is getting old and does not produce much milk. I will take another nanny for milking and perhaps a kid for food," stated Eleazar.

Levi answered, "I will leave you with Goshen and her kids: Sinai and Midian. This is her first birthing and she will not travel well tomorrow. The others are ready to leave now if I would let them. I plan to leave in the morning."

"I must return to the house to prepare our midday meal. Thank you for allowing me to name your new goats," stated Adva politely. She bowed slightly and left the barn. Each man watched her go. Each noticed her poise and gait. Eleazar was so proud of his daughter and the woman she was becoming. He looked at the men beside him and noted the expressions on their faces. Malachi was irritated and bothered by her behavior. Levi was relaxed and had a smile of delight on his face.

Malachi snorted, "We best get back to shearing these sheep."

Before she entered the house, she could smell that Tamar had already started preparing the meal, simmering potatoes, lentils, and leeks. Tamar would do a good job at keeping the food cooking. Adva stirred the pot and added some cinnamon, rosemary, and more water.

Exiting the house, Adva gathered her wool and hauled it to the spice garden. She returned to the barn for her washing pot. She added wood to the fire pit and built it up high. As the fire turned to hot coals, she pulled the coals into the middle of the ring of large rocks. She added more wood around the coals, making sure to leave room for the fire to breathe. Then she placed the large round pot on top of the stones and added her rainwater. When the water began to simmer, Adva took some of the black wool, added it to the water, and stirred it with a large wooden paddle.

Adva laid out some linen cloths across the high grass of the unplowed field. She put a rock on each cloth to prevent it from blowing away while the wool was washed.

Some dirt and brambles bubbled to the top of the pot. Adva used a netting fabric to catch some of the dirt and pull it away from the wool. She stirred it again, picked up this batch of wool with the paddle, and carried it to the drying mats. She laid the lump of wool there for a moment.

When Adva returned to the fire, she removed the bowl from the flame and dumped out the dirty water. She added more wood to the coals and after wiping down the pot with a cloth, Adva placed the pot on the fire. She added more water and her next batch of wool. She returned to the wet lump of wool and used large wooden combs to pull it apart so it would dry better, and she picked out some remaining burrs. She returned to her firepit and repeated the process.

Adva had been at this for hours when Malachi came to fetch her for the midday meal. Malachi saw her dirty, sweat-soaked face and admired her hard work. She had almost finished washing all the black wool.

"What are you planning to weave with this wool?" asked Malachi, trying to start a conversation with her. In truth, he was jealous of the ease of conversation that she and Levi had earlier that day and wanted that ease for himself.

"I want to weave a black and white blanket for my future husband and me to share," admitted Adva.

"I thought you didn't want to marry," Malachi inquired.

"I do not want to marry now. But I will be married one day as it is our custom."

Malachi could not think of anything else to say. "I do not converse as well as others because many months often pass between my conversations with people," he admitted plainly. "Eleazar sent me to escort you to our midday meal."

Adva smiled at Malachi. "Let me get this batch to the drying cloth and I will put out the fire with the water in the pot." Adva lifted the wool from the pot and stretched it out on the drying cloth. She felt the wool batches to see which ones were dry, and she placed those into a sack to carry back to the house. The wet ones were left to dry in the sun. She would have to eat quickly and return to the task.

"How do I keep the drying wool from blowing away while we eat our meal?" she asked Malachi.

Malachi looked over her tools and gave his assessment, "You can place your paddle over these three and place your bowl over those two. I suggest you take this one back to the house to dry on the roof. Is that where you will put your sack of clean wool?"

"Yes, the clean wool will go on the rooftop. I think your method of anchoring the wet batches will work. Thank you, Malachi," she said happily.

"I am quite hungry. I will carry this sack for you. Can you carry the other batch?" Malachi said as he threw the sack over his shoulder.

"We can go up the outside stairs to the roof so that we do not disturb the table. Yes. I will leave the rest for this afternoon. I should be able to finish washing the wool today."

5
To Market

During the midday meal, the conversation turned to events at the well. "Today there was a caravan of merchants and camels coming into town," said Tamar.

"We left quickly," added Ziva. "It takes a long time to water camels."

"That may have been the group I met in Jerusalem," said Levi with excitement. "If so, they are traveling to Damascus with their products from Egypt. They said that they would rest here in Sychar. They were the ones that told me about your village. Bah-Tin is the patriarch of the group. He is a merchant on the Silk Road. Malachi, if you sell some of your wool in the market tomorrow, you may get a better price. Be sure to take your best!"

"Papa, may I go and sell the rest of my soap?" asked Adva.

"I think I should go too," stated Eleazar. "I think I have a few wooden boxes for sale."

"Yes, can we all go?" asked Ziva.

"No, someone will need to stay here to help Tirzah and Abigail," insisted Eleazar.

"Papa, if you will get a good price for my soap, I can stay behind with Mother and Abigail. Tamar and Ziva could go with you to learn about the market," said Adva. "Levi, do you have more goats to sell?"

"I have a few more to sell," said Levi, "but I am not sure that I want to leave the women here alone."

"If you would like, I can take your goats with me," said Malachi. "They can carry the wool."

"How many can you handle and also sell your wool?"

"How many do you have left to sell?"

"Eight, no twelve."

"That will be my limit."

"Don't forget there will be four goat herders," replied Eleazar, wanting to give the girls a job to do. He hoped that would keep them from wandering off.

"Adva, do you have thirty sacks that I can use to put the wool in?" asked Malachi, whose deep voice boomed in excitement. Adva's eyes widened with worry. She did not have even ten sacks made and could not have that many by morning.

Tirzah, seeing the dilemma, replied, "Perhaps you should harness Shem to the cart and fill the cart with the wool, wooden boxes, and soap that you want to sell. Adva's soaps will add a lovely scent to the wool. It would also give you a place from which to do business in the marketplace." Admiring her mother's wisdom, Adva breathed a sigh of relief. Everyone seemed to like that idea.

"My goats are good at following after a cart as well, if someone walks behind them," replied Levi.

"I, the master herdsman, will bring up the rear. Tamar and Ziva can ride with Master Eleazar in the cart," said Malachi pridefully.

Eleazar replied, "We will go to Jacob's well first. We will water the animals and fill our jars for the day, then return with our remnants by sunset. Will you be okay that long, Tirzah?" Tirzah smiled and nodded.

Everyone had their fill of food, and the talk of tomorrow's trip to Sychar filled the house with excitement. Levi borrowed a brush and went to groom his goats and pick the best to sell. Adva made her way back to washing wool. Havilah watched the last of the births. Agnes was indeed the last to birth her twins. Havilah called Levi because the poor goat was so noisy during the process that Havilah thought something was wrong.

"No, Agnes just likes to tell the world about her new babies," said Levi. "I'm glad it isn't the middle of the night. She is quite loud."

"Will it be well with you waiting another day to return home?" asked Havilah, trying to quell her excitement about another day with the goats.

"Yes, it will be very well if I sell my goats," stated Levi. "It will give the little ones another day to be stronger."

Tamar and Ziva finished their chores and helped Mother with Abigail.

"Mother, what should I wear tomorrow to the market?" asked Ziva.

"Yes, Mother, what scarf should I wear to get my future husband to notice me?" asked Tamar.

Tirzah smiled and shook her head. She secretly wished it had been Adva that had asked to go to the market for that reason. But she was glad that Levi, Adva, and Havilah would be here at home to keep her company.

Eleazar and Malachi went to the workshop to pick out the best of Eleazar's work to sell and returned to the barn to shear a few more choice sheep.

Adva rebuilt her fire and quietly returned to washing more black wool. She was confident that her soaps were ready to go to the market.

The sky was getting dark as Adva finished the last of her washings. Havilah was the one to come for her at the end of the day. They gathered up the drying wool and hauled it to the roof for tomorrow's sun. "Thank you for your help, Havilah. Is everyone getting ready for tomorrow?"

"Yes, everyone is excited," stated Havilah.

"I don't want to leave this stuff out here overnight. Can you carry that wool?" Havilah tried to pick up three bags of wool. The wet wool was heavy and she shook her head no.

"I can carry the wet wool in the pot and put the paddle over the top, like this. There. Now we can make our way to the house and barn."

When they arrived back at the house, Adva pulled her bag from the pot and placed it by the door. She was about to enter the barn when Havilah spoke. "Adva, I wouldn't go in the barn tonight. We have men sleeping there, remember."

"Yes, thank you, Havilah. I will set the pot here out of the way. Now we need to get these bags up to the roof."

At that moment Levi and Malachi stepped out the door of the house. "Here, let me help you with this," said Levi.

"Oh, they can handle this. They are strong women," said Malachi.

"Yes, that is true, Malachi. But kindness wins the heart," said Levi as he hoisted the bag of wet wool over his shoulder. "This is heavy!"

"It is still wet," replied Adva. "Thank you for your kindness."

Not to be outdone, Malachi took the other two bags of wool and asked, "Where do you want these?"

"Up the back stairs to the roof, please. Havilah get a lamp to light the stairs. I will put the pot in the barn since the guests are on the roof," said Adva. She took the pot and paddle to the back wall and hung them on their hooks. Adva was leaving the barn as the two men entered. "I'm sorry. Please excuse me," she said.

Both men stepped back to let her pass but they did it in a manner that made her pass between them. Adva hurried across the courtyard knowing that the two men were watching her. Both men watched the sway of her hips as she briskly walked to the house and they continued until they heard her latch the door behind her.

As dawn arrived, Adva was awakened by the cry of Abigail from the corner of the room. The cry was soon muffled by Tirzah's breast as she began to nurse the wee one. She heard the men around the table, their voices low and resonating in their chests as they spoke. It was a pleasing sound to Adva, comforting.

"Don't you think you should wake your girls to begin cooking our breakfast?" asked Malachi, anxious to get the day started.

Eleazar answered his question, "I think I hear my girls stirring now. Why don't you two get some wood from the shed so that they can dress in private?" Levi and Malachi left quickly. "The room is clear, Adva. I will be with your mother. Let me know when you girls are finished."

"Yes, Father," yawned Adva. "Come on you two. You have only a few minutes to get dressed before Malachi and Levi return. You do not have much time to make yourselves beautiful. Havilah, you best dress quickly and come with me to the firepit." Adva dressed quickly and tied her hair back. She realized that her breasts were getting too big to be tied tightly. She would ask her mother what to do about it later today. Adva had a fire going and most of breakfast on the table when Levi and Malachi knocked at the door.

Havilah opened the door as Adva brought a second plate of flatbread to the table. *Shakshuka*[28] made with beans, tomatoes, and leftovers from yesterday filled a bowl in the middle of the table. There was also a bowl of goat

---

28 *Shakshuka* is a dish made of poached eggs, onions, green peppers, garlic, and spices.

curd with cucumber, apples, and raisins. It was a hearty breakfast that would help to hold their appetites until they returned tonight.

The men ate their fill, went to the barn to hook the cart to the donkey, and gathered the goats for the market. By the time they finished, Tamar and Ziva were ready for a day of selling at the marketplace. Mother Tirzah had given them some words of advice and a stern warning not to get separated from their father.

Adva had put some apples, nuts, and cheese in two sacks for them to nibble on during the day along with a few carrots for Shem. The wooden chests, soap, and wool were loaded into the cart. Shem was braying at the heavy load already. They were pulling away just as the sun peeked over the horizon to light the way. Levi went to check on his goats and Malachi's sheep.

"I think everyone has been fed," Levi said. "I think Mother Tirzah wants to wash Abigail's dirty laundry today. Where does your family wash their clothes?"

"We usually do it here in the courtyard," explained Havilah, "but I think Adva has more rainwater stored where she washed the wool yesterday. We can move the kettle out to the woodshed and start a fire. I will go and tell her to join us soon."

Havilah entered the house and told Mother and Adva that Levi was moving the washing pot to the woodshed to do the wash there.

Adva went to the door and watched as Levi's strong arms rolled the kettle toward the woodshed. "It is nice to have Levi here to help us today. Mother, have you and Father spoken about having Levi work here this winter?" asked Adva.

"Yes, we have talked about it. The fathers will have to make the decision. Levi is a good man. I hope your father can make a deal of securing him as a husband for one of my daughters," said Tirzah.

"Oh no, here we go again."

"Adva, you must begin to think of your future husband in a good light. You know you are fond of Levi."

"Yes, I do think he will make a good husband, and I do enjoy his company," Adva confessed. "Our house has not been the same since he arrived. I mean that in a good way."

"Then let us begin to make a request for him as a husband for you or Tamar. I do not want to miss this opportunity. Now take these dirty cloths to the washing pot." The soiled cloths were piled high and very pungent.

"Yes, right away," Adva said, grimacing at the stench. "I will use some of my good soap on these. They will smell better for a while."

"I will bring Abigail out with us as soon as she finishes eating," said Tirzah.

"Havilah, take these things out and ask Levi to get the fire started. I am coming right behind you with these cloths," requested Adva. Havilah left the room, and Adva sat with her mother for a moment. "Mother, I have something to ask you," Adva declared, then paused to gather her words. "I need your help."

"What is it?" Tirzah asked, her face showing deep concern for her daughter.

"I can no longer tie my breasts into place. What can I do to conceal them?" asked Adva.

Tirzah laughed out loud in relief and then stifled her laughter. "Oh, Adva, I am not laughing at you. Your sisters, Tamar and Ziva, were trying to find ways to make their breasts larger this morning and my eldest daughter wants to hide them." Adva laughed at that too.

"You are becoming a woman. Please do not hide yourself any longer. You must learn to use your beauty and womanly qualities. Just as men are warriors, a woman is soft and comforting, and not just for children. You will be a comfort for your husband as well and your breasts will play a part. So as Malachi, Levi, and Benjamin are searching for a wife, they want to know they could be comforted by you," Tirzah instructed. "Let me see how you are tying your breasts now. We will see if we can find a better way to tie them so you will be happy." Tirzah laid Abigail into her basket. The wee one let out a sigh and drifted into sleep smacking her lips.

Adva lifted her tunic and let her mother loosen the cloth bands that were tied around her chest. Her skin was red and sore where the bands had been tied too tightly. With a couple of knots and a crisscross, Tirzah had secured them in a much more favorable light. Adva put her tunic back in place and took a long-overdue deep breath.

Tirzah smiled. "Doesn't that feel better now?"

"Yes. But I will have to get used to it. I look quite different. I may be able to weave and sew something that will help keep my breasts more secure," said Adva.

"We will work on that as soon as the barley is harvested. We are hoping Malachi can stay for the harvest, as I do not think I can help this year."

Tirzah took another look at her daughter's silhouette. She laughed and shook her head.

"Levi will not know what to do when he sees you. I had better walk out with you. Abigail is sleeping."

"Thank you for your help, Mother. It is not easy to be a woman."

"You speak the truth," Tirzah said. "We may have to beat Malachi off with a stick." The two women shared a laugh. Tirzah grabbed Adva by the shoulders and looked at her closely. "You are becoming a young woman, Adva.

We may have to find you a husband sooner than you would prefer. We do not want your honor stolen from you."

"Mother, I will be more careful."

The family returned with only a few goats, a cart with filled water jars, four happy people, and one tired donkey. Adva helped unhitch Shem then washed him with the left-over wash water.

Eleazar and Malachi spoke to Levi about the goats, the caravan, and how much money they made. As they counted out his payment, Levi's eyes widened with surprise and joy. "My parents will be greatly blessed by this extra income. You were better at bargaining than I would have been. I should pay you some of this."

"No," replied Eleazar, "I am hoping to win your father over so that you may return to work with us this winter. I plan to visit your father as soon as the barley is harvested."

"I would stay to help, but I have been away for more than a month. I know my mother is worried. I need to leave in the morning."

"I can stay for the harvest," replied Malachi. "I am not expected at my Uncle Kenan's house for a while."

"Malachi, that is good news. I do not think my family can help as much this year. You, Adva, and I will have to do the whole harvest ourselves. Tamar and Ziva will have to go to the well for water. Havilah and Tirzah will be in the house with Abigail. This will not be an easy year of crops. The barley will need to be harvested and the vegetables need to be planted. Thanks be to *Elohim* that the goats have cleared the other pasture. It will be much easier to plow. I am a blessed man."

Eleazar patted the two men on the shoulder and smiled at his wife, who was herding Tamar and Ziva into the house as they chattered about the who and what of the marketplace.

Adva liked the quiet of the barn but could hear the discussion in the courtyard. After washing Shem, she dried him off and gave him an apple with his barley. She climbed into the loft to shovel clean straw for Shem's stall. The mice skittered off as she swept several large clumps of straw. She could hear the men entering the barn as she climbed down the ladder. It was Levi who ran to assist her off the ladder. "Here, let me help you," he said, "You should have asked me to get that for you. You have worked tirelessly today."

"Levi, leave her alone," spouted Malachi. "It is good for women to work hard. They are built to be beasts of burden."

"Oh, I respectfully disagree. Women are gentle creatures who need to be honored for the work they perform," said Levi, giving Adva his hand with a bow. Adva blushed at his attention and acknowledgment of her work.

"Levi, you are a kind man. I thank you," Adva said, returning his bow.

"Pffft," snorted Malachi. Eleazar watched the two men and knew that Levi had won his daughter's heart that day. They would make a good match, and he would be delighted to have Levi in the family. Havilah ran into the barn and called the crowd to a late meal. Eleazar and Malachi followed Havilah to the house.

"Levi, you go with them. I will be a few more minutes. I need to finish here in the barn."

"May I help you?" asked Levi.

"No, that is not a good idea. Shoo, before Malachi gets more angry." Adva finished in the barn and returned to the house. She was too tired to eat much of her meal, but she sat with the others.

"Adva, your soaps were a great help today. All the sheared wool smelled of sage and cedar. The women fought over it and made high bids for the wool. They also wanted to buy the soap so they could make other things as fragrant.

You made a large profit today, too. I was afraid to drive home after sundown for fear of being robbed so we drove to the well again and came home early," stated Eleazar proudly.

"I am glad you did," said Tirzah, "I would have burnt your dinner had you been much longer." As laughter filled the room, Adva's eyelids became heavy as she rested her head on the table. Overtaken by fatigue, Adva fell asleep then and there, even amidst the gleeful conversations.

"Adva, it is time for bed now," said Eleazar, his voice gently waking her from her spot at the now-cleared table. Eleazar slid six denarii coins to her.

"Oh!" exclaimed Adva wiping the sleep from her eyes.

"It is what your soaps brought today. Ziva is skilled at sales and the marketplace. She could read people well, knowing exactly whom to entice to buy your soaps and whom to attract to fight for the last one. She did this several times during the day and brought you top price."

"Has she been paid for her service?" Adva asked.

"No, I thought you would want to do that."

"Thank you, Father. I will do so in the morning. Goodnight." Adva rose and hung her scarf by the door.

"Adva, Levi will leave in the morning and Malachi and I will begin to harvest the barley. After you have finished the morning meal, I will need your help in the fields. Havilah will have to help your mother. Tamar and Ziva will go to the well."

"Yes, Papa. I will be ready. Goodnight."

"Goodnight," replied her father with a tender smile.

Tirzah sat in the corner nursing Abigail. She smiled at Eleazar as he drew the curtain closed. "Was Adva pleased with the money?"

"I am not sure. She was very tired. What did she do today?" asked Eleazar curiously.

"We did all of Abigail's laundry, cooked our meal, and ground flour. Then Adva and Havilah planted some herbs while Abigail and I napped. Most of everything fell to Adva. She could run this household if she needed to. Abigail takes most of my time and energy," Tirzah sighed. "Levi was also a wonderful help today. He rolled the washing pot to the woodshed, kept the fire going, and split and stacked the logs in the shed. He is a hard worker and so pleasant to be around. He and Adva were inseparable. I think they will be a good match. Do you see it?"

"I have seen it. So has Malachi. I will give Malachi a chance to work with her tomorrow in the fields. We will see how it goes with them," he said with a stretch and a yawn.

"That is a good idea. You are so wise, Eleazar," said Tirzah, her eyes glowing with admiration.

"Your love light shows in your eyes," Eleazar observed, smiling. "Is Abigail asleep yet?"

Tirzah laid Abigail in her basket as Eleazar snuffed out the lamp.

6
Womanly Rest

Adva woke to the sound of voices around the table. It was difficult for her to move; even her breasts seemed sore from yesterday's work. She arose and dressed in the dark by the steps to the roof. She tied her hair and made her way to the firepit to begin making a breakfast that could sustain a full day of reaping and properly send Levi to his home in Sebaste.

With Levi and Malachi at the table with Eleazar, she went to the barn to milk the goat. When she returned with a full bucket, Levi jumped from the table to meet her at the door and take the bucket from her hands. As he placed the bucket on the table, Adva smiled, silently thanking him. She kneaded flour into flat cakes and placed them on the hot stones. She wiped the sweat from her brow.

The men talked and waited patiently for their food. Abigail cried from behind the curtain just briefly. Tamar and Ziva arrived at the table fully dressed and ready to take their trip to the well. They would not be traveling with Shem today because he was needed in the fields, so they would have to carry the water all the way back from the well for the first time. Adva knew they would be gone for several hours.

Adva was very tired. Her arms and legs felt heavy. She was glad that she did not have to go to the well this morning, but she dreaded going to the fields for harvest. Thankfully, the water that Papa brought home last night would provide enough water for everyone while the girls were gone. It seemed everything done on the farm required water, and it had not rained for weeks. She hoped they could get the barley harvested before it rained, but rain was needed.

After breakfast was finished, Tirzah emerged from behind the curtain. Abigail cooed from her basket on Tirzah's hip, which Tirzah then placed on the table. Levi gave Abigail his pinky and she grabbed it and tried to suck on it.

"She likes to suckle all the time," he said.

"Tell me so," laughed Tirzah. "She demands much from me."

"She will be drinking from a cup and eating at the table soon," said Levi. "You will see. I must be going. Eleazar, I will tell my father that you will come to visit within the month. We will prepare a place for you."

"Here is a sack for your journey Levi," said Adva. "I have given you cheese, figs, and an apple."

"Thank you," he said as their eyes locked. "I hope to return for the winter."

"Yes, Father will make those arrangements," said Adva. Malachi cleared his throat or grunted; Adva could not tell which. She stepped back, rubbed her back, and turned to wash the dishes.

Eleazar, Levi, and Malachi walked out the door to help Levi gather his herd and begin his trip. Havilah ran after them to say goodbye to her goats. Adva's eyes filled with tears. She rarely cried, and she became irritated by her emotions as she wiped her eyes on her scarf. Tirzah watched Adva as she gave Abigail an apple slice to gnaw on.

"Are you feeling well?" Tirzah asked.

"I am acting like Ziva today. I do not know why," Adva retorted.

"You have been working hard for days. Make sure you drink water before going to the fields. Why don't you sit and drink for a few minutes while I get Tamar and Ziva off to the well?"

"Yes, Mother. Thank you," she replied as she sat down to eat some cheese and drink the cool water.

Tirzah placed two large jars on the table for the girls to take to the well.

"Mother, they will not be able to carry those jars once they are filled with water. They will have to take the smaller ones until they gain their strength. Papa filled four large jars yesterday. We will have enough if they bring back the two smaller jars. They must also carry a bucket skin to draw with. Tamar, take my market pouch with you to hold the skin and rope," urged Adva.

"One of the other women will let us use their bucket," said Tamar.

"Maybe, but what if they do not? Are you going to come all the way back home to get it?"

"Why do you have to be so wise?" Tamar asked, annoyed. She did not see Adva tear up at her remark.

"Come on, Tamar. We need to go," said Ziva. "How did you carry all this stuff by yourself, Adva? This is silly. I am going to stop drinking water in protest."

"You will do no such thing," Tirzah scolded. "You both need to take a drink before you head for home. Be careful, I have a feeling there will be more strangers at the well today. Do not talk to any strange men today! *Elohim* watched over you when you met Levi."

"Yes, Levi is a good man. He will make me a good husband," bragged Tamar.

Tirzah looked at Adva. “Yes, Levi is a good man. *Adonai* will help us choose who you will marry.”

“Adva, you must marry Malachi and I will marry Levi. Mother, will you talk to Papa?”

“Yes, now get going!” Tirzah nudged.

Adva got up from her seat and went back to washing the dishes.

“Adva, drink more water then go to the fields. Havilah and I will do the dishes and fix the midday meal.”

“Yes, Mother.”

At midday, Malachi and Eleazar had a full cart of barley to stack in the pen behind the barn. They dismissed Adva to go to the house. Adva, drenched in sweat, sat while drinking three cups of water. When she got up, the chair looked damp. With a sweep of her hand, Adva brushed across the wet spot. It was red. She looked at her tunic.

“Mother, I am bleeding! It is on my chair. I don’t think I did anything to harm myself.”

“I should have known. You had all the signs at breakfast.”

“Signs?” asked Adva.

“Adva, don’t be so surprised. You knew your day was coming. Today is your day. Welcome to womanhood. Now take some of Abigail’s cloths, a jar of water, and go up to the roof. I will come up in a moment to help you. I must wash and remove your stool.”

Malachi and Eleazar entered to sit at the table.

“Eleazar, may I speak with you for a moment?” Tirzah asked as she took the stool outside.

Though he was hungry, he recognized the concern in her eyes and relinquished, “Yes, what is it?”

“In private,” she whispered, as the couple stepped outside in the courtyard, back into the heat of the sun. “Eleazar, Adva has become a woman today. She is bleeding and has

gone to the rooftop to wash and rest. I have removed her chair and I will make her a tent on the roof for her confinement. You and Malachi will have to finish the harvest without her."

"Very well. I will leave her to your capable hands. Tamar and Ziva should be back soon and can help in the fields this afternoon."

"Yes, I will send them. I see them walking this way now. Now you go eat with Malachi. Eat everything on the table. I have some food back for me and the girls. I feel rain is coming, so you must finish in the field today. I will send Ziva and Tamar as soon as they have rested and Abigail is down for her nap." She rubbed her belly.

"Is the baby kicking today?"

"Eleazar, it is too soon for kicking but I feel this child's presence. This one takes all my energy. I fear I have nothing else to give."

"Adva is right. It is difficult to make one baby while nursing another." He kissed her forehead and went into the house.

Tirzah managed a weak smile and put her hand above her eyes so that she could see her daughters returning. They were struggling to hold the water jars, the rope, and the bucket. *They are so young to make this trip to the well*, Tirzah thought to herself. *But now that Adva has come into womanhood, I know they too will soon come of age. Their honor depends on finding good husbands. Adonai, please help me to prepare them.*

Havilah stepped outside with Abigail perched on her hip. The baby was crying. "I changed her cloth but she still is not happy, Mother," she explained.

"Yes, she is hungry again. Go to your sisters who are on their way back from the well. See if you can help them carry their load." Tirzah went inside the house as Abigail's

whimpering turned to a wail. "I am going to the roof to nurse. Havilah has gone to help Tamar and Ziva. Do you need Shem in the field right away? I can have the girls bring him out when they join you," said Tirzah to Eleazar.

"Shem needs to rest for a while in the barn. He will do better if he comes with Tamar and Ziva. Malachi, my wife tells me that rain is coming and we must finish today. Adva will not be coming back with us," Eleazar stated matter-of-factly.

"Why isn't Adva coming? She is a good worker," complained Malachi.

Tirzah sighed. She took Abigail and left for the roof before she lost her temper. Eleazar noted Malachi's lack of concern for his daughter. "Yes, she is. I am glad that you see how hard she works. She is needed at home this afternoon," Eleazar stated with some disappointment in Malachi's response.

"Do you think that is wise, Eleazar? You are too easy on her," continued Malachi with a bite of food in his mouth.

"Malachi, please do not challenge my wisdom in this matter," Eleazar said sternly.

"I am sorry if I overstepped my bounds. But if she were my wife, she would be working with us this afternoon," proclaimed Malachi.

"Again, you give me a reason for her not to marry you. You are not helping your cause." Malachi clamped his mouth shut and grunted in anger. Eleazar continued, "This is how it shall be. I will work beside Tamar and you will work with Ziva. I think her temperament will better suit you. She sings while she works and it is lovely."

"Yes, Master Eleazar," Malachi relinquished.

On the roof, a hot wind blew in from the sea. Adva had found a way to secure a blanket to protect herself from the

hot sun. Tirzah sat under the tent with her back against the roof's wall and began to nurse a very hungry Abigail.

"Did you get cleaned up?" Tirzah asked tenderly.

"Yes," she spoke. "I don't feel like myself. I am exhausted, tearful one moment and grumpy the next. And I have not yet eaten anything."

Tirzah smiled, "Havilah will bring you something to eat. Did you drink your water?"

"I am on my fourth cup of water. How long does my confinement last?" Adva asked.

"Most women rest for seven days. When I came into womanhood, I was out of the way for a full seven days. We will make you a better tent for your rest. You will come to enjoy your time away from the family. But don't get used to it because your sister Tamar will soon join you."

"Mother," Adva inquired, "is it permitted for me to weave while I am resting? If I have nothing to do, I will go crazy."

"Yes, I will have your sisters bring the loom up to you in the morning. You will have to immerse the cloth you weave in water for the cleansing ritual after your rest. But you worked hard yesterday and today, and I think you should nap this afternoon. How was it working in the fields with Malachi?" Tirzah asked.

"Mother, the man grunts and snorts like a bull." Tirzah laughed loudly, covering her mouth with her hand. Adva laughed too, then continued: "He is an unrelenting worker. But he is so quick to criticize and show me all the things I am doing wrong. At first I got angry, but I realized that his advice did help me get more barley cut. He also taught me to use a sickle instead of a knife. Father had sharpened it for Malachi to use and it cut quickly in one stroke. My knife was not as sharp, and I know that Father did that to protect me. When I returned the sickle to Malachi, I explained to

him that his strong arms could make a bigger sweep than mine and I returned to using my knife."

"Very good Adva. You did not insult him and you gave a good reason for him to use the sickle. *Adonai* is training your tongue," Tirzah praised.

"Yes, and for once we did not argue. I can see the wisdom in this method, Mother. You must teach me some more ways to honor a man. I believe those words served me well today."

"We will have much time to talk this week. I will nurse Abigail, and you can ask me questions. We can have 'wife lessons,'" Tirzah said with a smirk.

"I would like that Mother," Adva said.

"Me too," replied Tirzah as she laid Abigail down on the blanket. "I do think it may rain tonight. We must find a way for you to be away from the family without getting wet. We do not have another room for you. During my time of womanly rest,[29] I hide away behind our curtains, and your father sleeps in the barn. However, with my pregnancies, we have not been separated very much. Your father may have to be banished to the barn when your sisters join us. Your poor father does not know how his life is about to change. He may betroth you just to reclaim his own bed." The two women chuckled.

"May I leave Abigail with you? I need to get your sisters to the fields to help with the barley."

"Yes, Mother," Adva whispered, as she stroked Abigail's hair, "I will enjoy a nap with Abigail." Adva curled up around Abigail with her back to the steps.

"Thank you. I will be back in a little while."

---

29 "Womanly rest" is a term created by the author to depict the Samaritan ritual of seven days of separation and uncleanness during a woman's menstruation..

Ziva, Tamar, and Havilah were eating at the table when Tirzah came down the stairs.

"Eat up. After you rest a bit, you must go out to the barley fields to help your father and Master Malachi. Your sister Adva is resting on the roof with Abigail."

"Is she sick?" asked Tamar.

"Did something happen?" asked Ziva.

"She is having her womanly rest. She will be away from the family for seven days," said Tirzah.

"Her *what*?" asked Havilah.

"She has crossed into womanhood. She must be away for seven days like I do when I am not having babies. Her away space will be on the roof for now."

"Ohhh," said the sisters in unison.

"You may visit with Adva. You can be in her space but you cannot touch her or use the things that she touches. I must remind Eleazar that you cannot use Adva's knife in the fields today. If you do, you must wash and remain unclean until sunset. Havilah, when you take Adva her food, you must not touch her."

"But she is upstairs touching Abigail now," Havilah replied.

"I will give Abigail a bath before I feed her," replied Tirzah. "Now, Ziva and Tamar, you need to take Shem from the barn and hitch him to the cart and ride to the fields where your father and Malachi will be waiting for you."

"Yes, Mother," said Tamar as she finished her bowl. "We had a tough time carrying the water jars this morning, but we will get stronger. We will do our part."

"Thank you, Tamar. Drink more water then get going. It will be raining before sunset. Ziva, can you bring me some olive oil from the vegetable pit in the barn before you go?"

"We have oil for cooking here," said Ziva.

"No, I will be oiling the cloth we used for Levi's sheep pen to prevent the rain from soaking through it. Please take the oil up to the roof for me. And bring me Shem's brush too."

"Mother, you are very wise," said Tamar, giving her mother a hug.

"You will learn these things too. Now go."

Malachi and Eleazar worked quickly to cut the barley. Even though the sun was hot, they were able to cut as much as they had in the morning. This time they did not stop to tie the barley into bundles. The girls could tie the barley into bundles when they arrived. After it was tied, they would load the cart and get it all into the barn today.

Eleazar was very thankful to have Malachi to help with this chore today. He worked hard and knew how to handle a sharp sickle. He was indeed grateful for this ox of a man; he would have to help Adva see Malachi's good side. In some ways, Malachi would provide well for Adva. "Strong men need strong women," Eleazar mused to himself as he swung his sickle across the grain. The two girls were heard before they were seen, disrupting the silence between the men.

"Father, where do you want the cart?" asked Ziva.

"Tie Shem to the oak tree there," said Eleazar. "We must tie the barley before we load it in the cart. Do you remember how to tie?"

"Yes, Father, but will you show us again?" Tamar asked. Eleazar took a drink from the water jar under the tree. He waved Malachi over to rest. Malachi lumbered over to the tree for a drink of water too. He wiped the sweat from his face with a cloth, then poured water onto the cloth and wiped his face again. Each man's tunic was soaked with perspiration and dirt. As Tamar and Ziva took in a deep breath of manly sweat and grain dust, they exchanged sheepish glances and giggled.

Eleazar asked the girls to come close to the cut row of barley. “Girls, we cut on both the right and the left, making a path between the cuts. Can you see the paths?” The girls nodded. “You will gather each clump with your hands and use two or three stalks of barley to tie the others to themselves like this.” He demonstrated how to tie the barley stalks without damaging the head of the barley with the tie.

“You will need to work together, but quickly,” said Eleazar. “Malachi, do you think you can cut the rest by yourself? I will help the girls tie off all that we have done. We will then be able to load the cart before the rain.” The sky had begun to turn grey with clouds, which cooled the air and made the workers quicken their pace.

“I think that is wise,” said Malachi, looking to the sky. He chugged down more water and wiped the dribble on his beard with his sleeve. As he returned to the field, his arms made wide sweeps with his sickle. He swept to the right and then to the left making the same rows as before. Shem brayed loudly at a fly that was tormenting him, and Eleazar unhitched him from the cart to allow him a short grazing area.

“Come on girls, we must get started!” declared Eleazar, taking another sip of cool water. “Ziva, have you learned any songs you can sing for us?” Ziva began to sing as she gathered the stalks and Tamar tied them tightly. The girls walked swiftly through the rows and time passed quickly.

The rain began to fall gently before the stalks were put into the cart. Eleazar had Tamar hold the cart while he and Malachi tossed the sheaves to Ziva for stacking. Even though they worked quickly, everyone was drenched by the time they pulled into the barn. Upon being returned to his stall, Shem was wiped down and brushed. His coat shimmered with the oil left on the brush, which Mother had placed back in his stall. Tirzah had also placed towels on Malachi's bed, and there were more towels on hooks where the sickles would go.

"Your mother is so clever," remarked Eleazar with pride as he took one of the towels and wiped his face.

"She has placed a bucket of clean water in my stall," added Malachi, "with another of Adva's soaps. You are a blessed man, Eleazar."

"Girls, go into the house and get washed before we come to the evening meal," said Eleazar. "I will finish feeding Shem, then I will be inside."

The girls ran to the house through the rain, which felt cold on their skin. Their wet tunics could no longer hide their female curves. Mother had prepared a place for the girls to bathe and dress. The water for their bathing was warm.

"Mother, thank you for the warm water. Father will come to our meal after he bathes and feeds Shem," said Tamar.

"Did you get all the barley in the barn?" asked Tirzah.

"It is stacked on the cart with the heads in the air to dry. Father said we would leave them in the cart until morning and then decide where they should dry," said Ziva.

"Very good. I have been praying. Is it finished?" asked Tirzah.

"Most of the crop is in the barn. We could not get it all cut but what we cut we have stacked," replied Tamar. "Father said the other would have to dry again from the rain. He said we saved this crop."

"It is a good thing you were able to help. After you are dressed, go up to the roof and say goodnight to your sister. Take her some food, and see if she needs another blanket," said Tirzah.

Ziva took a bowl of soup to the roof for Adva. The rain was gently falling on the small, lamp-lit tent that Mother had erected. As Ziva pulled open the flap and entered, she was struck by the pungent smell of warm olive oil. Adva had arranged some bags of wool up against the roof's edge to provide support for her aching back. She invited Ziva into her home.

"I like this place," said Ziva. "I wish I could sleep up here tonight."

"Your time will come soon enough. Mother says that she misses her 'away time' when she is with child. I thought I would be lonely, but I have not missed the hustle yet. Abigail has kept me company today. I think mother was pleased that I was able to watch her all afternoon."

"Here, eat," said Ziva pushing a bowl in her direction.

"Wow, your braid makes a perfect crown for your head. You look different and lovely. I am jealous," said Ziva. "I wonder if Malachi will figure it out or if Father will have to explain things to him."

"I don't think Malachi understands women very well. He may not remember his mother and he had no sisters. His father sent him to watch sheep not long after his mother died. Sheep are all he has known for over ten years," replied Adva.

"I do not think he will know the customs for women," Ziva whispered.

"I think you are right," Adva said. "Will you tell Mother to talk with Father so that he can explain these things to Malachi?"

"I will do that for you. This is most important," said Ziva. She took Adva's bowl and left the tent quickly.

Adva was thankful for her sisters. She prayed that *Adonai* would keep them close as they started families of their own. Again, her eyes filled with wistful tears as she blew out the lamp and laid down to sleep.

The family was waiting for Ziva before beginning their meal. Abigail cooed in the corner near the small fire. A lamp had been lit and sat on the lampstand. There was only one lamp tonight because Adva had the other one. It gave a soft glow to the meal. All the chairs were filled with tired and weary people. After the meal, Eleazar read a short passage from the scroll and everyone retired to their beds. Ziva had spoken with Mother after dinner so that she could talk with Father about the matter with Malachi.

Malachi lit a lantern from the fire and left to go to the barn. He took a scarf from beside the door to cover his head and protect him from the rain. As he held the scarf, he wondered about Adva, but he did not dare to ask about her at dinner for fear that he would say something wrong. But as he left for the barn, he pulled Eleazar aside. "Eleazar, everyone seems to know and understand why Adva is on the roof but me. Is she being punished, or am I?" asked Malachi.

"No, Malachi. I will walk you to the barn so we can talk. I have forgotten that you grew up without women in your home." Eleazar grabbed Tirzah's scarf from the door and both men held the scarves over their heads and ran for the barn. After taking shelter, the men discussed the Law of Moses and the rituals required by Moses for women.[30]

Malachi spoke with urgency, "Eleazar, you must allow Adva to marry soon to preserve her honor. She is indeed a woman now."

"Malachi, nothing has changed. Adva's honor is protected so long as she lives in my house. *Adonai* will watch over her and my other daughters. He will tell me when it is time for Adva to marry. I do not take this choice lightly," declared Eleazar.

---

[30] Leviticus 15:19-23. NET.

"I respectfully disagree. With Levi coming this winter, I fear for your daughters' purity and I fear that I will lose the woman I have chosen as a wife," Malachi stated. He began to pace within the barn. "Eleazar, I will help you empty the cart of barley and I will leave for my uncle's home. I will not return until next spring. I hope at that time you will allow me to marry Adva. I have made my intentions known." Malachi stopped pacing directly in front of Eleazar and looked at his face and stated, "If you say, 'no' or 'not yet' at the next shearing, I will no longer burden your family with my presence." There was a long thoughtful silence between the two men. It was a declarative silence that changed a friendship.

"I hear you and I understand. Thank you for helping today. I could not have done this harvest without you. I have come to depend on your visits. Sleep well, my friend." Eleazar said as he patted Malachi's shoulder. He did not feel Malachi twitch.

"Do you know where you will stack this barley in the morning?" inquired Malachi.

"If the rain stops, I will stack it by the woodshed to dry. If it is still raining in the morning, I will use Shem's stall and put him in with the goat for a few days."

"With me gone, you can put the barley in my stall."

"I had not realized you were leaving so soon," said Eleazar. "But I could use that space."

"Then until tomorrow," said Malachi coldly.

Eleazar walked back to the house. Though he was disturbed by Malachi's words, he would not be pressured into making a betrothal promise for Adva. He entered his home and blew out the lamp without a word to Tirzah, who knew not to question him further.

7
Change Coming

It had rained most of the night. Adva enjoyed the relaxing drone of rain on her tent on the rooftop, and she awoke while it was still dark. Hearing the bleating of sheep in the distance, she knew Malachi was leaving and wondered why he would depart before the family was awake. She stood on the rooftop with her head cocked to one side. She watched as Malachi took his sheep out the back gate and into the pasture of freshly-cut barley stubble. The sheep grazed as they walked. Adva heard him call his sheep, herding them northeast toward Mt. Ebal. Jaspar was fully loaded with blankets and gear and she knew it had taken him a while to pack the goat. The bell around Jaspar's neck clanked as he darted ahead of the sheep. He and Malachi made a good team, moving the sheep along.

While closing the gate to the pasture, Malachi turned to the house. He could see Adva's form on the rooftop, but he did not wave or acknowledge her. He just turned and went on towards what would soon be the sunrise.

Adva did not wave to him either, but she felt a sense of sadness upon his departure. Something had changed and she did not know what it was. For the first time, she felt like she would miss his presence at the table with her family. It was the first time that she felt Malachi was truly part of their family.

In about an hour, she heard Tamar knocking at the barn door for Master Malachi. Adva came out from her tent to tell her that Malachi was gone. Instead of going into the barn to milk the goat, she turned and went back to the house. Eleazar came out and called to Adva on the roof, "Adva, are you there?"

"Yes, Father."

"Did Malachi leave?"

"Yes, Father. He left well before sunrise with Jaspar and all the sheep."

"Son of Anak!" And he stormed to the barn in disbelief. It was the only time that Adva heard her father swear.

Eleazar found the cart empty and the barley stacked neatly in the stall that had served as Malachi's bedroom. Shem's stall had been cleaned and new straw was in its place. Malachi's blankets were folded neatly on the bench and Adva's scarf was placed on top with soap to keep it from blowing away.

Moments later Eleazar left the barn and yelled up to Adva, "He didn't sleep all night. The barn is spotless and the barley that was in the cart has been stacked in his stall. Shem's stall is clean with new straw. What do you think of Malachi now?"

"I think he is a hard worker with a temper that he uses well," Adva called back. "He's a wild donkey of a man." Eleazar nodded, carefully considering his daughter's words. He walked into the house to tell Tamar she could go to the barn.

After the days of confinement passed, Adva returned to her usual routine. Her time on the rooftop had not been in vain; she had mastered the weave of her loom and made cloth from last year's flax crop. Her mother was quite proud of her progress. If Adva could continue to weave, she would have enough linen for the whole family to have new tunics. Adva knew her mother needed a new tunic because this baby belly was beginning to swell sooner than the other pregnancies. This tunic would be the first garment that Adva would make. She would weave more cloth on her next visit to the rooftop, where she had secured and covered her loom carefully.

Eleazar would leave in the morning to travel to Sebaste. Adva prepared two scented soaps, each tied in linen cloths for Levi's family to inspect. She hoped this would show her value to his family. Tamar, who had been crafting cheese for a few years, sent cheese to also show her interest in Levi. Ziva and Tirzah had made a basket that would hold the cheese Tamar had aged. The whole family wanted to join with Levi's family.

Tirzah and Eleazar endeavored to understand their girls' natural gifts. Havilah was developing a gift for healing and was good with animals and herbs. Ziva was dramatic and could sing like a beautiful bird; with her, there was never a dull moment and the songs she sang made the workdays pass more quickly. Tamar was quick and often bored with long or tedious tasks. She liked to get things done and was a hard worker, but she did not have much patience for things or people. It was a surprise to Eleazar that she could even wait for the cheese to age. Adva was skilled at many things due to necessity. She did love to weave. However, it was her love of learning and reading the Torah that had driven her early life. Adva dreamed of new adventures and seeing the great sea. She was obedient and compliant to the wishes of her parents, and she would make any man an excellent wife. Eleazar would share stories of each of his daughters to encourage a betrothal arrangement for their families. Adva, the first-born, was the most likely match for Levi, but *Adonai* would lead his decision. Eleazar was certain that *Adonai* would show him the right daughter when Levi came to live with his family.

During Eleazar's time away, Havilah cared for the animals. Tamar and Ziva made sure there was enough water for the family. They were better at carrying well water now that Eleazar had made them each a yoke for carrying two smaller water jars. This not only helped the growing family, but it would also serve the girls in their own families yet to come. The water bearers grew in strength and beauty, and they attended "wife learning" sessions with Adva while Eleazar was away.

When the midwife came to visit, she recommended beef to help Tirzah build up her strength for the next child. Therefore, Benjamin brought beef and veal to the women. He met Tamar and Ziva at the well and escorted the girls to their home, protecting them from animals and other men.

Adva helped Tirzah with daily chores and baby Abigail. Abigail, now fully weaned, ate food from the table. She would soon have her first birthday. For Tirzah, the child growing inside her was taking all her strength. Tirzah had a cloth wrap to tie Abigail to her body but had no energy to use it. She gave the wrap to Adva and tied Abigail to her. Adva carried Abigail everywhere. If she went to the garden or the barn, Abigail went with her. Even around the house when she was not tied to Adva's chest, Abigail began follow Adva on her own. Tirzah was pale and rarely left the house. Even the act of simply standing to grind grain or make a meal left Tirzah breathless. More of the motherly tasks fell to Adva.

While Eleazar was gone, both Adva and Tamar had their womanly rest. Havilah and Ziva were tasked with water carrying for a few days. Tirzah, who had spent the morning making breakfast for all her daughters, had gone back to bed to rest for a while.

Eleazar returned just before Sabbath. He had already unharnessed Shem from the cart and settled him in his stall, and he was curious why no one had yet greeted him. He could hear laughter coming from inside the house. He opened the door to see Benjamin sitting at the table with all the girls. Benjamin had escorted Tamar and Ziva home from the well.

"Hello, Master Eleazar," he said shyly, standing as if to leave.

"Papa!" the young ones cried. Havilah ran to give him a hug.

"Benjamin, don't go. I have something to tell you, but first, let me say hello to my family."

"Mother is in bed resting," said Adva bluntly, as she continued to peel some apples for their mid-meal. Abigail loved eating apples. They felt cool on her new teeth and gums.

"Oh. Is Mother sick?" asked Eleazar upon seeing Abigail perched on Adva's lap.

"Go talk with her. She will be happy to see you," replied Adva.

Benjamin sat at the table with the other girls. A few moments later Eleazar escorted Tirzah to the table, her swollen legs and ankles making it difficult for her to walk. He wanted everyone to hear what had transpired in Sebaste.

After Tirzah was seated, he sat next to her. Abigail climbed down from Adva's lap and toddled over to Eleazar. She lifted her hands to him. He scooped her up onto his lap and reached for Tirzah's hand.

Eleazar began, "Family, I want to tell you about my visit to Sebaste. I met with Levi's family, and we have an agreement that Levi will be apprenticed to me for farming and crafting wood furniture."

The girls giggled and clasped their hands. Tirzah sighed as though she had been holding her breath a long time.

Eleazar continued, "Levi and I felled a few trees from their property to make some furniture for his father and Levi's future family. Levi aspires to be a master craftsman. He is also interested in marrying one of my daughters."

This time there were squeals of delight and another deep sigh from Tirzah. Tamar glanced over at Adva, who continued to peel her apples. Tamar thought Adva was disinterested. Adva said a silent prayer.

"Mother, your prayers have been answered," Eleazar said, squeezing her hand. A smile broke across Tirzah's face as she wept with relief.

"During Levi's visit, he will get to know our family. Together, your mother and I will choose a daughter to be his bride. Levi and his father will join us in a few weeks for a visit and bring the trees that were too big for our cart. Levi will bring some goats to be sold or used for food this winter. Benjamin, I may need your help building a new pen for the oxen they must bring with them."

Benjamin nodded but squirmed in his seat a bit. He didn't know how to express joy for Levi without also wondering when he might be given a chance to wed one of Eleazar's daughters.

Seeing Benjamin's discomfort, Eleazar continued, "In the same light, Benjamin's father, Joseph, has consented to join our families. During Levi's visit, we will also choose one of you to be a wife for Benjamin."

Tamar and Ziva smiled at each other then looked at Benjamin, who blushed and tucked his head, hiding a smile.

"Father, the joy is too much to bear," said Ziva.

"I am honored, Master Eleazar," Benjamin announced with relief. "I am glad I will not have to choose one of your daughters."

"Well, you cannot marry them all," Eleazar teased.

The girls giggled again, adding more fire to Benjamin's face. "That is not what I meant. I meant they make it too difficult to choose," Benjamin explained.

Eleazar continued, "Benjamin, Tirzah says you have been extremely helpful while I have been away. Thank you. I have a gift for you in the barn. It is your own grinding stone with which to sharpen your butchering knives. I will teach you how to use it here, and then we will move it to your home. We will have to make a stand for it out of the wood I've set aside. We will figure that out very soon. I will speak with your father after our Sabbath. Well, what do you say to all that Benjamin?"

"Will you show me how to sharpen other tools as well? Many people come to my father's shop asking for someone to sharpen their farming tools. Many take them to the blacksmith for sharpening. I could feed a family on those wages," Benjamin said with excitement. "However, I really must get home to help prepare for Sabbath. Thank you. I will come back soon." He stood from his stool and prepared to leave.

"May I request one more thing, Benjamin?"

"Yes, of course, Master Eleazar."

"Will you ask midwife Zipporah to visit us after Sabbath? Will you carry that message to her today?"

"Yes, Master Eleazar. I will go there immediately. Is there anything else I can do for you and your family?"

"No. Give greetings to your father. I will be by to see him soon."

Benjamin stood and bowed low, hitting his head on the edge of the table. Rubbing his forehead, he backed out the door, bumping it as he went. After he closed the door, they heard him bellow, "Praise *Adonai*!" The entire family laughed but covered their mouths so Benjamin would not hear.

"Adva, Tamar, and Ziva, are you pleased with these agreements?" asked Eleazar. "The two young men will make good husbands for any of you and each will have a way to provide for you and your children."

"Father, you are a wise man," said Adva, rising to give him a hug and kiss. She seemed relieved to think of herself marrying Levi and having Tamar marry Benjamin. "Oh, but what of Malachi? Are you going to make him an offer?"

"I learned some things about Malachi from Master Baruch, who is friends with Master Lamech, Malachi's father. Malachi and his brother, Caleb, went to live with his Uncle Aaron in Damascus after Malachi's mother died. Malachi did not like living with his uncle and moved out to keep sheep when he was only ten. Malachi has been taking care of himself since age ten," Eleazar said with compassion, pausing to recall what he was doing at age ten. "We have a few months to think about Malachi. His temperament is troublesome, but he has been good to our family. He is not lazy and will be a good provider for his family. I will continue to ask *Adonai* for guidance. But you women are not to worry over this matter. *Elohim* will provide for my daughters."

"Father, will the betrothals be for Adva and Tamar only?" asked Ziva, who secretly pined for Benjamin. Eleazar looked at the three oldest daughters carefully. They indeed had grown in strength and beauty.

"The young men would be blessed to have any of you. Your mother and I will decide in time."

"Father, where will we put everyone?" asked Tamar.

"Benjamin will not be living with us, only Levi. And Malachi will shear his sheep in the spring. Levi will stay in the barn where Malachi usually sleeps. Levi and I can add a bed and a door to that area, and perhaps we can divide it to make two separate rooms for our male guests. Oh, and we must have room for Levi and his father, Baruch. I will have to think on this a little." Placing a large sack on the table Eleazar continued, "I have some things in my bag from the market in Sebaste. Adva, I think your mother could use one of your special teas. Do you or Havilah have a spice for swollen feet? Oh, wait! Levi sent some of his mother's spices. See if any of those might work for the tea."

Havilah and Adva dug into their father's sack. They found cheese, beans, grain, and spices. Levi had written the names of the spices on each bag. There were new spices that they did not have in the garden, like mustard and cloves. The two sniffed each bag, looking forward to experimenting with new remedies and flavors.

"Mother, smell this one!" said Havilah. She put the bag to her mother's nose.

"Havilah, I do not think I shall put it up my nose," she replied, pushing away Havilah's hand.

"But do you like it?" Adva asked.

"Yes, but I do not think I want to drink it for tea. Perhaps we should wait for the midwife or Levi to tell us how to use them. The midwife will know what I should do for my legs and feet. Would you make cinnamon tea for me? I am going back to bed to rest until our meal. Eleazar, would you help me back to bed? I would like to speak with you in private," said Tirzah.

During her visit after Sabbath, Zipporah, the midwife, was concerned about Tirzah's paleness and swelling. She told Tirzah to stop eating the beef that Benjamin brought to her. She feared the salted beef was making her worse instead of better. Zipporah had a long discussion with Adva and Eleazar in the courtyard before returning home. "Tirzah needs to drink dandelion and lemon tea. Add dandelion leaves to her cucumber-tomato salads, and add more lemon to your olive oil. No more salt in your soups. Make sure that Tirzah sits outside in the sunshine for an hour in the morning and an hour in the evening. And send for me if the swelling gets worse or if she faints."

Eleazar walked with her to ask some other questions and to see her to the city limits. Zipporah would return every week until the baby came.

Adva had taken over the household duties that her mother had performed. While Tirzah watched and instructed her with "wife learning" from a chair, she had little energy to help or do the tasks herself. Merely walking across the room took her breath away.

As Adva took on more and more of the household responsibilities, Tamar and Ziva complained to Tirzah about their sister becoming bossy and prideful. "I know this is hard for you both," explained Tirzah. "But listen to me and listen well. Adva is managing this house right now. Most women learn to assume this great responsibility a little at a time, but your sister has had to learn it all at once. If she gets bossy, ask her if you can help not only with the task she has given you, but also with another. Ask to take Abigail with you to the woodshed or the barn. Levi and Master Baruch will be here soon. They will help with the flax harvest. But there is much to do to get ready for them to arrive. Please help her as much as possible." It was difficult for Tirzah to watch Adva take over these duties, but she did it all without complaining or grumbling. Tirzah knew Adva's womanly rest was coming soon and there was so much to do to prepare for guests.

This time Tamar went first to the rooftop. Adva followed her the next day and Ziva joined them the day after. The tent on the rooftop had to be expanded to receive them all. The girls had prepared food and gathered water for their time away. Eleazar and Havilah took Shem with the cart to the well on the first day of Tamar's rest. They filled every pot with enough water to last them the whole week. Maybe this was a better way to fetch water from the well. Ziva made a big pot of soup that Havilah could manage for a few days. Tirzah laughed at Eleazar's bewildered expression when she told him that three of his daughters were women now and next month he would have to live in the barn with Levi and Baruch. "I must marry off these daughters of mine. They are too beautiful to keep to myself," Eleazar replied, kissing Tirzah's hand.

Levi and Baruch came for a visit the next week, and they helped to harvest the flax. Baruch had never grown flax and did not think that it would become a favorite crop of his. But he did love the fine linen that Adva wove, and the blanket that she was weaving from the black and white wool was quite beautiful. Master Baruch thought that Adva would be the best match for Levi.

Master Baruch greatly enjoyed the visit with Eleazar's family. The two men wrote a declaration of betrothal for Levi but left the daughter's name blank. The dowry was set and the agreement would be finalized with names in six months. Baruch promised that Levi would return in a month to begin his apprenticeship.

Levi tried to convince Adva to try weaving some goat hair blankets. "Many in Syria love goat hair blankets," he told her. When he brought her some of his goat's hair, Adva promised to try using it for her next weaving project. But she found the fiber to be coarser than sheep's wool and it felt scratchy in her hands.

"Levi, am I doing something wrong? This fiber seems more difficult to spin," said Adva with frustration. Levi came close and smiled at her, deeply inhaling the scent of her hair. When Adva shoved the small piece of yarn into his hands, he redirected his attention to the yarn to please her.

"I see what you mean," said Levi. "May I have this piece? I will ask my sister when I return to Sebaste." Using a finger to pick up her chin, he replied, "I like that you tried a new thing just to please me. Thank you. I prefer your flax linen weavings the best, although I love the black and white wool blanket that you are weaving to share with your husband. You are a master weaver and it is a beautiful thing that you do to serve your family while Tirzah is awaiting the next child."

Adva bowed her head in appreciation. She thought it would be good to be Levi's wife.

After adding mud walls and a thatch roof to the women's resting room, Levi began building an extension to Eleazar's woodshed to make room for bigger projects. Many days, after working in the fields in the morning, Levi would go to work in the workshop after the midday meal. Eleazar saw that Levi had a gift for creating things from wood; he knew how to get the material to bend and change colors. Eleazar was pleased and enjoyed having another man in the household.

8
Another Child

As Tirzah's time to give birth came near, Eleazar and Levi took Shem and all the water pots to town where they would get water, pick up supplies from the market, and retrieve the midwife to return to the farm. Once the men had left, Tirzah gathered her daughters around the table.

"This month during your womanly rest, I will join you to have this child," she announced. "We must work together to make sure we have all that we need on the rooftop. Today we will put things in place and get ready for the birth. Now that you are old enough, your father will not be permitted to attend this birth. Tamar, Ziva, and Adva will be my attendants. You will be unclean from your own bleeding so we can serve each other easily. You will also need to know how a baby is born as you prepare to wed and have children of your own. We will need about six cubits of cloth of various sizes. We will need olive oil, water, and a tub for washing cloths. We need soap, wood, and a firepit on the roof to heat water. Adva and Havilah, I want you to gather herbs needed for the birth of your brother. Today the midwife will tell you which plants to have ready. Havilah, you will care for Abigail. You will need to take her with you to the barn to care for the animals. Levi and your father will help you with the animals." Tirzah paused to go through the list in her head of the things needed. "We will prepare a nice place for us all during our time away." She continued assigning tasks to her daughters in preparation for the days to come. She knew her child would soon arrive.

"Adva and Havilah, please make a nice tea for us to have with our midday meal. Tamar, get some vegetables and beans from the root pit in the barn. Would you like to share your cheese with us? We will also have a wineskin available to us during our time on the roof. Ziva, would you make the bread? Your father and Levi are selling some things at the market and they will bring home cucumbers, tomatoes, onions, lemons, oranges, and beans. We will prepare food for the week. Adva and Havilah, take these sacks, stuff them with straw, and take them to the roof."

"What is the straw for, Mother?" asked Adva.

"It is to give us a better bed. It can be burned when we are finished. I will watch and play with Abigail while you get those things and return to the table," said Tirzah.

Ziva stepped to the firepit and got the things she needed to make bread. She began by getting the fire hot. "Mother, should I cook outside?" asked Ziva.

"No. If it gets too hot in here, I will let you know."

Tamar came back with a sack of vegetables and cheese. She laid them out on the table before returning to the barn with the sack.

A few moments later, Tamar came back with a sack of straw in each hand and dashed up the stairs to the rooftop. As Tamar came down from the rooftop, Havilah was dragging her sack.

"Here, take these, and I will take this one up top," said Tamar.

"Thank you, Tamar," replied Havilah.

Havilah took the empty sacks back out the door.

"Wheeee!" squealed Abigail, clapping her hands.

Tirzah laughed. "Yes, this is quite a busy place."

Adva entered the house with two sacks full of straw. She met Tamar on the stairs. "Let's look at the room together, Tamar."

The two young women planned where everything would go, determining which items could be stored uncovered on the roof and which needed to be inside their small room.

"What if we pile the straw over here on this side and leave this straw in the sacks as pillows? What do you think Tamar?" asked Adva.

"I like that idea. The birthing chair that Zipporah is bringing could be placed here and we can easily move in and out of the room as needed," said Tamar.

"I think mother will like that. She can see out the door and get fresh air also," said Adva. "I am glad Levi gave us more protection from the weather."

There was an unspoken urgency in the air, and the women worked quickly to get everything in place: wood, cloths, oil, straw, and blankets. Lamps were brought from downstairs. A week's worth of flatbread was prepared and a pot of vegetables began to simmer.

"Tamar, I hope the men bring back something from Joseph. I would like some meat in our stew," replied Tirzah, breathing heavily as she crossed the room.

"I am sure they will think of that, Mother," replied Tamar. "I have not seen Benjamin in a few days."

"Mother, please sit down while we finish up the things needed for the meal," suggested Adva.

"Yes, I think I will sit down. Please get me some water." Just as Tirzah crouched over her stool, her water broke, spilling onto the seat. Adva was quick to come to her side.

"Oh good, we needed this stool," Tamar said with a smile. "I will clean this up and bring it to the roof."

"Mother, I will help you change your clothes," Adva said. "Are you having labor pains yet?"

"No, not yet. Just hard to catch my breath."

After Adva helped to clean and dress her mother, the two women took the stairs one step at a time and reached the roof just as the men arrived from town.

"EEY-HOW!" Shem brayed, alerting Adva that he had returned. "I am glad the men are back, but someone else will have to get the carrot for Shem," replied Adva as she helped her mother get comfortable in her room on the roof.

Eleazar entered the house with the midwife, Zipporah. Levi carried the birthing chair.

"Not a moment too soon. Mother's water broke a few minutes ago. She and Adva are on the rooftop," said Tamar, who was stirring the pot of vegetables.

"Levi, take the birthing chair to the top of the stairs and return. You will remain clean and Adva will put it where it needs to go," stated Zipporah.

"Father, Mother has asked Adva, Ziva, and me to attend the birth this time. You must now stay away as most men do," Tamar directed. "Zipporah, I will take you up as soon as Levi returns. Mother is not yet laboring."

When Levi arrived with the chair, Adva thanked him graciously. "Mother really appreciates your help," she told him. "I will see you in a few days. Please help Havilah with the animals and with Abigail."

"After this, you will be ready for your own children, Adva," said Levi.

"Yes, I suppose I will." Adva smiled at his kindness and turned to place the chair in their rooftop room.

Levi stood savoring her smile for a moment before descending the stairs. He whistled all the way to the barn, where he met Shem. "Come Shem, I will get you your carrot," he exclaimed. "Adva is quite busy right now."

Tamar carried the unclean stool and followed Zipporah up the stairs to tend to Tirzah. Zipporah seated Tirzah on the new birthing chair and began to examine her. "Adva, get a fire started! This child will be born quickly." Zipporah stepped over to the roof and asked Levi to bring two pots of water to the rooftop. She examined the cloths and prepared the olive oil.

"Tirzah, are you comfortable?" asked Zipporah. "Is there a bowl that will fit under this chair?"

"Yes, I am comfortable for now. The bowl hangs in the back of the barn," replied Tirzah.

"Adva, ask someone to bring that for us."

Adva leaned over the rooftop and saw Havilah with Abigail. "Havilah, get the bowl from the back of the barn, have Ziva bring it to the roof quickly."

Zipporah took the bowl from Ziva and placed it under the chair. She added water from one of the pots Levi had brought to the roof. "Ziva, heat water from the other pot!"

There were many trips up and down the steps as everyone scrambled to prepare for the birth of this child. Zipporah checked on Tirzah's progress even though she was not yet in labor. As Eleazar made trips back and forth from the shed to fetch more wood, he was very concerned for his wife, his beautiful Tirzah. "Thank you, Father," said Ziva each time she received a new armload of wood, "but you must return downstairs."

"Adva, it is time to help your mother out of her tunic," commanded Zipporah. After Tirzah was washed and a blanket placed over her shoulders, the first contraction squeezed her abdomen.

"Ooooh! I feel the first contraction. Adva, help me to the chair. This child wastes no time," Tirzah said.

"Breathe deeply, but do not push," directed Zipporah.

"I'm not pushing but the child moves anyway," Tirzah exclaimed.

"Tamar, come!" commanded Zipporah.

Tirzah was fully gripped in a contraction. Her eyes widened, her breath caught, and she grabbed Adva's arm as she sat upon the birthing chair.

"Adva and Tamar," instructed Zipporah, "I need you each to hold your mother's legs, bent at the knee, and have her foot on your thigh, like this."

"Ahhh, another pain."

"Yes, it is time for you to push, Tirzah. On the next pain, grip the seat of the chair, lean back, and push downward. I will catch your baby."

As they braced themselves for another push, Adva and Tamar were amazed as they began to see the top of a black, fuzzy head.

"We are almost there, Tirzah. One or two more pushes."

"I am having trouble breathing," said Tirzah, who did not push as she struggled to take a breath.

"You can do this, Tirzah. One, two, three, PUSH," commanded Zipporah. "Ziva come stand behind your mother and push forward on her shoulders," exclaimed Zipporah.

"Okay, Tirzah. Let's try again. Deep breath in and PUSH!"

Tamar and Adva watched in awe as the baby's head emerged through the opening. In one motion, Zipporah turned the baby, cleared the shoulders, and pulled the baby into the air. She wiped the baby's face, eyes, nose, and mouth with an olive oil saturated cloth and cleared the mouth and nose of all fluids.

"Ziva, you can relax her shoulders now. Tirzah, you have another beautiful daughter. Adva, give a hard pat on the baby's back while I hold her. She is slippery," said Zipporah. Adva gave the infant a timid pat. "Try again, harder this time. You must get her to cry. It will help her breathe." Adva whacked the baby harder this time and the baby began to cry. "Very good, Adva. You did well."

Tamar staggered and was feeling woozy.

"Tamar, don't you dare abandon me now!" Zipporah chastised as she placed the child in Tirzah's arms. "You can begin to feed her if you would like."

Tirzah's eyes filled with tears as she held the child tight and she began to sob. Her chest felt heavy and she continued to find it difficult to breathe. She had wanted a boy child for her husband so badly. She was beyond sad; she felt disappointed and defeated. Ziva tried to console her mother. "All is well, Mother, we have another sister. What do you want to name her?"

"She is Mara," Tirzah spat.

"Mother, that means bitterness. She is a blessing and very healthy. Listen to her cry," said Ziva.

"This was my last chance for a boy. I will have no more babies. She is Mara to me. You can call her what you like," Tirzah whispered in disgust.

Zipporah took and cradled the child in her lap to cut and tie the cord. As she finished, she returned the baby to Tirzah who did as she knew to do. The child began suckling without trouble. "Girls, I need you to help with one more thing. We must take the afterbirth. Tirzah, can you give me one more good push? We need to make sure you are clean inside. Tamar, stay the course. You must finish this task. You cannot quit now, do you understand?" Tamar nodded, determined but queasy. As Tirzah pushed and Zipporah pulled at the cord, Tamar fell to the ground. "Ziva, come take your sister's place!" Ziva went around the chair and dragged her sister out of the way so she could hold her mother's leg in position.

As Zipporah finished delivering the afterbirth, the baby continued to feed at Tirzah's breast. Tirzah was pale and sad. Her tears had stopped, but she had a dark countenance about her. Zipporah tried to pull the baby from the breast, but she could not pry her loose as the milk bubbled in the corners of her mouth. "Your child eats right away. This is good, Tirzah. She will be another strong woman. *Elohim* has blessed you again."

Soon Zipporah was able to wash the child and fully examine the fingers and toes. She wrapped and gave the babe to Adva. Zipporah moved to examine Tirzah by pushing on her belly. With this gentle pressure, blood and fluid began to pour from Tirzah's body. As a large clot fell to the bowl beneath the chair, Zipporah looked concerned. "Adva, have you touched any blood? Are you clean?"

"Yes, I am clean. I have only touched Mother."

"Take the child to your father for his blessing. Tell him Tirzah will return in eighty days, then get some yarrow leaves for the tea that your mother needs," directed Zipporah.

Tamar stirred. She made it to the waste pot and vomited. She also looked pale. "Tamar, lie down on the straw. I will make a different tea for you. Have you started your womanly rest? You are usually first," said Adva.

"Not yet," Tamar replied. Adva looked down at the baby and smiled. The baby gave a hiccup. Adva laughed and she gripped the baby tightly for the descent to the house below.

"Father," Adva spoke tenderly, "You are blessed with another daughter."

Eleazar opened his arms to receive the child. He opened her blanket and looked her over then returned to her face. He smiled as her eyes opened to behold him for the first time. "How is your mother? What does she want to call the child?" he asked with a tender voice.

Adva squirmed a bit and replied, "Mother calls her Mara and is very upset that she did not give you a son."

"I cannot call her Mara. It is not this child's fault that we did not have a boy. I think we will call her Miriam, the name of Moses' sister, the prophetess. What do you think of that name?"

"That is a beautiful name. I need to get some herbs from the garden for Mother. Can you hold Miriam?"

"Yes, it would be my pleasure," doted Eleazar, mesmerized by his new daughter.

Levi came from the other side of the room. Adva had not noticed him there, smiling at her. "May I help you in the garden?" Levi asked.

"Yes, Havilah and Abigail can come with us," she replied seeking permission from her father. Eleazar nodded his approval. As Adva stepped out the door, Havilah ran to her. Adva held up her hand. "We have a sister, Miriam. Mother is doing well, but I need some herbs to help with the bleeding. Do we have fresh lemons in the house or in the barn?"

"They are in the house, fresh from the Sychar market," said Levi. "The lemons are on the table."

"Do you need my help?" asked Havilah.

"Yes, follow us to the herb garden. I will show you the leaves we use for Mother's tea."

Adva and Levi headed quickly to the herb garden, leaving Havilah and Abigail behind them. It wasn't until they got to the garden that they realized they were alone. Adva noticed how natural it felt to have him by her side, but she tried to focus on the yarrow leaves so they could return quickly. Levi brushed a strand of hair from her face and gazed at her with longing in his heart. Her hands trembled as she grabbed the leaves she needed. "Levi, we must return," Adva said. "We should not be here alone."

As Havilah came walking up the path with Abigail, Adva pointed to the plant she was picking. "Oh, the yarrow plant. Of course, I knew this from the birthing of Levi's goats. You could have asked me to get them for you."

"I will send you next time. Always take leaves from three different plants. Never the same plant," Adva directed.

Abigail held up her arms. Adva gave the herbs to Havilah and brought Abigail to her hip, placing the child between herself and Levi. They walked quietly back to the house. "Levi, when I go back to the rooftop I will not come back down until eight days have passed," Adva said when they approached the doorway.

"I will talk to you from the courtyard every day," promised Levi.

"Tamar and Ziva will not return either. We made enough soup to last most of the time we are away. But a butchered lamb would be nice. Or perhaps if you take Zipporah back to town, you could visit Benjamin and his father for some beef. How much water did you get today? Will you go to the well tomorrow? You could take the cart. Ask Father. Here, you take Abigail. I must go."

"Adva," Levi said, pausing to look at her again. Adva looked at him, puzzled. "I love saying your name. Adva, do not worry. I will take care of things with your father. The time will pass quickly."

When Adva entered the house, there were five bowls of soup and a cup of hot water on the table. Miriam was in a basket on the table sleeping and sucking at her fist. Havilah and Abigail looked at the baby in amazement. Adva washed the yarrow leaves and cut a lemon. She put the yarrow leaves in the cup of hot water and squeezed the half lemon into the water. She put the other half lemon on the tray. In another cup, she combined dried mint leaves and some honey for Tamar.

"Who is the other tea for?" asked Levi.

"Tamar," said Adva. "She fainted during the birth. You know she does not do birthings very well."

"Yes, I remember," laughed Levi.

"How is your mother?" asked Eleazar.

"She is doing well. I will take our tea. Levi, will you carry the tray with the soup?" Levi bowed low to her request and followed her up the stairs. "I will return for Miriam because she will need to eat soon. Zipporah will come down when she is finished with Mother."

When Adva stepped out onto the rooftop, it was scattered with drying cloths and Ziva was busy washing others to add to the collection. She wrung out the cloths and laid them to dry. Then she proceeded to pour the bloody wash water over the back of the house and refill the wash bowl with new water.

"Come Ziva, take a moment to eat your soup. Levi, you must not come any farther. It is unclean." replied Adva.

Levi looked about the rooftop and saw the tasks at hand. He put the tray next to the doorway and turned to descend the stairs. "I will bring you some more wood," he offered.

"How are Mother and Tamar?" asked Adva.

"They are both resting. Tamar has now started her time of rest," replied Ziva. "I will take her tea to her."

A short distance away, Zipporah continued to care for Tirzah. "Tirzah, drink this tea. Tirzah! Adva, help me wake her," stated Zipporah.

"Mother, I need you to wake up, eat, and drink," Adva begged. Tirzah's eyes opened slowly. She tried to focus on who was speaking to her.

"Adva, hold the cup to her mouth and make her drink the tea. She has lost a lot of blood."

Eleazar walked up the stairs with the crying infant and knocked at the door. "Adva, Zipporah," he said. "Someone needs to get this baby to her mother."

Ziva replied to her father, "I am coming!"

"Adva, keep your mother drinking," said Zipporah. "She must finish it so that she can nurse. Try to wake her." Zipporah placed the afterbirth in a bag for Ziva to give to Eleazar for burial. Ziva carried it to the door and gave the bag to her father, receiving the crying baby in the basket in the other hand. Miriam began to wail, which woke Tirzah.

When Tirzah finished her tea, she was more alert and ready to nurse. She opened her blanket to allow the child to suckle. The child fought to latch onto the breast, and Tirzah helped Miriam to get a good fit. The baby whimpered, then sighed. Tirzah huffed, "I would like to lie down after she is finished. I am cold."

"Mother, you can have some hot soup which will warm you. Then you can rest," said Adva, looking at Zipporah.

"Tirzah, we will get you dressed and you will have to walk around the roof a few times. We need to reduce the swelling in your legs. Your body will begin to adjust soon."

Zipporah added ashes from the fire pit to the bowl of blood below the birthing chair to absorb the liquid and to study the blood clots, for there were many. She was concerned for Tirzah but did not tell the others on the rooftop. It was in *Elohim's* hands. "Tirzah, are you feeling pain anywhere?" Zipporah asked as she stirred the bowl.

Tirzah took a moment while nursing Miriam to take inventory of the child's fingers and toes. "I am exhausted. My chest is tight and I am still having difficulty breathing. But my pain is minimal. I just need sleep."

Miriam had finished eating and had fallen asleep. Zipporah took the baby and laid her next to Tamar for warmth in the corner of the rooftop room. Tamar smiled and played with her little fingers and toes.

"Adva, get your mother's clothes and help me clean and dress her. Ziva, wash the chair and put it over there to give yourselves more room to lie down. I will use the chair to examine Tirzah again tomorrow. I do not need it for another family at this time," said Zipporah. After a walk around the rooftop, Zipporah and Adva helped Tirzah lie down in the western corner of the room, away from the door and the steps. They placed a sack of straw to raise her legs and a blanket under her head. Once she was comfortable, she fell asleep.

Zipporah pulled Adva away from the others to talk on the other side of the roof. "Adva, make sure that you walk your mother around the roof at every feeding. Continue to elevate her legs during this night. I will be back to visit tomorrow morning. You have been helpful today; you are a strong woman. Continue to be brave and vigilant. I am going to have Levi take me home so that he knows the way to come for me if you should need me."

"Thank you," replied Adva. Zipporah picked up her things and proceeded to the floor below. The room was dark and empty, and the hearth was cold. She stepped out the front door. Havilah was playing with Abigail at the front of the barn. Adva watched from the roof.

"Where is your father?" asked Zipporah.

"He and Levi went to bury something."

"Yes, of course."

"Is Mother well? I saw you walking her around the rooftop."

"Your mother is needing to rest and heal. Abigail and Miriam have been hard on her. *Adonai* will restore her, but it may take a while. Serve her well."

Eleazar and Levi were walking back into the courtyard. Giving his tools to Levi, Eleazar spoke to Zipporah. Havilah, Abigail, and Levi went to the barn to give the adults time to themselves. "You are finished so soon. I am glad we did not tarry at the market today," said Eleazar.

"Your wife will take a while to heal from this child. She should not have any more children, but I told you that after Aaron was born. I will be back tomorrow, and I have given instructions to Adva for her care. We must reduce the swelling in her legs and feet. The tea that Adva makes is good for that, but Havilah may have to help get the herbs, as Adva is now unclean. Keep hot water going for the first day. She must continue to drink the tea. She should not be left alone with the baby during her eighty days, as she is very ill and distressed about not having a son. I pray the angels attend her while I am gone. Please have Levi take me home so that he can come to get me if I am needed. You may come day or night. There are no other women in Sychar who are ready to give birth."

Levi returned from the barn with Shem and the cart to take Zipporah home. Eleazar offered to help her onto the cart. "Eleazar, I am unclean until sunset," stated Zipporah. "I will sit in the back of the cart on some straw. Since I will need the chair for my visit tomorrow, it can stay with you until then." Eleazar put straw in the back of Shem's cart and brought a stool to step on. Zipporah smiled at his kindness as she put her bag in the back of the cart and stepped onboard.

"Zipporah, if you could scoot to the front of the cart, it would help Shem to pull you better and we can talk without shouting," stated Levi.

"The cart will be unclean until sunset. Burn the straw in the fire when you return. Eleazar, my son will bring me out tomorrow, but the next day is Sabbath. Be vigilant," Zipporah said to the two men.

Adva watched from the rooftop and Ziva came to stand beside her. "Everyone is sleeping inside our room," said Ziva.

"This is good," said Adva. They watched as Levi pulled away, and Eleazar sat down on the bench by the barn door. Havilah and Abigail joined him. He drew them close in a hug. He then tickled Abigail and made her giggle. Smiling as he looked up to the rooftop, he was surprised to find his daughters watching him. He waved and then rose to come closer to chat with them.

"How is your mother?" inquired Eleazar.

"She is sleeping. So are Miriam and Tamar in the room that Levi built for us," answered Ziva.

"Yes, praise *Elohim* for Levi's carpentry. His gift was right on time," praised Eleazar.

"Father, I need Havilah to go to the herb garden for me, and we need more wood on the roof for the night. When Tamar wakes up, I will rest so that I can be awake for the night and help Mother. Ziva or Tamar will be awake to receive food in the morning. We will need water for laundry tomorrow. Can Levi go to the well for the family tomorrow? He can fill the water jugs again," stated Adva.

"It sounds like you have a good plan, Adva. *Adonai* has blessed you with wisdom. Go and rest. I will have Havilah come up in a moment and I will bring your wood."

"Thank you, Father," answered Adva.

During the night, Adva changed Miriam and made sure that Tirzah fed the baby. Her mother's breath was labored. Adva remembered to have her walk about the rooftop after every feeding. After each walk, she rubbed scented olive oil on Tirzah's feet and legs, helping her to go back to sleep. The swelling seemed to be going down slowly. In between feedings, Adva washed Miriam's and Tirzah's cloths. There were still large blood clots on her mother's cloths. Miriam's output was good and seemed healthy. The cool night air made Adva's hands chapped and red as she wrung out the cloths and hung them to dry, but the smell of her soap made the chore more tolerable.

Very early in the morning before the sun came up, there was a faint knock on the rooftop door soon after Adva had put her mother back to bed. Adva opened the door to find Havilah with a tray of fruit and hot bread.

"What are you doing up?" asked Adva.

"I can hear you walking about up here on the roof. It is louder when Mother is walking too. I know you have had a long night, and I wanted to feed you so that you can sleep. I will stay with you a moment before going to make breakfast for the men," said Havilah.

"Thank you. I am sorry that I am making so much noise," replied Adva.

"I am worried about Mother," stated Havilah.

"She seems to be healing. Her feet are less swollen. *Elohim* will be her healer."

"Yes, how is Miriam?" asked Havilah.

"She is beautiful. You're going to love her. I just hope that Mother loves her too."

"What do you mean?" asked Havilah.

"Mother has rejected Miriam because she is not a boy child. I have talked with Zipporah about it. She is praying that she comes to her senses. It is too soon to tell if it is causing problems for Miriam. Just pray about it with me. I do not want to tell Father. It will be a long eighty days," said Adva.

9
Celebration

Finally, the eighty days had been fulfilled. Adva, Tamar, and Ziva decided it was a day for celebration and planned a feast for the evening meal to celebrate Tirzah's return. Levi had cured a lamb for the event. He had chosen the branches from pruning the apple trees to smoke the lamb. Zipporah had arrived early in the day and was performing an exam with Tirzah and Miriam on the roof.

"Adva, could you have your father come join us on the roof please?" Zipporah called from the door at the top of the stairs.

"Yes, of course," replied Adva.

Adva went to the barn to look for Father. She did not see Levi or Father. Shem was in his stall and brayed at her, hoping for attention. "Not now Shem, I must find Father."

Adva walked out back and looked toward the fields and saw smoke from the workshop. It was hard to think of that space as a workshop now, full of tools and large pieces of wood for the men to craft into furniture. She walked toward them. The door was wide open and she stood there unnoticed for a few minutes. It was a beautiful thing to watch her father and Levi at work.

"Adva, do you need me?" asked her father.

"Yes," she replied, shaking herself back to attention. "Zipporah wants to talk to you on the roof."

"I will be there right away," he said as he washed his hands in the bowl nearby. The scent of one of Adva's soaps mingled with the musk of sweat and sawdust. At that moment, Adva decided that she liked the smell of men at work.

Levi came close and smiled at Adva, wiping his hands on a cloth. "Are you curious?" he asked.

"Yes, I am," stated Adva.

"Good, but I will not tell you. You must go away. Shoo. Now go with your father." Levi shut the door behind Adva and her father, who was also smiling at the two of them.

Zipporah and Tirzah were watching them walk from the woodshed. Tirzah usually loved coming back to her husband after the eighty days, but today there was a fear and reluctance that suffocated her. Although Zipporah had given her a clean bill of health, Tirzah knew something was not right. The swelling had almost returned to normal. She needed things to do. She was glad to return to her kitchen and her duties on the farm.

"Eleazar, bring another chair with you, please," said Zipporah. "Adva, can you take Miriam down with you to the kitchen?"

"Yes, of course," replied Adva.

"Bring the baby sling we used for Abigail," Tirzah added.

Adva went to the rooftop first. Miriam was sleeping soundly.

"Come close so that we can put the wrap around you."

"She is sleeping soundly, why must I carry her?"

"Adva, Miriam needs to be close to you. She is not eating well. Your mother is not able to carry her right now," stated Zipporah. They put the wrap around Adva and placed Miriam in the sleeve next to Adva's heart. Miriam shifted and sighed. "You and Tamar can take turns carrying Miriam like this when she isn't feeding, Miriam will tell you which one of you she prefers," Zipporah continued. Adva adjusted the baby's weight across her chest. The baby sighed again.

Eleazar came to the roof and Adva walked down the stairs carefully. Her balance was off with the added load.

"May I hold her?" asked Havilah.

"We will let her sleep, and when I change her, you can hold her for a while. What is left for us to do for our feast? Tamar, you get to wear this wrap after dinner. Miriam needs to hear a heartbeat. Zipporah says she is not eating well. I don't think I want to be a mother yet."

"I know I am not ready to be a mother yet," said Tamar.

"I think you both will be ready when the time comes," Levi chimed in from the doorway. "How do you want to cook the lamb?" he asked. "She is ready for the pot."

"I think that pot over there will work well," said Adva.

"Show me which one," said Levi.

"Oh, my word, this one," Adva replied. Levi stepped in front of her and tossed the lamb into the pot. With a playful smirk, he grabbed her hands and turned her about. "Be careful, Levi. I have the baby."

"I know. That makes you even more beautiful," Levi said, then whispered in her ear. "One day you will carry our baby and we will celebrate in many ways on our eighty-day reunion."

Adva wrapped her arms over Miriam and her face turned crimson. At that moment, the roof door opened and Adva turned to stir the pot. Everyone else stood around the table to witness Tirzah's return. Zipporah descended the steps first, followed by Eleazar who held Tirzah's hand. Tirzah blinked her eyes to get used to the darker room. Levi pulled out her stool at the table. "We are preparing you a feast, Mother Tirzah. I hope you are hungry," announced Levi.

He glanced at Adva, who blushed once again thinking about what he whispered to her, then back at Tirzah.

Tirzah was wearing the tunic Adva had made for her, which was skillfully embroidered with leaves, vines, and grapes. When Tirzah reached the bottom of the stairs, Eleazar kissed her forehead. "You made it back to our home," said Eleazar. "I am blessed indeed."

"Zipporah, would you like to stay to celebrate Tirzah's return, or would you like us to give you a ride home now?" asked Levi.

"I would like to go home if that will not delay your celebration too much," said Zipporah.

"I will hitch up the cart and we will be on our way," said Levi. "Who would like to go with us?" he asked.

"Me!" squealed Abigail.

"So be it, princess! Anyone else?" asked Levi.

"I would," said Tamar.

"I would like to go, but I have the baby," replied Adva. "Ziva, will you stay and help me with the meal?"

"Yes, of course," Ziva replied, doing a spin and a bow to Adva.

"I need some more wood for the fire," said Adva.

"I have an idea. Tirzah, do you want to ride to town and back?" asked Eleazar.

"No, I better not. The child will want to feed again soon. I'm sorry, Eleazar," Tirzah replied tenderly.

"Well then, will you walk with me to the woodshed? I will show you the new things in the workshop and retrieve the firewood that Adva needs. Besides, I would love to have some time alone with you. I have missed you," courted Eleazar.

Tirzah looked at her husband tenderly and spoke, "Yes, I would enjoy that." Eleazar got Zipporah's shawl and one for Tirzah. He opened the door and gave the wraps to the women.

Levi had the cart pulled into the courtyard. He gently lifted Tamar to her place on the other side of Abigail, who sat in the middle. Tamar squealed at Levi's strength. "Tamar, I must ask that you sit in the back until Mother Zipporah has arrived at her home," stated Levi.

"Yes, of course," she said climbing over into the cart.

"Havilah, do you want to come?" asked Levi.

She asked, "Father, may I?"

"Yes, go and get back soon," answered Eleazar. He grabbed Tirzah's hand and escorted her to the woodshed.

Levi helped Zipporah onto the seat of the cart, then lifted Havilah into the back with Tamar.

"Adva, we will be back soon, and we will be hungry," said Levi, as he waved to her.

"Yes, of course," Adva said, then turning to Ziva, "What can we do to make this place more beautiful while everyone is gone?"

"I'll get the lamp from the rooftop and the other chair for cleaning. Adva, do you have a cloth for the table? Get some fruit and put it in a bowl on the table. Do you have some scented oil we can add to the lamp?" asked Ziva, her creative juices flowing.

Miriam stirred in her wrap as her fist found its way to her mouth. "We best hurry with preparations. Miriam will want attention soon."

Adva took a sharp knife and cut some meat and fat from the loin of the lamb. She added some rosemary from her dried herbs. She added seasoned olive oil to the stew and stirred the vegetables that had settled to the bottom of the pot. She added more water to the stew as it would take another hour for Levi to return. She also got Tirzah's tea steeping for her return from the shed.

When Eleazar opened the door to the house, Tirzah was laughing. But her countenance instantly changed when she heard Miriam crying. "Mother, we have changed her for you. You may rest in your nursing chair behind the curtain," stated Adva.

"The child calls for me," said Tirzah. "Mara, my child." Eleazar watched his wife take the child from Adva and bitterly make her way to the separate room. Miriam cried louder at the touch of her mother.

"Father, what shall we do?" asked Adva once Tirzah had left the room. "It isn't Miriam's fault, and it makes me so sad to see Mother this way."

"I will try to talk with her. I do not think feeding time is the best time to do that. I hope they will work it out," said Eleazar. "*Adonai*, help us."

After a while, Tirzah came back into the kitchen and Miriam was crying softly. "She won't eat anymore. Here you take her," said Tirzah, thrusting Miriam into Adva's arms. "I will finish dinner."

"Dinner is finished. We are just waiting for the cart to return. Would you like your tea?" asked Adva.

"Here Mother, rest yourself. Look at the table we have set for you," said Ziva. "Isn't it lovely?"

"Yes, you did a wonderful job in dressing this home and making it beautiful," Tirzah said as she sipped her tea and closed her eyes, trying to drown out the sound of Miriam's cry.

Adva took the baby outside for a walk around the courtyard. She could see the cart in the distance heading towards them. She talked and cooed to Miriam who stopped crying and let out a big sigh.

Eleazar stepped outside to check if he could see the cart returning. He noticed that Adva had calmed the child quickly. "You are this child's lifeline. Do not take this role lightly.

She will die without your help, Adva. I have seen the ewe reject her lamb. Your mother is doing the same thing. The next thing to happen will be that her milk will dry up. I pray that does not happen with your mother, as I do not know of a wet nurse in Sychar who would take our child. Zipporah left some herbs to keep her milk flowing if we need to use them. Do you think that is why Miriam is crying?"

"No, she is not sucking her fist. She is now resting," said Adva. "Father, she is beautiful. I do not know how a mother can reject her own child."

"Adva, I do not understand these things either. I thought I had your mother back, but when we returned from the woodshed, the cloud of darkness came over her instantly. It is in *Adonai's* hands."

Abigail was laughing as the group returned from town. Adva and Levi exchanged smiles. Eleazar saw the love light in the eyes of Adva and Levi, but there was also a love light in Tamar's eye. Levi would be a great husband to either of his daughters, but which daughter should be his wife? In any case, he was pleased to have him at the family home. In a few months, Malachi would return and things would get difficult again. But for now, he had to focus on the work in front of him. Tirzah needed him.

"Who is that in the cart with Havilah?" asked Eleazar.

Ziva came running out of the house, "Benjamin!"

"Well, now we have everyone," said Adva, "Let the feast begin."

Adva went inside and added a chair to the table and told Mother that Benjamin had come. Adva laid Miriam in a basket near her chair. She and Tamar would care for Miriam.

"Hello, Mother Tirzah," said Benjamin. "My family sends their congratulations. You are blessed indeed. We will send some beef once the lamb is finished."

"Your family is too kind. Thank you," Tirzah replied, biting back the bitterness that welled up in her throat.

The family dined and danced until late that night. Benjamin would stay in the barn with Levi for the night as was discussed with Benjamin's family. When the lamps went out, everyone was tired and ready for sleep. Tirzah fed the child and gave her to Adva to keep close during the night. Adva looked at Tamar, Ziva, Havilah, and Abigail all piled together in the middle of the floor. She took a blanket and Miriam in her basket up to the roof. The baby slept for five hours before beginning to squirm. Adva changed her on the roof before taking her to her mother.

Tirzah rolled over in the bed and placed Miriam under her breast. Miriam held onto the breast with both hands. She ate her fill quickly, then Tirzah returned the child to Adva.

"She should sleep another four hours if you want to sleep on the roof. I will tell the others not to disturb you."

"Thank you, Mother. It is getting crowded on the floor."

"Yes, I think it is. Good night, Adva."

"Good night, Mother."

10
Damascus

During the next monthly confinement of all the women of the house, Eleazar thought it would be a good time for him to visit some merchants in Damascus. He would stay with Master Lamech, Malachi's father, and get to know them better. During this time, Levi would also take a trip to Sebaste, leaving the women to enjoy the whole house to themselves. Before departing, Eleazar and Levi filled every container in the house with water. Benjamin sent some beef and promised to look in on the family every day while the other men were away.

Havilah enjoyed feeding the animals and tending the herb garden. No other crops needed attention; they had either not yet been planted or were not ready for harvest.

Abigail liked having a younger sister. Each day she would brush Miriam's hair for what seemed like hours. Miriam loved it too, and the two sisters bonded in ways that no one yet understood. Abigail talked gibberish and Miriam seemed to understand. Levi and Eleazar had made a crib for the two young sisters to share. It was their private space. Often Abigail would be on her side with Miriam next to her. Miriam's ear would be close to Abigail's chest, and Abigail would twirl her sister's hair in her fingers as they slept. Abigail's closeness helped Miriam sleep through the night, and during the day Abigail rarely left Miriam's side. It was Abigail who let Adva know if Miriam needed something and most times before Miriam even began to cry.

While on the roof, Tamar and Ziva made a few new baskets to sell in the market. Baskets were good to weave during their womanly rest because the reeds were frequently immersed and made clean. After their rest, the three oldest sisters and Tirzah decided to process the flax in the barn. They worked from dawn to dusk, and by the time Eleazar returned there were large empty spaces in the barn and several large sacks of thread for Adva and Tirzah to weave into blankets and fabric. Adva had begun her black and white blanket. Tamar and Ziva wanted one for their own.

Adva teased, "If I don't like this one, you can have it. I'm not sure how I feel about it yet. If so, I will buy more wool from Malachi and make another one." She knew that she was going to keep this one.

Eleazar returned with gifts for the women. He had sold everything he had taken to market, and he was pleased that he was able to buy Tirzah a gold bracelet.

"I met with Malachi's family," said Eleazar at the midday meal. "You will love his father, Lamech, and his younger brother, Caleb, who still lives at home. Unfortunately, Malachi was not there during my visit. They are such kind people. Master Lamech is a merchant in Damascus very well known for gathering items from other countries. The marketplace there is huge. There were camels and donkeys, and I even saw an elephant.

"Father, what is an elephant?" asked Havilah.

"I am so glad you asked. Here is an elephant for you." Eleazar handed Havilah a soapstone carving of an elephant.

"Oh my! Father, this is the most beautiful thing I have ever seen," squealed Havilah. "What is this part called?"

"That is the elephant's trunk. *Elohim* knew that the legs and feet of the elephant would not allow him to reach and grab his food so *Elohim* gave the elephant a trunk to reach and grab for things like our arms and hands do."

"That is amazing," gasped Havilah.

"The merchant said it was carved in Asia. The elephant's feet are this big around." Eleazar held his hands apart as big as his plate. "I have something for everyone. I gave your mother a gold bracelet, did you see it? I brought a hairbrush for Abigail. Isn't it lovely? It is made from a gourd that sounds like rain when you brush your hair."

"Papa. Ooooh," Abigail said, loving the sound of the new hairbrush.

"Abigail said my name. When did that happen?"

"She has been talking more now that Miriam is here," said Adva with a smile. "They are inseparable."

"I am a blessed man!" exclaimed Eleazar, clutching his heart.

"Ziva and Tamar, I have silk scarves for you. You may choose one or share them all."

One scarf was sea blue. Another was orange. Another one was red. The last was of a courser fabric with embroidered leaves and beadwork.

The girls grabbed at the scarves and ran their hands over the smooth fabric. They had many questions about the material and how it was made from worms.

"I could learn an Egyptian scarf dance," declared Ziva, dancing around the table with the red and orange scarves.

"I'm not sure that Benjamin would approve," stated Tamar, snatching the orange one.

"Let me see that one," said Adva, as she grabbed the one with embroidery and beadwork. "This is beautiful workmanship. Father, I want to learn how to do this kind of work."

"That fabric is made from a small goat's undercoat and the embroidery is done with dyed wool fibers. That is a shawl for your mother. But the gift I bought for you is this."

Eleazar handed her a small, wooden box. Adva rolled it over and over in her hand trying to figure out how to open it. Finally, she found that the lid slid open, and inside were seven needles of various sizes. Some were carved from soapstone like Havilah's gift and the smallest were carved from bone.

"Father, these are perfect!" Adva exclaimed as she leaped from her chair to hug her father and kiss his cheek. "Mother, we can sew more quickly with these needles. Father, thank you. Did you see we processed the flax while you were gone?"

"I did notice the barn was clean of flax. You have been busy. Did you have any trouble while I was gone? Did Benjamin come and visit?"

"Yes," Tirzah replied. "One day Benjamin came with Joseph and his wife, Deborah. We were a mess from the flax that day. We invited them to stay for the midday meal. It was a lovely visit. We should visit them one day soon."

"Yes, we should. By the way, I gave a message to one of the merchants going on to Sebaste to let Levi know that I have returned home. I am sure he will return soon if things are well for his family."

Tamar replied, "Thank you for doing that. I have missed him, haven't you, Adva?"

Eleazar looked at Adva. She thought for a moment. She had not missed anyone. Her life had been so busy that she had not even missed her father. It was hard to believe that Miriam was now four months old.

"I suppose Malachi will be back soon to shear his sheep. It will be good to have everyone back," Adva replied, avoiding Tamar's question. But she did not fool her father.

Eleazar would speak to her soon about betrothal options. He had not told her about Malachi's ultimatum from his last visit, and he did not think Adva understood that he had gone to Damascus to inquire about a betrothal.

"Yes, Lamech seemed to think that we would see Malachi before he came to Damascus, saying he was rarely in Damascus and always eager to leave for Mt. Ebal when he was there," said Eleazar. He watched for Adva's reaction, but she was more interested in tending to Abigail and Miriam than thinking about Malachi or Levi.

"Master Malachi likes the outdoors. Do you think his wife will have to travel with his sheep?" asked Ziva.

"Oh no, that would be terrible! However, Adva does like to sleep under the stars on the roof," said Tamar, still assuming Adva would marry Malachi.

"What? I heard my name," asked Adva. "What are you talking about?"

"Never mind," said Eleazar and Tamar simultaneously. They looked at each other and laughed. So did Tirzah, Havilah, and Ziva who had been listening. Adva blushed and went back to tending Miriam and Abigail by the table. Abigail was gently brushing Miriam's hair with her new brush while Miriam sucked at her fist.

"Mother, I think Miriam is going to need to nurse soon," said Adva.

"Yes, it is close to that time. Eleazar, will you join us so that I may talk to you in private," requested Tirzah.

"Yes, of course. Girls, can you take everyone outside for a visit to the barn, please? Go ahead and feed Shem and make up the barn for Levi's return," said Eleazar. "I will come to get you when we are finished talking." In a short while, Eleazar brought Miriam out in her basket and gave her to Adva and returned inside the house without saying much at all. Ziva and Tamar were busy making Levi's bedroom clean and comfortable for his return.

Adva asked Havilah if she would like to go to the herb garden with Abigail and Miriam. Adva sat Miriam's basket in the shade and Abigail climbed into it. The two snuggled into the blanket for a nap. Miriam instantly got less fussy and went to sleep. Havilah and Adva went over the plants that Adva had added to the garden and weeded out things that did not belong or had overgrown the area. After a short time, Abigail woke from her nap. Havilah got her out of the basket without waking Miriam.

"How did you do that without waking Miriam?" asked Adva. "Let's go back to the barn. I'm thirsty."

As they approached the house, Eleazar met them on his way out. "I'm sorry girls, I fell asleep. Your mother is still sleeping," he said. He ruffled his hair and tugged at his beard and appeared deep in thought. "Let me see what you have done to welcome Levi."

The next morning Eleazar woke the girls and prepared the fire for breakfast. The girls dressed while their father milked Goshen and returned to the house.

"Adva, today you and I will go to the well to fill all the water pots for our laundry and we will purchase a few things from the market," he declared. "Tamar, you will help your mother with Abigail and Miriam. Do not let them out of your sight. Ziva, you will prepare our midday meal. Havilah, you will tend to the animals and the barn. Your mother is resting. We will wake her when breakfast is ready."

Adva began to collect the water pots to take to the well and placed them by the door. She also braided her hair and prepared herself for a trip to town. It had been a long time since she had been to town. To her surprise, she was excited to be going and eager to have a morning with her father by herself. She had missed those times so much.

Tamar dressed Abigail and Miriam. She took Miriam to feed with Tirzah. Havilah helped Ziva with breakfast and gathered some apples from the root cellar in the barn. She fed and watered Shem and the goats.

Eleazar took the pots to the bench by the barn and gathered more pots from the barn. He brought wood from the shed, stacked it by the wash area, and brought another load of wood into the house for cooking.

Tirzah joined them for breakfast. Tamar had shared some of her cheese with the family and Havilah's bread was sweetened with honey, apples, walnuts, and raisins. It was delicious.

Soon after breakfast and while the sun was beginning to rise, the cart was loaded with water jars and Eleazar and Adva rode to the well.

"Father, it has been a long time since I walked to the well to fetch water. I have been caring for Mother and the little ones for two years."

"Yes, it is true that life has taken much of your childhood away. I am thankful you were able to do all that you have done. I brought you on this trip to ask you some important questions." Adva looked at her father with questioning eyes. He sighed, "When Malachi was with us last spring, before Levi came to stay with us, he and I had just finished putting up the barley for the night. It was raining. Do you remember?"

"Yes, I had just begun my first womanly rest. He left without saying goodbye to our family," said Adva quietly.

"Well, the night before he left, he was concerned that you were in danger of losing your purity by coming into womanhood without a declared husband. He was concerned that he would lose you to Levi in his absence. He told me that he would return in the spring to ask for you once again. And he said that if I refused him, he would leave and never return. Adva, I went to Damascus to speak with Malachi's father, Lamech. I wanted to see if a betrothal was an option for you. Malachi's family is willing to welcome you to their family."

"Oh. I should have realized that was the purpose of your trip," said Adva.

"Adva, do you feel that Malachi is the husband for you? I am not sure that Malachi has stolen your heart. I have seen a look of love in your eyes for Levi, but I also see that you have not missed him during his time away. What is your heart telling you?"

"Father, I do not get a chance to listen to my heart. My day is filled with household chores and children that are not mine. I do not have a husband to share these things with. I do not have time to dream. I do not sit and giggle with Ziva and Tamar about a life with Levi or Benjamin. In some ways, it feels as if I am already married," confessed Adva.

"Yes, I see that. Hopefully, Tirzah will be able to return to her role as mother and matriarch. Then you will be free to marry. However, I promised Baruch, Levi's father, that I would choose a daughter for Levi by spring. My time to choose is upon me. He may be on his way to our home to demand an answer and finish the betrothal. I want to know your heart. You are my first-born. You have a right to help decide your future husband."

"In some ways, Malachi has pursued me and declared that I am his for so long that I do not feel I have a choice. Even my sisters believe that I will marry Malachi. He has convinced almost everyone." There was silence between the two as they made their way to the well. The sky was beginning to turn red and gold.

"Father, I saw Malachi leave last spring. I could make out his figure in the dark as I stood on the roof. There was an eerie understanding that passed between us. We did not wave goodbye or acknowledge that we saw each other, but I knew he was coming back for me. And now I find myself looking for him. On the roof, I look toward Mt. Ebal and search the hills for his sheep. I am expecting him to show up any day. I do not know if I fear the day or look forward to it."

"What about Levi?" asked Eleazar pensively.

Her face glowed as she spoke, "Levi is a delight. He adds so much love to our family. I enjoy having him with us. But I have not missed him as Tamar has stated. I wonder if I treat him as the brother that I never had. During the birth of Miriam, I relied on Levi as a partner. He will make a great father to his children. I see a good man in him. I desire a good man who follows the Samaritan traditions and who will provide for my family, a man who loves my family as his own. I see those qualities in Levi. But I see them also in Malachi, in a different way. Malachi is a hard man to love."

"Malachi has given so much to our family. Last year we could not have managed the barley harvest without him. We would have lost it all to the rain," said Eleazar. "I am grateful to Malachi for showing up at our farm when I need another man's help. He is a hard worker. He chose you for his wife very early. I think he chose our family first then he selected you. He knows what he wants and pursues it tirelessly."

"What does Mother say?" asked Adva.

"We believe that *Elohim* has a special calling for you and we see His spirit upon you. You can calm Miriam with a touch. You know the Law of Moses. You read, you write, and your wisdom abounds. You remain calm in a crisis.

Your mother prays but does not know which man should be your husband," confessed Eleazar. More silence passed between them and they were deep in their own thoughts as they arrived at the well. As a team, they worked hard to fill all the vessels with water. Eleazar hauled water from the well and Adva kept the pots coming until they were all filled. They were leaving the well just as most of the women were arriving.

When they arrived at the market, the merchants were just opening. A rooster crowed from near the blacksmith's shop. Adva enjoyed picking over the fruits and vegetables. She smiled at the merchants, speaking kindly to them, and was surprised that she remembered their names. "Adva, I must go to the blacksmith shop. I will find you soon and we will need to return home," said Eleazar.

Eleazar saw a joy in her face that had not been there yesterday. He watched as the town interacted with her and he noticed how quickly the young men came to talk with her. *She does not see the interest in their eyes. She is so innocent*, thought Eleazar. *She doesn't know how beautiful she is*. Adva spoke with the tailor and admired some cloth from Egypt. She looked at a wool blanket and remembered the blanket she was working on at home. For a moment, she caught herself being prideful; she knew her blanket was a treasure and a work of art.

"Good morning, Asa. Who has made this lovely blanket?" asked Adva.

The merchant beamed. "My daughter, Rebekah, made that one. It is beautiful, yes? It is six dinars," Asa replied.

"Rebekah does good work. May she be blessed," spoke Adva.

"Hello, Adva. Master Asa," said Benjamin with a nod.

"Good morning," replied Asa.

"Adva, may I ask you a question?" asked Benjamin, walking closely beside her.

"Yes, of course," Adva replied walking out into the market.

"Do you think that Ziva will want to live in town when we are married?" asked Benjamin.

"Have you set your sights on Ziva?" inquired Adva with a smile.

"Yes, I think she has set her sights on me as well."

Adva nodded her head in agreement. "I think you are right. Ziva loves all the excitement of town. She would enjoy living here."

"I have made enough money to rent an apartment here on the main street, just above the market. It may be loud and noisy at times."

"Does my father know this?" asked Adva.

"Do I know what?" interrupted Eleazar.

"Hello, Master Eleazar. I was telling Adva that I have money enough to acquire the apartment on the corner for my future bride."

"Do you know which of my daughters has caught your eye?"

"It is no secret that Ziva has stolen my heart. Do you think she will want to live in town?"

"Ziva is going to love living in town. Where will you set up shop?"

"I have asked to rent from the blacksmith, Jacob. We are preparing a place for me to work. I can sharpen knives and farm tools. I can also sharpen the things the blacksmith makes and uses."

"You have chosen an excellent location," said Eleazar, patting him on the shoulder.

"I am hoping that Levi can assist me in building a small shop in the front stall and we will put in a window or door that faces the main street. Do you know when he will return?"

"He will be back any day now. Levi and I will bring supplies and help you set up shop. Have you worked out the final details with Jacob?" They stood in front of Joseph's butcher shop. Joseph stepped out from the back and wiped his hands on a cloth.

"My father and I are still in negotiations with Jacob. I will let you know very soon," replied Benjamin.

"I hear that my son has told you the recent decisions that have been made for him and his future bride," interjected Joseph.

"Yes, this is very exciting news. I will bring Ziva to town and we can finish the betrothal documents. Benjamin, come home with Ziva and Tamar this week and we will talk more. Adva and I will not tell Ziva of your news. Your secret is safe with us," said Eleazar.

"We need to buy a cut of veal," said Adva.

"I will get that for you. It is very fresh. I will double wrap it for you," replied Joseph.

"Thank you, Master Joseph."

"Adva, are you finished here in Sychar?" asked Eleazar.

"Yes Father, we need to return home. There is much to be done," answered Adva.

"Goodbye, Benjamin. Joseph, I will return this week with documents," said Eleazar.

"We will see you soon," said Adva. They hitched Shem to the cart and began their journey home. "I had forgotten how much I enjoy the marketplace. Thank you for the trip to town today." Adva leaned over and kissed her father on the cheek. Eleazar enjoyed making Adva happy.

The whole family was in the courtyard when they arrived. Tirzah sat in the shade by the barn nursing Miriam and Abigail sat by their side. Havilah raced to find a carrot for Shem. Ziva and Tamar stood up from their wash and straightened their backs.

"Where did you find water to wash the laundry?" asked Adva.

"We took the stored water from Shem. I will take your jars to the barn to replace what we took earlier," said Ziva. "We were able to finish in the cool of the day."

Adva took a water pot and the sack of fruit into the house. Tamar followed with another jar of water.

First Eleazar kissed Tirzah on the forehead as he passed, carrying water into the barn. On the second pass, he kissed Havilah who was unhitching Shem. On his third pass, he kissed and tickled Abigail, who giggled loudly, startling Miriam from her feeding. The baby looked up at him with a smile as milk dribbled down her chin.

"Oh, I am a blessed man," exclaimed Eleazar, lifting his face toward the heavens and thumping his fists to his chest.

"What happened in Sychar today?" asked Tirzah.

"Nothing much. I just feel blessed by my house of lovely women. Let's get out of the hot sun and have some refreshments at our table. Adva bought some lovely fruit, and we have fresh water and a new skin of wine from town."

Eleazar poured a cup of wine for Tirzah, Adva, Tamar, and Ziva as Adva poured a cup of water for Havilah and Abigail. He raised his cup and offered a blessing.

"Daughters, it is time to pick your husbands. I can wait no longer. Say you this day whom you choose," demanded Eleazar, drinking from his cup.

Tirzah took a deep drink from her cup and whispered a prayer. She and Eleazar had talked much of the day yesterday about this decision. She had spent the morning praying for a good decision.

"This is good wine. It is sweet," said Tirzah.

"I thought it a good idea that our daughters taste wine with us on this special occasion."

The daughters raised their cups to their mouths. Adva sipped her wine but added water to it. Ziva drank hers like drinking milk. Tamar drank hers quickly because she was thirsty. It wasn't long before they felt the warmth in their stomachs.

"I shall not drink any more of that now. I am too thirsty," said Tamar, pouring water into her cup and drinking it down.

"Yes, I think I will drink water too," said Ziva.

"Well, our girls are not partial to strong drink, Tirzah. Tell me Ziva, to whom do you wish to be betrothed?" asked Eleazar abruptly.

Ziva tucked her head to one side, "I would like to marry Benjamin, Father. He is so sweet. He plans to live in Sychar. I will be close to you and Mother, but I will be able to live in town with the sounds of the market every day. It will be exciting to live there with Benjamin."

"I agree. It will be exciting for you. Does anyone object to Ziva marrying Benjamin?" There were no objections to that match. "Tamar, you do not wish to marry Benjamin?" asked Eleazar.

"Father, I do not feel for Benjamin the way I do for Levi," she said as her voice carried on dreamily. "Levi is so strong and yet kind. He is a delightful man. Did you know that Levi plans to be the master carpenter in Sebaste? He plans to make his home there. I will have to move away, but I plan to visit often," interjected Tamar. "If I can steal him from Adva, I choose Levi. But I love my sister more than I love Levi."

"I did not know that Levi wanted to live in Sebaste. Did he share that with you?" asked Adva.

"He told me that when we took Zipporah home from her last visit with Mother," stated Tamar.

"If he is sharing with you secrets of his heart, it sounds like he has made his choice too," said Adva.

"You have been so busy caring for everyone that you had no time to listen to Levi. We talked only when in the company of Havilah and Abigail. You know, I always ask questions," replied Tamar. "This is why I know these things and you do not."

"Yes, you always ask questions," replied Adva taking a large drink of her wine. "Father, it appears the only one left for me is Malachi," she sighed.

"That is not true, Adva. Did you see anyone in town who caught your eye?" asked Eleazar. "You talked with several young men. They all found a way to talk with you. I watched them all. Any of them would be willing to bid for your hand. Some spoke to me today and said so. They followed me to the blacksmith shop."

"I was so focused on being in the market that I did not notice anyone in particular," stated Adva, thinking about the young men she had met on her trip to town. "All of those men were strangers to me. I do not know their character. Do you know them or their families? Have they sought to invest in our family in any way? I do not know them like I know Malachi. He is a strong man in might and personality. Malachi says what is on his mind and pursues what he wants at all costs. It may not be easy to be Malachi's wife, but I feel it is my purpose."

"What happened to 'Malachi smells like sheep'?" asked Havilah.

Adva laughed, "Well, I guess I will need to make more soap." They all laughed with her.

"Tirzah, what do you have to say about these decisions?" asked Eleazar.

"I have seen these things take place in our home. I have seen the love light in the eyes of our daughters and their future husbands. I am concerned that Levi will be confused at first. He has pursued Adva from the start. However, I honestly believe that Tamar is the better match for him. Who will tell Levi?" asked Tirzah.

"I will tell him when the time is right," said Eleazar.

"Adva, do we know where Malachi will choose to call home?" asked Tirzah, taking a sip from her cup.

"I do not know. I hope that I will not become a Bedouin," she laughed. "Perhaps I can continue to live here until a home is built for us. Perhaps he has already made arrangements that I do not know of."

All were startled by a knock at the door. "Enter, my friend!" exclaimed Eleazar, feeling festive and thinking that Benjamin could wait no longer. Havilah opened the door. There in the doorway stood Levi and Baruch, behind them was a cart pulled by two oxen and a load of items for the workshop.

"Welcome! *Shalom*! Your timing is perfect! Adva, get more cups and let us pour the wine. We now have guests. Tirzah, have you put the meat in the pot yet?"

Baruch embraced Eleazar at the door, "Eleazar, my good friend, we would like to unload the cart and let our oxen rest in the shade before we sit to eat or drink with you."

"Yes, of course," replied Eleazar.

As the men exited the house, Levi turned to wink at Adva. They walked the oxen and the loaded cart back to the workshop.

"Mother, may Ziva and I return to the barn to fix another bed for Master Baruch?" asked Tamar.

"Please do. And be sure to take the blanket from our bed for our guest," said Tirzah.

"Yes, we will make them very comfortable. Adva, do you have more soap?" asked Ziva.

"Yes, the soap is in the root cellar," Adva replied. After the room had cleared, Adva spoke to Tirzah, "I hope the men speak of the betrothal before they return. I cannot continue to lie to Levi."

"I hope so, too. I pray that *Adonai* has already begun to change his heart's desire."

"Let's make the midday meal with Levi's favorite spices," suggested Havilah.

It took a long while for the men to unload the cart and make the oxen comfortable in the goats' stall and pen. The goats were moved to the outside pen. The oxen were almost too large for the pen but it would do.

When the men had finished their tasks, Eleazar and Baruch entered the house to drink their wine and talk around the table. "Adva, Levi has asked to speak with you by the barn," said Eleazar. "You may talk outside the barn on the bench. Baruch and I will watch you from the table here."

"Thank you, Father," she said, wiping her hands on a cloth and bowing to her elders. Putting her scarf about her head, she propped the door open with a chair and walked to the barn where Levi was waiting for her.

"Hello, Levi," she said quietly.

"Adva," he sighed. "I do not know what to say. Your father says that you have chosen to marry Malachi."

"Are you disappointed?" asked Adva gazing into his green eyes.

"Yes," he said quickly. He began to pace back and forth as she sat on the bench and watched his torment. There was a pause between them.

Adva tried to comfort him and explain, "Levi, when you came to our family with your goats, we all loved you instantly. You belong in our family. I was comfortable with you. I could tell you anything. I could ask you to do anything. You were like one of the family, a brother perhaps.

Mother had been praying for more men to come to our farm so that all of us would make better wives. My sisters and I needed to understand the temperament of men. You were an answer to my mother's prayers."

"Your family was an answer to my prayers," he said coming to sit beside her. "I needed to learn from a master carpenter. Your father has taught me much."

Pausing to change his focus, Levi continued, "Adva, I loved you from the moment you opened the door not so long ago. I love your quiet manner always seeking to do what is right. I loved the care you gave your mother and the young ones. It is difficult for me to change my affections to Tamar."

"Levi, I believe that feelings for Tamar are already in your heart. You have told Tamar about your wanting to live in Sebaste and be a master carpenter. You have told her stories about your sister and mother. She knows the spices you like in your food. She knows your favorite color. She knows how old you were when you started keeping goats. You told her secrets of your heart. I do not know these things."

Levi stood in protest, but then realizing the truth of her statement, he tucked his head down and shuffled his feet in the dust. "Are you truly going to marry Malachi?"

"If that is still his desire," she said with reluctance.

"You do not know?" Levi asked, his voice trembling with the hope that she may change her mind.

"I have not seen Malachi for a year."

"Is there a chance that you would accept my betrothal if he no longer desires you as a wife?"

"Levi, that is not fair to you or Tamar. It does not change that I feel you are like a brother to me. When you marry Tamar, you will become my brother-in-law. I hope you will continue to be my protector and advocate. I love that you challenge Malachi's understanding of women. I may need you to continue to do that. Will you do that for me?"

"Yes, I will continue to do that for you," he promised.

"Thank you, Levi." Adva changed the subject, "Now tell me how you feel about Tamar. What do you like about her?"

"Tamar . . ." he sighed as he looked to the rooftop and found Tamar, Ziva, and Havilah staring back at them. He smiled at the trio on the roof. "We have so many eyes on us. Everything we say and do is being watched."

"Yes," Adva smiled to the ones on the roof, "it is our lookout. We sisters are a package deal. You marry one and you get the others as a bonus."

"I see that," Levi nodded. He took a deep breath and turned his back to the house. "Tamar is beautiful in a different way than you. She likes my jokes when she understands them. She is so inquisitive. It is hard to keep a secret from her. Yes, she knows secrets I have told no one else and I trust her with those secrets. She is blunt in all her remarks and does not hide her feelings. She is the reason I came to your family that day at the well. I do not think Ziva would have suggested that I come to your farm with my goats. I am so thankful to her for that invitation."

"We are too. I trust you to take good care of my sister. You are so kind and tenderhearted. I could not think of a better match for her. You will keep her blunt remarks from being hurtful. You two are like the oxen in the barn and once yoked together, you will pull evenly."

"Adva, again you amaze me with your wisdom. You and I would not have pulled evenly, would we have?"

She shook her head, "I think not."

"Perhaps you are right, and you have saved us from great sorrow," he replied sadly.

"I do not think it was me, but *Elohim* and my mother's prayers. Shall I get Tamar for you?"

"Yes, please," he said, offering Adva his hand to get up from the bench and savoring the opportunity to touch her hand one more time. He raised it to his lips for a gentle kiss.

"Levi, tell Tamar what you think of her. You will win her heart all over again," said Adva as she walked to the house. She paused and yelled up to the rooftop. "Tamar, will you come down please!"

Tamar ran down the stairs and was at the doorway putting on her scarf by the time Adva said "please." She wore the blue scarf that Father had brought back from Damascus. It elegantly framed her face, and she was radiant.

Tamar turned to her father and Master Baruch, "May I talk with Levi now?"

"Yes," replied the two men in unison.

"We will be watching from here. Do not walk off anywhere," said Eleazar.

"Thank you," she said as she bowed low in respect.

Tamar began to run out to the barn, but she tripped on a steppingstone between the barn and the house. As she started to fall with her arms outstretched, Levi's strong arms caught her and he used the momentum to spin her around.

Eleazar and Baruch had jumped from their places and stood in the doorway. "I do not think she needs to be spun to be dizzy," laughed Master Eleazar.

"Are you safe?" called Baruch, showing some tenderness to his soon-to-be daughter-in-law.

"Oh yes, very safe," she said looking into Levi's eyes as he placed her firmly back onto the ground. Levi smiled at her. The two elders went back to their seats at the table laughing at the two young lovers.

Adva went to the herb garden to have a moment away from the house and to escape all the eyes that were watching her. She felt the breeze, smelled the blooms, and listened to the birds. She looked off in the distance to Mt. Ebal. She listened for sheep and Jaspar's bell but heard nothing. But she knew Malachi would be there soon. She remembered his words: "Adva, I am not a bad man. I desire you as my wife and I will never give up on having you as my own." Those words that had once filled her with fear now filled her with hope. More than anything, she wanted a man that would fight for her and never give up. If Levi had truly wanted her at all costs, he would have put up a fight for her. She needed someone with strong convictions of purpose. She hoped her budding love for Malachi would bring some softness to his rough edges. "Malachi, where are you?" she whispered out loud. She picked fresh basil, rosemary, and mint for their meal.

Adva walked back to the house just as Levi and Tamar were returning. When Baruch witnessed his son's seamless transfer of affection, he began to understand what Eleazar had meant earlier in the workshop. *Shalom* fell over the house. Mother Tirzah had prepared a beautiful meal, praying as she cooked. *Adonai* had answered her prayers yet again. She was thankful.

When the table was set, the family raised their voices in prayer: "*The Lord bless you and protect you; the Lord make his face to shine upon you, and be gracious to you; The Lord lift his countenance upon you and give you peace.*"[31]

[31] Numbers 6:24-26. NET.

11
Tirzah

Baruch and Levi returned to Sebaste to prepare a home for Levi and Tamar before they both returned to Sychar for Passover celebrations. After Passover, Levi would stay and continue to work with Eleazar.

Adva's birthday passed with a quiet celebration with the family. The next day everyone worked on the barley harvest as there were no extra men to help this year. It was essential to get the barley harvested before Passover and before the women had their next womanly rest. It would take three days with everyone working at full capacity. On the first day, Tirzah's feet and legs were swollen by the fifth hour and she returned home with the young ones to rest. It was the same on the second day. On the third day, she was breathless at breakfast and did not go to the fields at all. Havilah stayed home with her to help care for the little ones. Eleazar and the older sisters were busy tying the last cuts, they would begin to put it on the cart and be finished by the sixth hour today. Shem brayed and fussed with the flies that bit him. Ziva sang a song to pass the time.

"Papa!" screamed Havilah in the distance. "Papa, it's Mother!"

Eleazar took off as fast as his weary body could take him. "Adva, take charge!"

Adva swallowed her fear and began barking commands, "Ziva, hitch Shem to the cart and bring him over. Tamar and I will finish tying until you bring the cart over." Ziva quickly hitched Shem to the cart and met Adva. "Tamar, get in the back and catch the stalks I throw to you. Stack them in the back of the cart. We will come back when we can do the rest."

The sisters stacked a half cart of barley before going back to the barn.

Eleazar was coming out of the house as they parked in front of the barn. "Who will run for Zipporah?"

"I am the only one who knows where she lives. I will go," said Adva. She took a large drink of water from a water pot and put her scarf about her head and left for town.

Adva ran and walked quickly. She could not go very fast because her body was weary from harvesting barley. As she approached Sychar, she saw Benjamin walking towards her. "Benjamin!" Adva screamed. He paused then started to run towards her. "No! Stop!" screamed Adva. "Go get Zipporah! It's Mother!"

Benjamin ran back to Sychar and alerted Zipporah that Tirzah needed her services and that Adva was coming for her. As Zipporah got her things, Benjamin borrowed Jacob's best horse and wagon. Benjamin and Zipporah met Adva at the city's gate and allowed her to climb aboard.

"What has happened to your mother?" asked Zipporah, as the horse galloped to Adva's home.

"We have been harvesting barley. Mother could not help because her legs were swollen. Today she was breathless and stayed home with Havilah and the little ones this morning. I do not know the rest," said Adva.

"Is she pregnant?" asked Zipporah.

"I do not think so. We are due for our womanly rest next week," replied Adva. "Benjamin, thank you for getting the cart for us. Who owns this cart?"

"It is Jacob's. He is the blacksmith and my new boss," said Benjamin.

"Congratulations," said Adva softly.

They rode the rest of the way in silence. Eleazar was quick to get Zipporah down from the cart and into the house. Benjamin helped Adva down from the cart. He led the horse to the shade and a water trough.

Tirzah was resting in her bed, her mouth pulled to the left and drool fell from her mouth.

"She tries to speak but nothing comes out. She had fallen when Havilah came for me. She cannot walk for her legs are weak," stated Eleazar. "What is wrong? Will she get better?"

"Do you know if she is pregnant?" asked Zipporah.

"I do not think so. She has not been sick as she did with other pregnancies. Her rest is next week."

"Havilah, was your mother having pain?" asked Zipporah.

Havilah closed her eyes and thought about the morning. "We were all seated at the table. Mother got up from the table and said she was going to lie down. She turned but did not make it very far before she fell to the floor. I could not wake her so I ran for Papa," stated Havilah. "When we returned, she was still not awake."

"Can you do anything for her?" Eleazar asked of Sychar's only doctor.

"It is in *Adonai's* hands. I cannot heal her heart. Only *Adonai*," said Zipporah. Hearing her breath rattling in her chest, "Let's try to sit her up in the bed. Do you have another blanket?"

Tamar got a blanket from the shelf. Eleazar raised Tirzah's shoulders off the bed by encircling his arms around her. Tirzah stared into the eyes of her lover and friend, mumbling, "I love you, Eleazar," but no one could understand her. Tamar slid the blanket into place beneath her shoulders and backed away. Eleazar held her close for a moment and whispered his love for her in her ear. Tirzah stopped babbling, gasped for air, then let go with a ragged sigh. She went limp in his arms. Eleazar laid her back against the blanket. He tenderly brushed the hair from her face as her lifeless eyes stared back at him. He studied her face as if trying to memorize it, and he gently closed her eyes as his own welled with tears.

"She is gone," he whispered, choking on the words. As he stepped away from the bed, Zipporah rushed to feel for her heartbeat. There was none. The girls watched in horror, frozen in time.

On his way out of the room, Eleazar was numb with disbelief. "Zipporah, my girls do not know how to dress a body," he said. "Please show them how."

"Yes, I will help them say goodbye and prepare her body for burial," she said quietly.

"Thank you," said Eleazar, continuing out to the barn. Passing Benjamin who was pacing in the courtyard, "Benjamin, Tirzah has left us. Can we use this cart to bury her today? Mine is full of barley." Eleazar did not pause to listen to his answer but continued to walk out to the fields and in a loud voice wailed to *Adonai* in the same way that he had cried out for his son, Aaron. However, there was no one to comfort him but *Ruach Elohim*.[32]

Zipporah and the sisters carried the body to the table using the blanket from the bed. All the girls played a part in washing and dressing their mother for the last time. Abigail lovingly brushed Tirzah's hair, babbling quietly to Miriam who seemed to understand that Tirzah was no longer with them. They placed the embroidered shawl around her

32 Ruach Elohim is the Hebrew name for the Spirit of God, first mentioned in Genesis 1:2.

shoulders. She wore her scarf around her head. She was ready for burial within an hour.

Adva went to the field to find her father. "Father, it is time," she said. Her voice sounded unfamiliar even to herself. "Benjamin has emptied our cart of barley and Shem is hitched to our cart to take mother to her final place of rest. Our cart will be unclean instead of the borrowed cart. Joseph and Jacob have arrived from town. They knew to come because Benjamin had not returned. Is there anything else I should do?" Adva asked.

Eleazar walked back to the house with Adva and beheld his lovely bride on the table. She still took his breath away. He held her lifeless hand, but there was no love there. "My sweet Tirzah," he whispered. He took the blanket and wrapped her tightly as one would wrap a baby in swaddling cloth. When he got to her face and before he covered her for the last time, he kissed her cheek.

The four men loaded the body into the cart. Eleazar, heartbroken and weary from the work in the barley fields, could barely move. His grief made the weariness unbearable. Jacob gathered the reins and led Shem out to the hillside where the family cave was located. Eleazar gave the directions as needed, and those were the only words spoken during their travels.

They had some trouble finding the cave's entrance. Eleazar had not expected to need to use the gravesite so soon, and he had not cleared the site for many years. It was overgrown with vines and blooming weeds. The men had brought some tools with them for moving the stone and lamps to light the inside. Eleazar had not thought to bring anything. Tirzah's body was placed inside very close to Joachim, Eleazar's father. Eleazar also moved Aaron's wrapped body to rest in the arms of his mother. The lamp was removed and the stone was put into place.

Although Eleazar's mouth was dry and his eyes sore from weeping, he spoke these words: "*The* L*ORD* *God said, 'It is not good for the man to be alone. I will make a companion for him who corresponds to him.' . . . The LORD God made a woman from the part he had taken out of the man, and he brought her to the man. Then the man said, 'This one at last is bone of my bones and flesh of my flesh; this one will be called* woman, *for she was taken out of man.*"[33]

Eleazar released a ragged breath then continued, "Goodbye my beloved Tirzah, my best friend, and the delight of my eyes. May you rest until we meet again." He then turned to go. His friends quietly let Shem guide the cart back to the farm.

While the men performed the burial, Zipporah taught Adva how to boil and then cool goat's milk for Miriam. So far, the youngest one had no problem drinking goat's milk from a cup. Zipporah said that she would get some ground rice for Miriam in town and bring it to them soon. Until then she could eat beans and lentils that were cooked and mashed up for her. She assured Adva that Miriam was old enough to survive without Tirzah.

On their return, Benjamin embraced both Ziva and Tamar who wept quietly against his chest. Havilah went to the barn to care for Shem. She brushed him for a long time. Adva sat in her mother's nursing chair holding both Miriam and Abigail. They both were sleeping in her arms.

The men ate the meal that the girls had prepared and drank the wine the men had brought from town. All the guests went back to town as the sun set in the sky behind Mt. Gerizim. Eleazar was beginning to pace while tugging at his beard. He felt the room collapsing around him.

---

[33] Genesis 2:18, 22-23. NET.

"Father, why don't we sleep on the roof tonight?" asked Adva. "Tamar and Ziva, will you be okay if Father and I sleep on the roof under the stars tonight?" asked Adva.

"I think we should all sleep on the roof tonight. Havilah, Tamar, and I can sleep in the room with Abigail and Miriam. You and Papa can sleep outside," said Ziva.

"We will do that," said Eleazar. "Let me take up a lampstand. I will come back for the crib for the little ones."

"Yes, Father. We will be up soon."

"Yes, thank you," he said numbly.

The girls decided not to take the crib up to the roof but took Miriam's basket instead. Adva latched the door and followed the sisters to the roof. Everyone carried a blanket, a basket, or a child. Adva brought the other lamp.

Eleazar was relieved that he did not have to bring the crib up the steps. He was proud his daughters could figure these things out on their own. As he stared at Orion's belt and the nothingness beyond it, he tried to imagine Tirzah's voice and the things she used to say. But nothing came. The sisters settled down for the night in their room on the roof. Adva brought out two blankets and handed one to her father.

"Do you want a fire?" he asked, "There is wood here for a small fire for a while."

"No, it is warm tonight and our lamp will be enough light," Adva assured him.

Ziva began to sing to Miriam and Abigail. It was a lullaby that Tirzah had sung many times to the little ones. Eleazar was grateful for the memory that came to his mind. Then all was quiet except for the crickets and the frogs. Eleazar huddled in the corner by himself. He was comforted by the scent of Tirzah on their blanket and for the wine, which allowed him to drift off to sleep for a short time. In the quiet, as the stars twinkled above, Adva wept.

In the week that followed, Eleazar harvested the rest of the barley, chopped wood, and replenished the wood piles in the house and on the roof. He then went to the workshop and sharpened tools and tinkered. He did not like being in the house for very long. Although he kept busy, he still found himself watching for Tirzah to enter the room.

Adva and Havilah cleaned. On the first day, Adva opened every window and door. She swept and washed: dishes, pots, baskets, chairs, and walls. Havilah emptied the fireplace of ashes and then cleaned the roof room. Tamar, Ziva, Abigail, and Miriam took Shem to the well. They stopped by Sychar and asked if Benjamin could help them at the well. He traveled with them and filled every jar. Benjamin asked to go back with them, but they refused. Abigail stayed close to Miriam and comforted her.

"We will see you again soon. We have much to do today," said Ziva.

"I sent word to Sebaste to Baruch and Levi," Benjamin said. "You should see them soon. There have been no travelers to Askar or Damascus. Perhaps Baruch can send word to Malachi."

"Thank you, Benjamin. You are so thoughtful," said Tamar. He bowed and watched them travel back home. Tamar and Ziva told Eleazar that Benjamin sent word to Baruch and Levi in Sebaste. Then they prepared the room in the barn for Levi and Baruch while the other sisters cooked beans and lentils.

Zipporah came by to bring the ground rice for Miriam and to see how she was doing. "Her eyes are bright and her skin is not showing a rash. She will do well," reassured Zipporah. Relieved, Adva relaxed her shoulders a bit, but fear still gripped her stomach.

The next day the sisters did laundry. They washed every item of clothing and linen in the house, except for the few items that Eleazar refused to let them wash. He did not want Tirzah's "presence" washed away. Those treasured items he put in a new wooden chest. He put a scarf on his belt and took it to the woodshed. He wanted her with him in any way he could still have her.

By that afternoon, Tamar had entered her womanly rest. "Father," Adva said, "Havilah, Miriam, and Abigail should probably join us on the roof for our seven days. Will you be able to be without all of us? You could travel to Sebaste?"

"No, tomorrow at sunset is Sabbath. Perhaps they will come after Sabbath," said Eleazar.

12
Malachi

Baruch and Levi arrived before the Sabbath. Eleazar was comforted by their arrival as they unloaded the cart. Ramah, Levi's mother, had sent a generous basket of food for the family for their Sabbath. Levi brought another tree trunk and a large leather belt to make a tool for the workshop.

As the men unloaded the cart by the workshop, Tamar watched from the roof. She was upset that she had to wait seven days to be with Levi. The men stayed in the workshop for a while. Eleazar had to show them his new creations and Levi wanted to show his ideas for the leather belt and the large tree trunk. They stayed so long in the workshop that the oxen began to stomp their feet, pleading for rest and water. The men finally came out and took the oxen to the barn for new straw and water. The sisters had moved the goats to their outdoor pen. With Sabbath coming, Adva had tried to get as much milk from the goat as possible to make sure that Miriam had enough. She was cooking the milk when the men came inside out of the hot afternoon sun.

The two older men sat at the table. Levi and Tamar talked from the roof. Adva, Ziva, and Havilah prepared the midday meal. Levi took Tamar her meal.

"Tamar, I have your food," called Levi.

She stepped out of the rooftop room. "It is good to see you. I have missed you. I am glad you have come."

"I am so sorry to hear about Mother Tirzah," he said quietly.

"Yes, it would have been good to have you here to help. I know it means much to Father to have you here now," she smiled. "You must go. I am unclean. I will see you in a few days. Thank you for my food."

"Yes. Of course. If you need anything, just ask," he said as he backed down the stairs and she shut the door.

"Eleazar, your daughters get more beautiful as the days pass. I am the luckiest man alive," said Levi as he stopped at the bottom of the stairs and looked up at the closed door.

"Baruch, I think your son is smitten," said Eleazar, smiling for the first time in days.

"Yes, as do I," Baruch replied as he patted Adva's hand on the table. "I am so sorry for your loss. Your mother would be proud of the woman you are becoming. All of you." A reverent and lingering silence befell the table.

Adva and the sisters cleared the table and showed Eleazar, Levi, and Baruch where the food was for Sabbath then they all moved to the rooftop for their seven-day rest.

The day after Sabbath, Levi went to the well and stopped in town. He returned with Benjamin and the four men worked on a project in the barn all day. Benjamin stayed overnight, and in the morning, they worked in the kitchen building something new. While the two young men worked in the kitchen, Baruch and Eleazar went to town to grind the barley at the mill. They traded some grain for two lambs for Passover week. Baruch offered to cook goat for their next Sabbath meal and they purchased a choice cut from Joseph, returning home by midday.

They were very impressed with Levi's idea and handiwork. The older men were convinced that there would be a high demand for kitchen worktables such as these in Sebaste. Levi also added a new shelf over the fire pit.

The men made plans to leave for Sychar early in the morning to work on Benjamín's workshop at the blacksmith's stable. Shem needed to see the blacksmith for some new shoes, and the ox-pulled cart would carry the needed supplies.

Eleazar was thankful for their handiwork in the kitchen and Benjamin learned much about carpentry in the process. After the sisters returned to the kitchen, they beheld their new wooden workspace, shelves, and a wash basin that drained to the outside of the house.

"Oh, Levi! This is beautiful!" Tamar exclaimed, running her hand over the smooth surface of the new workspace.

"Benjamin helped," Levi replied, looking to Ziva.

"Benjamin, will you build one of these in our home?" asked Ziva, wide-eyed with delight.

"There are rules we have to follow while we live in town, but I will ask," he replied, realizing that he would have a difficult time saying no to Ziva.

"Mother would have loved these things. I love them too," Adva said. "Thank you for your gift."

"Adva, will you join me in the barn for a moment?" asked Eleazar. She took her scarf from the doorway and covered her head.

"Come sit," spoke Eleazar. "I have arranged for Tamar and Ziva to spend a month with their future families to learn their customs and ways. Adva, until my mourning has passed you will be the female head-of-house. You will manage Havilah, Abigail, and Miriam. For Abigail and Miriam, you will be the only mother that they will remember. At the end of the year, I will choose a new wife. You will then be free to marry."

"What about Malachi?" asked Adva.

"I have not heard from Malachi or his father. I am beginning to believe that he has chosen a new plan for his life."

"I see," she said with disappointment. "Tamar, Ziva, and I were making plans to be married on the same day."

"A triune wedding would be lovely, but we have not heard from Malachi, and I must assume that he no longer wants to join our families. Levi sent word to Damascus when Tirzah passed," Eleazar said. "We have heard from no one. None of the shepherds passing through have seen him on Mt. Ebal. I was planning to travel to Damascus again next month, but I cannot leave you here by yourself."

"Father, I would like to go to the well in the morning to have some quiet time to think. The others will be here to help you and take care of the little ones," requested Adva.

"That sounds like a good idea. *Adonai* will tell you what to do," replied Eleazar. "Yes, of course." Eleazar pulled her close and kissed the top of her head with tears in his eyes. "I will come inside in a few minutes. You go prepare for our midday meal."

She returned to her tasks, but in a fog of confusion, her head filled with more questions than answers. Eleazar paced about the barn tugging at his beard and he wept again for his loss.

In the morning Adva woke up early, milked the goat, and prepared the milk for Miriam. She fixed breakfast and had it all laid out on the table before sunrise. She drank water and ate some cheese and left for the well before any of the family or guests had come to the table.

She took her yoke, her bucket, and two water jars. The equipment felt heavier than she remembered. It had been a long time since she walked to the well, but she wanted to get there before the others arrived and the gossip began. She began to feel her spirits lift as the songs she used to sing returned to her memory. Deborah, Benjamin's mother, arrived while she was filling her last jar of water. They talked for a while before Adva left for home. Anna, Ziva's age, and Sarai, about Havilah's age, were walking to the well as she passed on her way home.

Adva was lost in thought as she traversed the dusty road to her home. She thought about making soap again soon, but she would have to wait for the next rain to collect enough rainwater. She also needed to finish her blanket and begin weaving more linen for the family's clothes. Perhaps that was something she could start today.

The journey home seemed long and hot. Off in the distance was an ox-pulled cart coming towards her. She rested under the last sycamore tree before home to wait for it to pass. She retrieved an apple from her sack and had begun to eat it when the cart stopped directly in front of her. Looking up, she tried to block the sun from her eyes but the glare still obscured her view of the driver. For a moment she was afraid and she held tight to her knife.

"Has it been that long since you have seen me? Have I changed that much?" said the man.

"Malachi!" she shouted. "The sun has blinded me."

She rose from the ground and he jumped from the cart. Both wanted to embrace but both were afraid at the same time. When he could stand it no longer, he embraced her and held her close, smelling her hair and enjoying her warmth. She savored his embrace and his new scent of rosemary and mint. He wore the tunic Tirzah had given to him that she had made for Eleazar. His beard was trimmed and soft. His hair was cut short. He had lost weight and his hands were not as thick as they were before. "I came to take you home. Are you ready?"

Adva confessed to him, "I did not recognize you. I was just waiting for the cart to pass." He placed her up on the cart and loaded the jars and equipment into the back.

They took their time returning as there was much to discuss. Malachi was so excited to see her and to tell her everything. “I have been living with my Uncle Kenan and Aunt Rue. When I left last spring, I decided I needed to win your heart, not just buy you as my bride. I went to the best family I knew for help. My aunt, Rue, has two girls and two boys. My nephew, Aden, is twelve. He has my sheep and is learning to be a shepherd. Uncle Kenan has a small farm and is a merchant in Beth-shean. Aunt Rue is a lot like you. She works hard, enjoys weaving, and makes soap too. Rue has been teaching me about women, womanly rest, and such. Also, I have been able to see the love between Kenan and Rue. It is a beautiful thing. Nothing like what I experienced as a child. Even when they argue about things, Aunt Rue is quick to forgive. I have also seen them stay angry for days, but they always find a way to work it out. Anyway, I have been trying to learn to be a farmer,” he said laughing at himself. He barely paused for air and continued.

“Adva, I tried to be a merchant but I kept insulting people so Kenan sent me home. I could not sell things like Ziva and Tamar did at the market. I sold nothing and made many people angry. Kenan talked to me about it, but I told him that my sheep did not complain as those people did. He laughed and said maybe I would be better at farming. I helped with their olive tree crops. It is hard work to pick olives and then extract the oil. That is how I became leaner. It is much easier to move about now that I am lighter, and I am not as clumsy either. Adva, I am not very good with olives but I can continue to learn on Uncle Kenan’s farm. If that is what you want?” he asked, taking a big breath before continuing. “However, I miss the sheep and sleeping outdoors. I get restless being inside all the time. I would go for long walks, but I had to return at midday. Soon it was time put the animals and children to bed. I don’t know what I have to offer but I know I want you as my wife.

Adva, I do not think I can give up being a shepherd. Can you love a shepherd?"

Hearing his torment, Adva asked, "Malachi, who told you that I would not marry a shepherd?"

"You said I smell like sheep," said Malachi sadly.

Embarrassed that she had said such a thing, "Malachi, I was ten years old! I was a child. Children say unkind things."

"Ziva and Tamar asked me many questions the last time I was here. 'Where were we going to live if we married? How would I support our family? Would I be gone all the time? Would I ask you to travel and live in a tent?' I had not thought about those things."

"Yes, this sounds like my sisters," stated Adva. "I am sorry these questions have caused you so much pain."

"Aunt Rue says I should not ask you to live in a tent. I understand that raising a family in a tent would not be ideal. I asked Kenan if we could live on their farm and I would raise sheep and help with the olives. He said he would talk with Aunt Rue and let me know. Adva, we must find a way to make it work. I cannot live without you in my life. It has been killing me not to have you with me. I will do anything to win you if it is not too late."

"Malachi, did you speak with Father before you hitched up the ox to our cart?" asked Adva quietly.

"No, I asked to speak to you first. He was reluctant, but eventually agreed," said Malachi, pulling the ox to a stop. "You are not betrothed to someone else, are you?" Malachi winced at just the thought of those words.

"No, Malachi. I am not betrothed to anyone." His relief was audible. "But things have changed since you were last here. Tamar is betrothed to Levi and Ziva is to marry Benjamin. Did you know that my father went to speak with your father, Lamech, in Damascus?" she asked.

He shook his head. "No one knew I was with Uncle Kenan. I suppose I should have sent word to my father. Kenan's farm is off the main trade route and I did not think to send him a message."

"Levi tried to get in touch with you after my birthday and I guess no one found you. But let us go home before I say more. Tell me more about your uncle's farm and Beth-shean," said Adva, amazed at the man who was now speaking with her so freely.

"You will love Beth-shean. It is green and beautiful and the olive trees whisper in the wind when they are in bloom. My aunt and uncle want to meet you. I talked about you all the time until they were sick of me," he confessed with a smile that lit up his face.

The cart pulled into the courtyard which was empty of activity. "We are home. What is it that I must know?"

"Malachi," Adva paused as she took a deep breath. "Mother Tirzah has died and the child she was carrying when you left us is now six months old."

Speechless for the first time since his arrival, Malachi looked at her in tearful disbelief. Adva could see the unanswered questions running through his mind. "Adva, I am so sorry," Malachi spoke tenderly. "And here I was babbling about my family. I am sorry. I am still not good at this talking thing. Sheep do not talk much. Rue and Kenan have been helping me to become more of a conversationalist."

"Well, I guess you were a good student," she replied quickly.

He chortled, then looked at her again. He ran the back of his hand down her cheek feeling its softness. She shut her eyes in response to his touch. "Adva, I am sorry. I did not know," he said with a renewed sense of purpose. "I will talk with your father and I will come to talk with you soon." He lifted Adva down from the cart and took the water pots inside the house for her.

With Miriam on her hip and holding Abigail's hand, Havilah was returning from the herb garden. Abigail ran and hugged Adva's legs while staring at Malachi. Miriam began squealing for Adva. Havilah quickened her pace and put Miriam in the arms of Adva. Upon returning to the courtyard, Malachi cupped Miriam's face in his hand, "What is her name?" he asked of Adva.

"Miriam," Adva answered.

"I see she is doing well. Praise *Adonai*." Malachi patted Abigail's forehead. "Abigail, you are getting so big. Where is Master Eleazar?" Malachi asked.

"He is in the workshop with the other men," answered Havilah.

"Thank you," replied Malachi politely. "Havilah, it is good to see you!" Malachi walked the ox and cart into the barn. He unhitched the ox, put him in his stall, and gave him water. He noticed the barley sacks in the barn, remembering that he had not been there for the harvest. He then looked toward the woodshed and saw the new workshop for the first time. He walked to the shed taking note of everything that had changed during his absence.

With the door open for the air to circulate, Malachi paused for a moment before he entered the workshop. Eleazar sat on a stool polishing a wooden box with oil. Baruch sat on another stool watching Levi who used his hammer and chisel with great skill. "I have returned your daughter to the house. The ox and cart are in the barn. Thank you for trusting me to bring Adva home," Malachi said with a bow.

"Welcome back!" said Levi, extending his hand and introducing him to his father, Baruch. Baruch extended a nod to Malachi ben Lamech. Baruch remembered his friend

Lamech whom he had not seen for many years. He would ask about his wellbeing at their evening meal.

Malachi bowed to the elder, “Master Eleazar, may I speak to you in private?”

“Yes, of course,” he said, wiping his hands on a cloth.

Adva watched the men embrace from the rooftop. She watched as Eleazar talked and paced while tugging at his beard. While she couldn’t hear the conversation, sometimes she could read the emotion in their gestures. Eleazar noticed that they were being watched from the rooftop and escorted Malachi to the apple orchard.

Havilah brought the little ones up to the roof. She opened the door to the room on the roof so the young ones could be out of the sun. She sat Miriam down on a blanket and Abigail began to brush her hair, which seemed to comfort them both. Abigail sang her a song quietly.

“How is it going between the two of them?” Havilah asked, seeing the two men in the field beyond the workshop.

“I have been spotted and they are walking to the orchard,” answered Adva quietly.

“Do you want me to spy on them?” asked Havilah in jest.

“No. I am afraid that things cannot be resolved,” she whispered as she turned towards Havilah, fear etched into her forehead. “How do I marry Malachi and stay here to take care of Miriam and Abigail? I am the only mother they will ever know.”

Not knowing how to answer her question, Havilah changed the subject. “What time did you go to the well? How did I not hear you?” she asked.

“I was quiet, arose very early, and traveled some of the way in the dark,” Adva answered. “It is easier to milk the goat from the back pen than from inside the barn, although Goshen did not like being awake that early. I will probably have to milk her again this evening. Perhaps we should sleep up here tonight and offer our space to Malachi. No, I will ask if he wants to sleep outside in a tent since he misses watching his sheep. Do you think Tamar and Ziva will mind if I watch the girls here in our room? I want to finish my weaving," said Adva sadly.

"I will tell them you are up here if they need you. I'm going to say hello to Jaspar who is out back with Goshen," said Havilah now that she no longer had to watch the little ones.

"Thank you," she whispered as she walked into the room on the rooftop and shut the door.

As Havilah raced down the stairs, Tamar and Ziva, who were making the midday meal, immediately asked Havilah many questions.

"Well, what did Adva say? What did Malachi say? What's going on now?"

"It appears that Malachi did not know Mother had died. He still wants to marry Adva. Father is talking to him in the apple orchard and we could not see them. Adva is afraid that she cannot marry Malachi and care for Abigail and Miriam. She is sad and is going to finish weaving her blanket. If you need her, she has Abigail and Miriam up on the roof. I am going to the barn. Did that answer all your questions?"

"Do you want to spy on Malachi and father?" asked Tamar.

"No, I do not think that is wise," she stated. "Father looked disturbed that we were on the roof watching them."

"Oh," said Ziva with great disappointment.

Just before their meal, Adva finished her weaving and brought Abigail and Miriam downstairs. She got them both a cup of goat's milk and sat them down at the table to wait for the men. She quietly went back upstairs for the blanket.

"Tamar! Ziva! What do you think?" Adva asked as she held her blanket from the stairs.

"Oh!" said Ziva. "It looks like our old oak tree in the east pasture."

"Yes, it does. It is beautiful, Adva," said Tamar.

Before she could fold it up and put it away, the men walked through the door, causing the sunlight to dance off the fibers of the blanket.

"Adva, your work is stunning," exclaimed Levi.

Baruch stood quietly marveling at the work of art on the far wall. Eleazar walked to the stairs and held the blanket in his hands. Tears came to his eyes.

"Your mother would be so proud of you, as am I." stated Eleazar.

But the person whose praise she most wanted to hear was not in the room yet. "Where is Malachi?" she asked.

"He went to the barn to check on Jaspar and to get some gifts he brought for the family," said Levi.

"Good! Help me fold this up and I can keep it a surprise for him," she said.

Baruch shut the door. Eleazar held the bottom to prevent it from touching the floor and they folded it quickly.

"I will put it away in the room on the roof. Did you and Malachi come to an agreement?" asked Adva wanting to hear some hope.

"No, we will talk more after our meal," stated Eleazar.

"Oh," she said and quickly raced up the stairs to put the blanket away.

After dinner, Baruch, Levi, and the sisters put their heads together to find a solution that would allow Adva to marry Malachi while continuing to care for Miriam and Abigail. Adva also wanted to find a way for Malachi to remain a shepherd.

"Are there laws stating that a woman *must* go to live with her husband's family?" asked Ziva.

"No, I think these are traditions. But the husband becomes the legal provider for the woman. Is that your understanding, Eleazar?" asked Baruch.

"Well, it is stated that '*a man will leave his father and mother and will be united with his wife, and the two will become one flesh,*'"[34] explained Eleazar. "But it does not declare where they will live."

"That's it! Eleazar, if we could live on your farm, I could work with you," Malachi exclaimed, pounding his fist on the table, causing all those in the room to jump.

Ziva, unbothered by his dramatic gestures, spoke first: "Since Adva and Malachi like the night sky, perhaps they could live on the roof?"

"Malachi loves keeping sheep. If I were to live here while he is herding sheep, I would be protected while he is away. I would be able to help Father with Abigail and Miriam," said Adva.

"I would not have to be away all the time," Malachi said. "I could come back for the barley, flax, and apple harvests. And perhaps my Uncle Kenan would gift us some olive trees."

"Perhaps you could process enough oil to have some left over for the woodworking oils that I need," said Levi with excitement.

"Uncle Kenan sells his good oil for cooking and the lesser quality is sold for lamp oil, but I bet there is a third quality of oil that could be used for woodwork."

"I need oil to make soap too," Adva chimed in excitedly.

"Yes, Aunt Rue uses his oil for her soap," stated Malachi, now overcome with joy.

"Malachi, it sounds as if we have found a way for you to marry Adva. The three sisters wish to marry on the same day in the spring when the apple trees are in bloom. On

34 Genesis 2:24. NET.

this Baruch and I have agreed, and we hope that Joseph will also agree. Do you think we can convince your father to agree?" asked Eleazar.

"I will convince him with Kenan's help. Eleazar, you have made me a happy man!"

13
The Wedding

The day came full of sunshine, bringing guests from Sebaste, Damascus, and other cities. Eleazar had borrowed every tent in Sychar to house the guests. The sisters had constructed a ceremonial tent from linen woven from their flax fields. The three sisters had wanted to marry on the same day, and the grooms all welcomed sharing the day. Each of them seemed relieved to have someone with whom to share the experience.

The men had come to know each other very well over the last month. Benjamin and Levi were closest in age. Levi had helped Benjamin build a few things in Benjamin's new home in Sychar for his bride. Malachi was the strong man of the group and the other two had come to depend on his strength for several things that needed to be done for the wedding. With all the arrangements in place, the grooms were moved to Sychar to live in Benjamin's home for a week. After a few days, Malachi grew tired of town and could not wait to be back in the country again. He was able to calm his spirit by sleeping on the roof at night, which Levi and Benjamin did not mind since Malachi tended to snore loudly. Jacob the blacksmith and his father, Master Gideon, were tasked with making sure that the grooms did not see their brides the week before the wedding. Even Jaspar had the work of carrying preparations to the field.

All the brides had been escorted to Levi's home in Sebaste for a week and would be back at their home today. For a treat, the women had spent a day at the Great Sea. Adva loved being at the sea, so this was a dream come true for her. Rich olive oil salves and creams, many of which were from Levi's family recipes, were lavished on the brides. The beauty treatments were a gift from Levi's family. Before leaving Sebaste, the brides were washed, oiled, and dressed, and today they would parade through Sychar. There would be a pause in the parade to visit with the midwife, Zipporah, who would certify their virginal status, give instructions for the marriage bed, and prepare the brides for welcoming their husbands. Zipporah gave each sister a special jar of scented oil as a wedding gift.

All three sisters were seated on the back of Jacob's cart with their legs dangling in the air. Adva leaned over to Ziva, the youngest of the brides at eleven, who was holding tightly to the jar on her lap. "I'm starting to feel like they are going to fry me in a pan," Adva whispered.

Ziva laughed and then confessed, "I am scared Adva. What have we done?"

"We do what every woman before us has done. We marry so we can live. We shall bear children so our husbands are honored. We move from our father's home to our husband's home. We are bought and sold like prized ewes," replied Adva, who is the eldest bride at fourteen. "Baaaah."

"Oh, that's awful," said Tamar, the middle bride at twelve. "We should be happy to marry the men that our father has chosen for us. He did not make bad matches for us."

"Aren't you scared?" asked Ziva.

"Yes, of course. But I have been scared before. When you and I went to the well for the first time, I was terrified.

I could not carry all the things that Adva had carried. How did you do it, Adva?"

"We do what we must do. You will find a way. I do not know how I will care for Malachi, Father, Havilah, Abigail, and Miriam, but I know it shall be done. After Mother died, I was simply told 'this is what we were going to do.' Havilah will be the next daughter to be betrothed, but I hope Father will not decide on that too quickly. Abigail and Miriam are not yet old enough, and I will probably have a child of my own by next year to grow up with them.

"Tamar, will you be happy to move to Sebaste? Did you like your new home?" asked Ziva.

"Yes, I am glad that Levi's workshop is directly below our home. He will always be nearby," Tamar sighed.

"Yes, well I am glad I do not have to move and very pleased that Malachi will continue to herd his sheep to Mt. Ebal," said Adva. "What about you, Ziva?"

"I am sad to see Tamar leave our town. I will have to find reasons to come and see you. But I love the home that Benjamin has selected in town. It is just above the market. I will love all the early morning sounds of the busy marketplace, and I will make things to sell there. Adva, you can bring me your soaps and blankets and I will get you a good price. Benjamin's knife sharpening service will take place at the blacksmith shop for now, until we can afford another place in town. We will try to buy the place directly below our home like Tamar and Levi. Benjamin will know what to do."

"I am just glad Benjamin has finally grown a beard," Adva said with a smirk.

The girls shared a laugh and watched the town drift into the distance and knew they were getting close to the farm. There would be a lot of people to feed and serve over the next few days. Eleazar was happy to have all the relatives there to help. It was Caleb, Malachi's brother, who helped the women off the cart.

"*Shalom*. My name is Caleb. I am Malachi's brother. I am here to assist you from your chariot. If you put your jar on the cart, I will lift you down."

"Here, Ziva. I will hold your jar for you," said Tamar.

Ziva was the first out of the cart. "I'm Ziva, the bride of Benjamin."

The sisters exchanged jars. "Hello, Caleb. I am Tamar, the bride of Levi."

Adva set her jar on the cart as the other two sisters moved on to the house while chattering with guests who were milling about their home. Adva swallowed hard but continued to stare at Caleb. He looked so much like Malachi that they could be twins. "You must be Adva, my brother's bride. It is an honor to meet you. I hope you had a pleasant ride to town," spoke Caleb, who lifted her from the cart and set her feet on the ground. "My brother is a lucky man," he said with joy, handing her the jar of scented oil.

Adva took the jar from him and cocked her head to the side, "Why do you say that? You do not know me."

"Yes, but Malachi has told me much of your beauty and your wit. I see that he was not mistaken about your beauty, so I trust that the other things he has shared must also be true."

Adva blushed as Caleb bowed, "I am at your service. If my brother misbehaves in any way, you just call on me."

Adva smiled at the charming man standing before her. At that moment, Miriam began screaming for Adva.

"She has been calling for you all afternoon. I think she was afraid you had left her again," explained Havilah. "You look like a younger version of Malachi. I am Havilah. This is the youngest sister, Miriam."

Adva remembered her manners, "Thank you, Jacob, for the ride home. Are you staying for a while or heading back to town?" His reply was drowned out by the turning of the cart's wheels; Jacob was already in motion as he waved behind him.

Instead of reaching for Adva, Miriam held her arms out for Caleb to hold her, which she had only ever done for her father or Levi. "Well, you've been adopted," stated Havilah. "It's a sign." Abigail ran to meet Adva.

"You are popular," Caleb said to Adva as he took Miriam into his arms.

"Yes, since our Mother died I have become their mother. That is why we will live here after the wedding," replied Adva as she hugged Abigail from the side since her hands were full.

"Well, that makes sense," replied Caleb, who galloped off to the house with Miriam on his hip squealing in delight. Adva stared at them, astonished that Miriam took to Caleb so easily.

Deborah, Benjamin's mother, met the brides at the door. There were people everywhere on the farm. "Hello brides," said Deborah. "Your things have been taken to your new homes. Adva, your things are here but will not be available to you until after the wedding.

"Where do we go now? Where will we sleep tonight?" the brides asked.

Deborah smiled, "You have your bridal tent. We have put some of your favorite things in the tent. There you will dress, prepare for your groom, and wait for his arrival. Eleazar will escort you there. You will not visit with your guests until after the wedding ceremony. Eleazar is currently entertaining the grooms' fathers. They have bonded well. You should be very happy that things are going so well. Did the midwife give you papers to present to your groom?"

"Yes, we put them inside our tunics," replied Adva.

"Well come inside and get those out. Your father will escort you to your marriage tent with your papers and your jar of oil," said Deborah. "Girls, you have never been to a wedding, have you?"

"No."

"And your mother was not able to tell you about our traditions."

"No."

"Well, it does not matter. I will go ask your father to escort you to your tent. He will be happy to see you," continued Deborah. "Caleb, have you seen Master Eleazar?"

"Yes, he is in the barn," said Caleb.

"Tell him the brides have arrived," Deborah said.

"Yes, of course," said Caleb, bowing low to the ground. Deborah giggled and waved her hand at him to go.

Excited to see his daughters, Eleazar came running from the barn. He was dressed in his finest tunic, his beard and hair were well groomed, and he smelled of cedar. He gave each daughter a hug and kiss on the cheek. "Your mother would be so proud of you three" he spoke, swallowing back tears. "I will now take you to your bridal tent," he said, clearing his throat. "We placed it under the apple trees and they are in full bloom. Havilah helped put the tent in an ideal spot. She and Deborah decorated the inside. I think it is lovely. I hope you like it. Your meal will be served to you in the tent. If you need anything, you must ask someone to get it for you as you will not be seen again until you meet your groom. Do you have your papers? You will hold the rolled parchment in your right hand and your jar of oil in your left as we walk past our guests. Did Zipporah explain our wedding customs?"

"Yes, Father," stated Adva, embarrassed by the conversation she had with Zipporah. "We will do as you ask."

"Adva, you will walk first, then Tamar, then Ziva."

The women had their parchments and their jars of oil. Eleazar opened the door of the house and there was a crowd in the courtyard exclaiming a loud "Hurrah!" Adva and her sisters did not know most of the people as they scanned the crowd for a familiar face. Eleazar led the procession, and after rounding the corner of the house, more people joined the procession. Directly in front of them were three large tents on the right of the path to the apple orchard.

Eleazar stopped at the doorway of the first tent, motioning for Master Lamech, who wore a fine white linen tunic and trousers, to step beside him. Lamech's shoulder length, black hair framed his kind expression. His beard was neatly combed and its great length rested on his chest. Adva stepped forward as Eleazar reached for the parchment in her right hand.

Eleazar unrolled the paper and read it aloud to the crowd: "I, Eleazar ben Joachim, swear that my daughter, Adva, is a virgin worthy of her groom. It bears the seal of our midwife, Zipporah." Eleazar allowed Lamech to look at the parchment.

"Where would you like to put your gift?" Eleazar asked Adva.

"What?" replied Adva, appalled by what was just read aloud to the crowd of witnesses.

"The oil," Eleazar whispered, "Walk inside and put your oil by the bed and come back to the doorway."

"Yes, Father." As she entered the tent, Eleazar took a hammer and nail to attach the parchment to the main tent peg. When she returned to the door, Lamech grabbed her shoulders and kissed both cheeks, thus welcoming her into his family.

"Hurrah!" chanted the guests.

This ritual was repeated with Tamar and her father-in-law, Baruch, then by Ziva and her father-in-law, Joseph.

Eleazar then escorted the daughters to the bridal tent where two unknown men stood guard at the doorway. With Abigail and Miriam by her side, Havilah opened the flap of the tent and welcomed her sisters inside.

As each daughter entered the tent, Eleazar whispered into their ear, "I will not see you again until you are married to your husband. *Adonai,* watch over my daughters and the ones they marry!" The daughters entered the tent and let the flap close.

Havilah spoke first. "Why do you all look so sad and pale?" Miriam held up her arms for Adva to hold her. Adva took the child and hugged her tightly and did the same for Abigail.

"That has to be the most humiliating thing I have ever done," spat Adva.

"I wish mother would have told us about that," replied Tamar.

"She would have if she had lived to see this day. She thought she had more time," said Ziva. "I think Father thought that Zipporah had told us. That was too dramatic even for me. Adva, if you had started crying, I would have lost it."

"It is hot in here. Can we open the door?" asked Adva as she threw open the tent door. She was met by the men at the door barring her exit. "I do not wish to leave I just need some air. Please, can you make a way for air to come into our tent? The grooms would not want to find us dead," said Adva, turning to allow the tent door to close. "Perhaps we can put out one of the lamps."

One of the guards went around the tent and dropped some of the tent walls from the top to allow for airflow.

"Thank you," Ziva responded through the tent walls.

"Do we get to sleep tonight, or do we have to stay awake waiting for our grooms?" asked Tamar.

"All I know is that I am permitted to stay until sunset then Miriam, Abigail, and I must leave," said Havilah. "When they bring you food, eat up. I do not think you will eat again until the wedding feast. Your dresses will be delivered to you soon." Havilah wrung her hands, feeling a nervous need to do something. "May I braid your hair?" she requested.

"Yes, please braid my hair into the crown you used to do for me. All my hair wants to do is curl and frizz. Do you have any of my oils in here?" asked Adva.

"No, there is only olive oil for the lamps," answered Havilah.

"That will do to tame my curls. Is there a brush?" asked Adva. Abigail handed her the brush that sounded like rain. "Thank you, Abigail." The sisters sat and listened to the swooshing of the hairbrush going through Adva's hair. Havilah stood behind her braiding the tresses into a crown that wrapped around her head.

"Oh, that is so beautiful," said Tamar. "Do mine next!"

"Yes, me too," said Ziva.

"Me too," said Abigail.

"Me too," echoed Miriam.

Havilah moved to braid Tamar's tresses. They were easier to braid and not as curly as Adva's. Adva braided Abigail. Miriam did not yet have enough hair to braid, but Abigail brushed it and put olive oil on her head. Havilah moved on to Ziva's hair and her hands were beginning to hurt from all the braiding. But all the sisters laughed together and enjoyed each other's company. Ziva was twirling about and dancing with her headscarf when there was a rap at the tent's door.

The tent flap opened and a young girl from Sychar came in bringing them a bowl of fruit and a skin of wine. Another had a large basket of bread and cheese. Yet another brought a bowl of curds and cucumbers. Two young women brought jars of water. Anna from Sychar brought bowls, cups, and towels and then the women were gone from the tent as quickly as they had appeared.

The sisters giggled at their royal treatment. They sat cross-legged on the carpets that covered the floor of the tent and ate from the spread before them until they were full. Miriam and Abigail had eaten and fallen asleep while the older sisters savored their last meal together. "I wonder what time it is. I don't know if the stars are out," said Ziva.

"Havilah, will you go look out the door?" Tamar asked. "Those guards are scary."

Havilah opened the door to the tent and motioned to the women who brought their food and were now waiting outside for them to finish. They came inside and cleaned up the leftovers.

"Please leave the bread, wine, and water," replied Adva.

"Of course, Adva," the girl replied and then left the tent immediately.

Deborah, Benjamin's mother, entered the tent to give the brides their dresses. "Blessings to the brides and sisters. Your grooms could come for you at any time this night or tomorrow so you need to dress yourselves soon. Adva, this dress is yours. It has the embroidered trim at the bottom."

Adva accepted her dress and ran her hand over the fabric and the fine needlework at the hem. Her eyes welled up with tears as she longed for her mother to walk through the door of the tent.

"The tailor in Sychar was paid by Malachi to make each of your dresses. The fabric has come from Damascus. Adva, your embroidery is from Malachi's wool and was made by his Aunt Rue in Beth-shean. Tamar, this is your gown. The embroidered trim is at the waist. Your trim is made of yarn from the goats of Levi's herd. It was stitched and embroidered by Ramah, Levi's mother." Tamar hugged the dress tightly in delight.

"Ziva, your needlework is on the collar of your gown. The yarn is also from the goats from Levi's herd. I have embroidered it around the collar to accent your lovely face. I tried to make it with many vibrant colors to reflect the many sights and sounds of your new home in Sychar."

Ziva accepted her dress, hugged Deborah, and twirled around in delight. "It is lovely! I love all the colors and that it came from Levi's goats. Thank you."

At that moment, the three young women appeared with sandals, silk scarves, and veils. "Malachi's father, Lamech, has given you each a white scarf of pure silk from the Orient to wear over your hair and a fine linen veil from Egypt to cover your faces." The sisters ran their fingers over the silk and linen. They were so beautiful.

Deborah continued, "Oh, I love your braided hair! The scarf will weave into the braid very nicely and stay put during the day. Do you need for me to stay or do you want to serve each other?"

"We will assist each other in dressing," stated Adva.

"Very well. The sandals are a gift from Joseph and Baruch. Joseph provided the leather from the butcher shop and Baruch tanned and formed the sandals. A few of the women of Sychar helped me with the straps and beadwork. The beads are gemstones from Lamech. Widow Tara and a few other women of Sychar also have a gift for you. Here are personal cloths made from a tunic that belonged to your mother. Eleazar asked us to make you something that you could hold during your day that would help you to know that your mother was close. He asked us to embroider, '*Il*

Raa'ee' in the corner." Each daughter gave Deborah a kiss on the cheek, thanked her, and asked her to thank the other ladies who helped as well.

"I am overwhelmed by all the gifts. Thank you for your kindness," said Ziva. "May Havilah stay to help us?"

Deborah bowed in response. "Yes, but she and the younger sisters will have to leave once you are dressed, and no one can claim you but your groom. They may come together or separately. I do not know their plans. More than likely the procession will begin in the morning before dawn. Very well, I will leave you now. Blessings to you all. May your wombs be filled with children." Deborah gave her blessing then left the tent.

"The sun is setting over Mt. Gerizim. It is a beautiful sunset," said Havilah wistfully, knowing it would soon be time for her to go.

The sisters dressed in their fine tunics and silk scarves. Their sandals had leather bottoms and beaded straps to go over the toes and around the ankles. There were bells on them that tinkled as they walked. It made a beautiful sound, but they removed them and placed them by the door so that people would not hear them walking about.

"I am reluctant to go, but I should probably leave you or they may find a groom for me," said Havilah. The sisters laughed. "I will take Miriam and return for Abigail." Havilah bent down to pick up Miriam and Abigail woke up. She carried Miriam and held Abigail's hand, and the youngest sisters left.

"I have been sad today," said Ziva. "I have thought about all the things that will never be the same again. I will miss sleeping in the middle of the floor with you both."

"Yes, remind me to tell Benjamin that you steal the covers," said Tamar. The sisters giggled.

"I have been afraid mostly. I try to be brave but I have been beset with fear all day," said Adva.

Tamar asked, "What are you afraid of?"

"Would you be afraid if you were marrying Malachi?" Adva asked with a small nervous giggle.

"Maybe. You are not angry with Levi and me for marrying, are you?" asked Tamar as she came close to Adva.

"No, Tamar. You and Levi are a perfect match. I can see that now. Levi is more like a brother to me, and we can continue in this way," promised Adva. "And Ziva, you will love living here in Sychar in the middle of the marketplace. Benjamin will be so good for you . . . now that his voice has finally changed." The sisters shared more laughter as they imitated Benjamin's once-squeaky voice.

"I think we should sleep in the middle of the tent," said Ziva. "Adva, I'm sorry we cannot look at the stars tonight."

"We could cut a hole in the tent if you like," said Tamar.

"No, that is not necessary. But I do think it is a good idea to sleep together. They can't have a wedding without us. Ziva, blow out that lamp," said Adva. "Tamar, get that blanket. I will bring this blanket and blow out this lamp."

The sisters curled up in the middle of the tent and slept until a shofar blew in the distance just before dawn.

"Sisters, wake up! The grooms will be here soon," said Adva.

Adva's braid had fallen during the night and needed to be re-braided. "I will do your hair," said Tamar. "How does my hair look?"

"Like you slept on it all night," said Adva smiling.

"What about me?" asked Ziva.

"I will do your hair after Tamar's. Oh look, Abigail left her brush!" exclaimed Adva. "Praise *Adonai*!"

Adva grabbed a lamp of olive oil and began to oil and brush her own hair. The other sisters undid their braids and waited. The shofar blew again, a little closer this time.

"Oooh, they are coming. Hurry, Adva!" said Tamar.

"Sit here, Ziva. I will do your hair while Tamar does mine. Tamar, do it as tight as you can." Adva winced. "Well, maybe not that tight."

"I'm sorry. I am so nervous," said Tamar.

"Drink some of the wine they left for us. It will calm you down."

"Good idea." Tamar went to the wineskin, poured a full cup of wine for herself, and drank it all.

Ziva raised her eyebrow, "I don't know if that was a good idea. You drank a whole cup on an empty stomach. You will be the first one drunk at your own wedding."

"Oh no, I had better eat something." She broke off a big piece of crusty bread and gobbled it down.

"Tamar, come back and finish my hair please," said Adva as she completed Ziva's crown of hair.

"Ziva, get your scarf!" The shofar blew again, now even closer. They could hear the beating of drums, one in the camp and one off in the distance. Ziva came back and sat at Adva's feet. Adva twisted the scarf into Ziva's hair. She took Ziva's hand and placed it just above her ear.

"This is where you should attach the veil," said Adva.

"Yes, I can tie it directly to the scarf in my hair. You are brilliant, Adva." Then she kissed her.

Tamar finished Adva's braid as Ziva brushed Tamar's hair.

"Ziva, can you make Adva's crown? I can't seem to get it secure."

"Adva, sit so I can see what I am doing." Adva sat down on the rug. Ziva undid some of the braid that was crooked, then wrapped it around her head and secured it.

"Tamar, get the scarves for you and Adva!" Ziva secured Adva's scarf just above her ears by tying a knot in the scarf. She left a tie for the veil to be secured, then she tucked the scarf under her hair so that none of her braid could be seen.

"Ziva, I love it! Thank you. You, too, are brilliant," said Adva. The shofar blew again.

"Adva hurry! I need mine done too," said Tamar in a nervous frenzy.

"Tamar, sit. What would Levi say to you right now?" asked Adva.

"He would be laughing at me," said Tamar.

"I think you are right. Calm down, please," said Adva. She enjoyed braiding Tamar's hair. She had the least amount of curl in her hair. It was very different from her own. She wished she had some lavender or mint for the oil. Perhaps there was a servant nearby who would go get her oils for her.

There was a knock on the tent's door frame. The three brides gasped. "Who is it?" asked Tamar.

"Havilah."

"Oh, yes, come in," said Adva.

"Oh, you all are so beautiful!" exclaimed Havilah.

"Havilah, can you go and get my scented oil?" asked Adva.

"You mean this?"

"May *Adonai* bless you! Which did you bring?"

"Lavender."

"Perfect!" Adva dipped her finger into the oil and traced a line from her neck down to her breast. She took another finger full and wiped it across her armpits. "Only one of us will smell like sheep today." The girls laughed as they followed Adva's lead and dipped their fingers into the oil. The tent filled with the smell of lavender.

"It reminds me of the teas we made for mother," said Havilah.

There was another knock at the door. "Oh no, I am here and I should not be. Hide me."

"It is Deborah. I have makeup if you want to do your eyes?" She opened the tent's flap and smiled at the brides.

"Oh, what is that lovely smell?" asked Deborah.

"Adva's oil," replied Ziva.

"The grooms do not stand a chance. They will rush to take you away to the wedding tent," said Deborah. "Here, I have a charcoal stick for your eyes if you would like?"

"I have never used it before, can you do it for me?" asked Adva.

"Yes, of course. Do you want it thick or thin?" asked Deborah.

"I think thin would be best."

"If I like it on Adva, I will try it," said Ziva. "Oh yes, I like it. You look Egyptian."

"I think I will do without it," said Tamar.

"Deborah, I do not think Malachi will like it. I had better remove it. What is the best way to take it off?"

"Your oil should take it off best. Here is a cloth. Brides, I came to make sure that you drank some water this morning before your long day. I do not want you to pass out from the heat."

The shofar blew again, this time very close to the tent.

"How do I look?" asked Ziva.

"You look like a painted Egyptian," said Tamar. "Too dramatic for me."

"Do you think that Benjamin will like it?" Ziva asked Deborah.

"I do not think so," replied Deborah. "It was a bad idea."

"I got mine to come off," said Adva. "I will help you get yours off too. Tamar, pour us all a cup of water, please."

"Havilah, we need to leave," said Deborah.

As she opened the tent door, Abigail and Miriam ran in. "That's the way it is with sisters, Deborah. Expect to see us all together for many years to come," said Adva as she scooped up Abigail and Miriam in each arm and twirled about in a circle dance. When Adva stopped, she gasped seeing Malachi in the doorway watching her.

"My bride," he said, as he extended his hand. Malachi was dressed in a white linen tunic, trousers, and a white turban. The embroidery around his collar matched the embroidery on Adva's tunic. He wore white boots of lamb skin on his feet. His presence filled the doorway and he exuded great joy.

"Come inside and place the veil over your bride's face, Malachi. We will help you if you need it," said Deborah.

Malachi inhaled a deep breath of perfumed air as he entered the tent. He took the young girls from Adva's arms and scooted them toward Havilah. "Such loveliness, it takes my breath away," said Malachi, touching Adva's face with the back of his hand.

"Here, drink first, Adva," said Tamar handing her a cup of water.

"Yes, drink my bride. I want you to enjoy this day," said Malachi in a soothing voice.

After Adva emptied the cup, Malachi gave it back to Tamar who watched him tie the veil above Adva's ears with such care.

All the sisters were surprised by Malachi's behavior. He seemed so happy and joyful. Adva did not know this side of Malachi, and she was mesmerized by his presence. Malachi took her hand and led her through the tent's doorway. The guests that gathered nearby applauded as Adva exited the tent.

"Oh, my sandals. Havilah, bring me my sandals," requested Adva. Havilah exited the tent and knelt to put the sandals on her feet.

"Oh, let me do that, Havilah," said Malachi.

"Is that allowed?" asked Havilah.

"I do not know, but I would like to place the sandals on my bride's feet." Havilah left the sandals on the ground in front of Adva and then retreated to get Miriam and Abigail from the tent and went to stand by their father.

Malachi knelt in front of Adva. She lifted her left foot and he slipped the sandal on and secured the ankle strap. The warmth of his hands on her foot caused Adva to shudder. He felt her tremble and smiled at her response to his touch. He put her foot back on the ground and retrieved the other sandal.

"Adva, raise your other foot, please." Adva raised her right foot but soon began to lose her balance. Catching herself, she placed a hand gently on Malachi's shoulder, causing him to quiver. He took her foot into his large hands and placed the sandal onto her foot and secured the ankle strap. When he stood up, he was distressed upon noticing that the crowd had been eagerly watching this tender moment; Malachi did not like being the subject of such interest. "There you go. Do you have everything you need?" he asked with a gruffness to his voice. This was the Malachi Adva remembered, and it snapped her from her trance. She smiled at him through her veil. "Yes, thank you, Master Malachi," said Adva.

"I think you should call me Malachi now," he said as he reached for her petite hand.

"Yes, of course," Adva answered. Eleazar looked on with a smile of relief. He had fretted most about this match. *Adonai* would watch over this marriage and the marriages of her sisters.

Levi was next to retrieve his bride. Flanked by Ramah and Baruch, he approached the tent and knocked on the doorpost. Deborah, who was still inside with the sisters, ushered Tamar to the door.

"Did you drink your water, Tamar? Do you have your sandals on?" asked Deborah. Tamar nodded.

Ziva put her sandals on quickly and gulped her water down at the far side of the tent.

"Levi, you may enter," spoke Deborah. "Your bride awaits." Levi opened the tent flap and gazed at his bride with awe.

Levi was dressed in a fine linen tunic and he wore an embroidered belt to match Tamar's dress. His hair and beard were neatly trimmed and not hidden by a hat or turban. Deborah helped Levi, whose hands were shaking too much to tie the veil to Tamar's scarf. The crowd cheered as Levi stepped from the tent with Tamar, and Deborah took her place behind Benjamin, the final groom.

Benjamin knocked and entered to tie the veil on his bride. He took Ziva's hand and escorted her from the tent. "Praise the name of *Adonai*!" rejoiced the crowd. "May these couples be blessed with many children!"

Malachi and Adva led the procession to the ceremonial tent, followed by Levi and Tamar, then Benjamin and Ziva. The crowd fell in behind them.

The ceremony was short. Each couple received a blessing from the High Priest of Sychar. Once each *ketubah*[35] was signed by the couple, the shofar sounded again to signal the start of the feast, music, and dancing.

As the flute, drum, and oud began to play, Havilah approached her newlywed sister with two little girls who were eager to hug Adva and say hello to Master Malachi. Malachi, so full of joy, lifted the girls, putting one in each

---

35 *Ketubah* is the Aramaic word for the official written marriage document.

of his arms as he danced around in a circle. Watching the young girls as they giggled and screamed loudly, Adva imagined their own children with him. It was the first time she had thought such things. Malachi met Adva's gaze and took her hand in his. "I think they are calling us to dance," he said cheerfully. After sharing their first dance together, the three couples joined hands in a line and invited the other guests to join them. There was much laughter and joy.

Eleazar watched his daughters closely as they danced. When widow Tara came close to Eleazar, he took her hand and joined in the revelry. Lamech then joined on the other side of Tara. They added Joseph and Deborah, then Baruch and Ramah.

During the mid-day meal, Eleazar gave a blessing to each couple. He then had a dance with each daughter before ceremoniously handing them off to their husbands to finish the dance. Then Eleazar danced with Havilah, Abigail, and Miriam.

"Lamech, are you enjoying our festivities?" asked Eleazar, wiping sweat from his brow and taking a long drink of wine.

"Yes. Sychar is home to some very lovely women. It does my heart good," said Lamech, taking his time to savor his wine.

"How is it that you have never remarried after all these years?" asked Eleazar.

"Although I have wanted a woman to share my bed, no one has stolen my heart," he said with a wink.

"I am afraid that will be true for me also," Eleazar confessed. "Tirzah would have loved today."

"Your wound is still fresh. It will get better with time. The pain will remain, but soon it will no longer take your breath away."

"That is good to know, my friend." Eleazar scanned the crowd for his youngest daughters and spotted them with Havilah and Caleb. "Your son, Caleb, seems to be enjoying himself." They watched the four children dance and laugh. Miriam squealed as she spun around, became dizzy, and finally toppled over.

"Yes, Caleb knows how to have fun and allow others to have fun with him. Perhaps Havilah can be betrothed to Caleb?"

"I am not ready to have another wedding any time soon," Eleazar said.

"Ah, yes. I, too, hope Caleb will stay with me a while longer," admitted Lamech. "He is a good lad, much like his mother."

14
The Wedding Night

The sun began to set and the lamps around the table were lit. Malachi gathered two cups and a jar of wine to take to their tent. He had arranged for Havilah to leave Adva's oils and hairbrush in their tent. There was a bowl and a water pot near the door, and Malachi took a moment to wash the sweat from his face and chest. It had been a long day and he could tell his bride was beginning to tire. As he turned to exit the tent, Havilah was there to enter.

"Oh, Master Malachi!" Havilah squealed as she put her hand to her heart. "I am sorry, I thought you were still at the feast."

"What are you doing here?" he asked sternly.

"Adva asked that I put a gift in your tent. She wanted to have it as a surprise for you for tonight."

"You may leave it here," he said, stepping aside so that she could enter.

"Adva told me to put it on your bed."

"Very well, then do so."

"You must go away so that it will be a surprise when you return," replied Havilah.

"I will bring her back here very soon. Do so quickly, and be gone," he commanded.

"Yes, Master Malachi," replied Havilah with a bow of respect.

He left to find his bride. The moment he had been waiting for since the day he selected Adva to be his wife was finally upon them. It did not seem like four years had passed. When he returned, he spotted her dancing with Caleb and the youngest sisters. He paused for a moment to watch, but his thoughts were interrupted by his aunt Rue. "Malachi, we are leaving for Sychar," she announced. "I am not able to sleep on the ground and Deborah and Joseph have offered us a place to stay. We enjoyed the day. Adva is a lovely woman and her family is wonderful. You are a blessed man."

"Thank you, Rue. It was good to have you here. Kenan, enjoy your visit to Sychar," said Malachi extending his hand to pat him on the shoulder.

"Our first time away without the children in five years," Kenan replied with a wink. "May *Adonai* bless my brother Eliab, who has our children."

Adva walked over to say goodbye. "Thank you for all the things you have done for Malachi over the last year," she said as she kissed Rue's cheek. "He is indeed a different man."

"Malachi, you be good to this woman! You will not be sorry." Rue smiled and walked away arm in arm with Kenan. They quickly joined a group of guests that were walking back to town with their lanterns.

Malachi playfully reached down and threw Adva over his shoulder, "Woman, the time has come. I will show you I have not changed that much."

Adva laughed, "Malachi, we are not Philistines; put me down. We have guests and must say goodbye." In jest, she slapped his strong arms with her flat hand.

He put her down. But as Adva started to walk away, he grabbed her arm and gently pulled her back. "Adva, we will walk back to the table but we will not stay. I am taking my bride to our marriage tent," Malachi commanded. "You have a moment to say a quick goodbye. If you do not come willingly, I will haul you off like a Philistine." Adva looked into his eyes and knew he spoke the truth. She held his hand and led him around the table, bidding goodnight to her guests and sisters. Adva then kissed her father goodnight.

Eleazar hugged her tight and whispered in her ear, "*Il Raa'ee*." She remembered the first time he whispered that in her ear; it was when Malachi had seized her in the barn so long ago. Eleazar grabbed Malachi by the forearms, giving him a blessing and instruction, "I have entrusted you with my Adva. Be kind."

Malachi looked carefully at his friend and father-in-law, "Do you regret the decision?"

"No," replied Eleazar, "not yet." He smiled and patted Malachi's shoulder. "Go."

Malachi took Adva's hand in his and they walked to their tent. The two other brides watched them go and took a long drink of wine to quell their nerves. Music still played for the guests who would linger a while longer. Tamar giggled loudly at something Levi whispered in her ear. Ziva asked Benjamin to dance another line dance with her friends from Sychar.

When Malachi opened the tent flap, a rush of lavender and heat billowed through the open door. "I lit the lamp so we would not have to fumble in the dark," he said to his wife.

"Thank you," Adva said as she followed him into the tent. To their right was a stool with a wash bowl for their feet.

As Adva started to walk across to the bed, Malachi took her by the hand. "Not yet. Sit here and let me remove your sandals. I do not want anyone to hear you tinkling about."

She looked at him curiously. "Your bell-ridden sandals," he explained. She nodded and sat on the stool.

Malachi knelt and removed her sandals then poured water over her feet. Adva squealed, "Oh my, that is cold!"

"Give me a moment and I will be through," he said wiping her feet with a towel. At that, they heard a group of children giggling on the other side of the tent. The couple looked at each other. Malachi held his finger to his lips and quickly threw open the tent door and growled like a bear at the young ones who went screaming off in the other direction. "They will not listen to us anymore tonight," said Malachi. They both laughed. He took her by the hand and helped her rise. Adva motioned for Malachi to sit on the stool and he allowed her to wash his feet. She untied his boots.

"Your feet must be very hot in these," said Adva as she unlaced his boots.

"They are very soft on the inside. I should make you some," Malachi responded. As Adva rinsed the dirt from his feet, Malachi noticed the beautiful artwork that covered their bed. "Is that the blanket you made?" he asked.

She smiled, "Malachi, do you remember the sheep shearing when Levi arrived at our farm?"

"Yes, the black and white sheep we sheared for you."

Adva nodded, "This blanket was created from that wool."

"It is a beautiful oak tree. Do you have some on the farm?" inquired Malachi. "In Damascus, it is called Tree of Life."

"Yes. The oldest one collapsed last year; it was hundreds of years old. But I tried to recreate it in my weaving. I had to do it in two pieces and then join them together in the middle, but the stitching is not noticeable."

"Adva, I am delighted that you made it for us to share. Is this what Havilah was bringing to our tent?" Malachi asked. "Although it is lovely, we need to remove your blanket. They will come for our bed linens in the morning to prove our union. I do not want them to take your blanket away. May I help you fold it up?" asked Malachi.

With Malachi on one side of the bed and Adva on the other, they folded it down the bed and put it by her personal items.

"Is there anything else you need to do?" asked Malachi.

"Yes, I need to relieve myself," said Adva.

"I best take a walk myself. I will knock before I enter," stated Malachi.

"Thank you," replied Adva.

Malachi walked around to the back of their tent. From the darkness, he saw Tamar and Levi enter their tent next door. Tamar was quite taken with the wine she had consumed. Levi was guiding her to their tent. Ziva was dancing on her toes as Benjamin pulled her off to their tent. The drumming had stopped and everyone was going to their own places of rest for the evening. Eleazar, Lamech, Baruch, Ramah, Joseph, and Deborah went off to the house for their rest. Malachi sighed as he looked to the heavens. Cassiopeia reigned supreme directly over Mt. Gerizim. He returned to the front of the tent and knocked gently.

"Yes, come in." Malachi stepped in and rinsed his feet again in the bowl. He rose from the stool and then placed it by their bed. Malachi watched as Adva let out her braid, pulling her small, oil-dipped fingers through her locks and following with the brush. Malachi was mesmerized. From behind her, he gently took the brush from her hand and began to brush her hair himself. As he finished, he grabbed a handful of hair and rubbed his face in it playfully.

Adva laughed. "Yes, let's put some oil on that beard of yours." Adding several fingerfuls of oil to her hands, Adva rubbed it onto his chin. Taking her brush, she began to soften and detangle his beard.

"You must teach me how to do this," said Malachi.

"I have wanted to do this for a long time," confessed Adva.

"Oh, have you now," Malachi said, raising his eyebrow. Adva's face reddened with her confession and her hands stopped. He took her by the hand and they walked around the bed to the other side.

"Can we blow out the lamp now?" asked Adva. "The tent is very hot."

"Everyone is going home for the night. We can open a flap."

Malachi took the stool to the west side of the tent. He loosened and then dropped a corner of the tent's side. The cool night air rushed in as Malachi returned the stool to the bedside. Adva blew out the lamp as the light of the moon shone in.

"Adva, did your mother explain to you what takes place in the marriage bed?" asked Malachi.

Adva bowed her head, embarrassed to confess. "No. Mother taught us much about womanhood, household duties, and marriage customs, but we had not yet reached that lesson before she left us," Adva said softly. "But during our visit yesterday, Zipporah explained to me and my sisters what is expected of a wife, and she gave us this special ointment to make our time of coming together easier."

"And have you applied the ointment as she instructed you?" asked Malachi.

"Yes, but it is sticky and I did not use very much."

The couple sat down together on the edge of their bed. Malachi reached for the small pot, dipped his finger into the potion and brought it to his mouth to taste it. "It contains honey and myrrh."

Adva dipped her finger into the pot and agreed. "I do not like that."

"We have your oil with us. Perhaps we can add that to it and create a recipe you do like?" suggested Malachi. Adva rose to get her jar of lavender-infused oil. Malachi dipped two fingers into the oil and stirred them in the potion. He then put his fingers to her lips and she tasted the new recipe. He then tasted for himself, "Yes, this is a good mix. Does it please you?"

"Yes, I like it better and it is less sticky now," Adva declared, still not fully understanding the potion's purpose.

Malachi stepped away to pour wine into their cups, then returned to her side.

"Let us leave the oil, the potion, and the wine here on the stool. We may need them during the night."

As Adva rose to place the jars on the stool, Malachi quickly removed his trousers and his tunic. She heard his movement behind her back and was afraid to turn around. "I have covered myself with our bed linens. You may turn around." But Adva remained frozen in place. "Adva, would you like me to remove your tunic or would you like to do that?" he asked gently.

"I will do it," she answered. Adva, with her back to her husband, pulled the tunic up and over her head. She stood there quietly after disrobing.

"Adva, what is wrong?"

"I am afraid," she whispered.

Malachi swallowed hard as a new tenderness for Adva developed in his heart. "Drink your cup of wine; it will steady your nerves." Adva obeyed and took a sip. "Drink it all at once, Adva." Obediently, she drank it all and purposely backed to her spot at the edge of the bed feeling vulnerable and frightened.

Malachi reached to pull the stool closer to the bed so the potion would be easily accessible. He wished he could do more to quell the uneasiness of his new bride, knowing that she had not yet been with a man. It had been Kenan who had explained that a young woman was vulnerable as one of his ewes. He advised that if their union was not handled properly on the wedding night, it would cause difficulties throughout their marriage. Malachi had waited four years for this moment, he could wait a while longer. He wanted a long and fruitful marriage with Adva.

Malachi gathered her long hair and laid it gently over her shoulder. He put his legs on both sides of her and slowly snugged up to her back. Although he desired to see his beautiful bride, he would wait until she was ready to show herself to him. He wrapped his arms around her waist and pulled her close to him. He tenderly kissed her neck then rocked her side to side to allow her to relax in his embrace.

As the fear subsided, Adva touched his arms. Timidly at first, she began to stroke the hair on his arms with her hands. Malachi could feel the weight of her breasts on his arms but did not dare to move from the comforting embrace.

Releasing Adva from his hold, Malachi spoke in a husky whisper, "Adva, do you trust me?" Malachi waited for her reply, but she did not give it. "I want to show you how a man loves a woman."

"Yes, I trust you," she whispered.

"Adva, will you stand in the moonlight by our bed and let me see you?"

In the golden light of the moon with her tousled hair draping her body, Adva stood and faced Malachi, whose intense gaze made her bow her head. Malachi, overcome by her beauty, spoke reverently, "Oh Adva, you are so lovely. More lovely than I had even imagined."

Adva was reminded of Adam's response to Eve in the garden when *Elohim* presented Eve to Adam for the first time. Malachi reached for Adva's hand. He dipped their fingers into the oil and rubbed their hands together. Adva stood before him at the edge of their bed as he placed her hand on his chest.

Feeling his muscles tighten, she asked, "are you afraid, too?"

"Yes, I am afraid that I will hurt you. I see you as the young woman that you are for the first time," Malachi explained. "I have shown you only some of the steps of our new dance. Come my bride, I will show you more."

Welcoming Adva to their bed, Malachi moved to the other side and generously applied the lavender-infused salve to ease Adva's pain in their union. Their final dance steps left them exhausted, and they slept well until morning.

When the morning light came, Adva was slightly embarrassed by their nakedness and sheepish about the pleasures of the previous night. Malachi, as he kissed each of her shoulders, wanted to start all over again. Both were startled by a knock at the door.

"Who is it?" Malachi barked, grumpy about the interruption.

"I have come for the bed sheets," said the servant.

"Come again in a moment, we are not dressed," Malachi replied.

"Very well," said the young servant, who scurried away quickly.

"Wake up, Adva. There is much to do today," called Tamar from the path in front of the tents.

"How are you awake already?" Adva called to her sister, clutching the sheets to her body.

"We are moving Ziva to Sychar today," replied Tamar.

"Okay, give us a moment. We are just waking."

Suddenly, Malachi sprang from the bed like he was on fire. He donned his tunic and raced barefoot past Tamar to the next tent.

"Levi, did you have relations last night?" Malachi inquired urgently.

"No, Tamar fell asleep too quickly," he replied. "Why?"

"I will explain later. Do not let the servant take your bed sheets!"

Malachi raced back to his tent where Adva was dressed and sat braiding her hair.

"Where is our potion from last night?" he asked in a panic.

"There on the stool by the bed."

Malachi grabbed his knife and the potion then returned to Levi's tent.

"Here cut your hand," said Malachi as he took the jar with the prescribed honey potion and smeared a spot on the linen. "Add some of your blood to this spot. I must go to warn Benjamin. Your parents will inspect the bed linens this morning."

Levi did as he was told. Malachi took the knife and knocked at the door of the last tent.

"Benjamin, did you have relations with your wife last night?" Malachi asked in urgency.

"We were both tired from dancing and fell asleep," replied Benjamin reluctantly.

"Quick! Cut yourself with the knife," Malachi commanded quietly as he smeared the honey potion on the bed linen. "Wipe your blood here in the ointment. Then wash your hand. The groom's parents always inspect the bed linens on the morning after the wedding. I have just saved you and your wife from much disgrace. Do not speak of this to anyone," he whispered.

Levi caught Malachi's arm as he passed. "Thank you, Malachi," Levi said. "I had forgotten about that custom!"

"Say no more to anyone. Not even your wife," replied Malachi.

He entered his tent and inspected their own sheets to make sure there was enough blood on them to please his father. He sat on the stool and rubbed his face. Adva came close and stood in front of him.

"What is wrong?" she asked.

"I cannot tell you of my deed. Please do not ask me again."

The servant knocked again for the bed linens. Malachi gathered them and took them to the tent's door. The servant bowed to Malachi and went to the next tent and the next. After washing his face and beard and drying his face with his tunic, Malachi walked over to Adva who was standing in the doorway. Standing behind her as she stared off in the distance, Malachi shifted her tunic to the side and softly kissed her shoulder.

"You are a beauty to behold, my dear wife," Malachi said before spinning her around and kissing her fully on the mouth. Adva returned his kiss. Malachi pulled away because they could not return to their bed. "My desire for you will never be quenched," he whispered in her ear.

"Come, put your boots on, and let us go to the house for our breakfast," offered Adva with a playful smile.

Tamar, who witnessed the kiss, was embarrassed; she regretted falling asleep last night. Levi approached beside her and squeezed her hand in anticipation. "Come sisters!"

called Tamar. "Let us make breakfast for our guests and husbands."

Ziva danced out in front of her sisters with a scarf over her head. Benjamin emerged from his tent tying a rope belt around his waist. The sisters led the way with the men enjoying the view from behind.

The sisters did not think to knock on the door to their previous home. Adva entered first followed by the other two. Once inside, they stood frozen near the doorway, bewildered both by the discussion at the table and the display of their bed linens.

"Adva!" cried the little ones. The in-laws were gathered about the table inspecting the linens, discussing the purity of the brides, and giving their consent that the marriages were good.

"Good morning daughters! I am surprised that you are awake so soon after all the festivities of yesterday," said Eleazar.

"Father, our table is unclean now," said Adva in disgust. Abigail grabbed her hand. Havilah held the squirmy Miriam.

"Yes, it is unclean until sunset," Eleazar answered earnestly. "We will have our meals in the tent we used yesterday. This room is not big enough for all of us anymore. Come, our breakfast awaits us there."

The young men backed out the door giving Malachi a look of thanks. The sisters huddled together as Eleazar led the way to breakfast.

"What were they doing with our bed linens?" asked Ziva.

"The groom's parents inspect the linens to make sure that the brides are virgins," stated Adva.

"How do they know?" asked Tamar.

"There is blood from when a woman's body is joined with her husband for the first time. I did not know this until Malachi told me."

"Oh," replied Ziva and Tamar. Tamar tugged at Adva's arm. "But we have not yet had relations," she whispered. "I passed out from the wine."

"Benjamin and I also fell asleep and did not have relations either," admitted Ziva.

"Well, the in-laws are happy with what they found, so someone did something. Ask your husbands, they seem to know. But do not say anything more until you are in private. Act like newly married women today and focus on pleasing your husbands." Adva knew in her heart that Malachi had saved her sisters from shame, and in that moment, she loved him a little bit more.

15
First Fruits

Adva and Malachi spent the first two months of their marriage planting olive trees from Beth-shean, which Uncle Kenan had given to Malachi as a wedding gift. They planted them near the apple trees in the area that Levi's goats had cleared. During the hot summer months, they had to use Adva's water yoke to haul water to their new plantings. There had been many trips to the well in the wee hours of the morning to fetch water in the cart before the plowing of the fields. They were thankful when the rains began. During the first year, Malachi worked hard and learned much about farming, but he truly missed just tending sheep.

Eleazar and Malachi had built a large pen for the sheep towards the west of the barn. The pen extended to the grove of oak trees but did not enclose them and would be large enough for a medium-sized herd of sheep.

Malachi's itch to return to the outdoors made him difficult to live with on the farm. Eleazar and Malachi devised a plan for Malachi to help plant the barley then leave with his sheep. Malachi would return for the barley harvest and flax planting, then again for the harvest of the flax and the shearing of the sheep. After selling the wool, he would take a third trip and return for the apple harvest. This seemed to make Malachi happy and he felt less confined. Everyone was happy when Malachi was happy. Both Eleazar and Adva looked forward to his time away.

Being a wife and daughter in the same house was difficult for Adva. Oftentimes, when tensions were running high, she chose to walk away, letting the men argue and talk it out. The words written by Moses told her to honor her father and her husband. She tried to do both, but she still had more to learn about men and their ways. Eleazar and Malachi could argue one minute and be best friends the next. She also noticed that the farm was doing much better with two men working hard on the crops. She had helped in the fields only on a few occasions.

Now that the rainy season had passed, the barley had been harvested and the flax planted. Eleazar returned from a trip to Sebaste without Shem, having purchased two oxen as a replacement. When Havilah greeted Eleazar, she noticed the new oxen in Shem's stall and the absence of Shem. "Where is Shem?" she cried.

Eleazar took a deep breath and replied, "Havilah, Shem has been sold to a smaller farm in Sebaste. Levi knows the family and Tamar will look after Shem. You will be able to visit him on your next visit to Sebaste. Shem was getting older and less able to plow."

"Perhaps it is a good thing he doesn't have to work so hard. I will miss him," she confessed.

"I am already missing him," said her father. "I really felt like he understood me. The oxen are not listening very well."

"What are we going to do with all the carrots we planted?" Havilah laughed. Eleazar joined in.

"What are you two laughing about?" Adva inquired as she entered the barn.

"Father had to sell Shem to a smaller farm in Sebaste," Havilah said sadly. "We were laughing about all the carrots we planted."

"I think Abigail and Miriam like carrots," added Adva. "How are Levi and Tamar?"

"Levi is doing excellent work in his workshop. I was able to help with a few orders, and he paid me enough to help buy the oxen. And Tamar is very happy. Their baby swells within her," said Eleazar. "She will give birth before the apple harvest in September."

"I am happy for her. She will be a good mother. I am sorry I did not get to see her. Does she have a good midwife?" asked Adva.

Eleazar replied, "Yes, I believe she does. Zipporah speaks highly of the midwife in Sebaste."

Since Eleazar had returned from his visit to Sebaste, Malachi could now leave for Mt. Ebal. He was traveling all the way to Beth-shean to visit Uncle Kenan and Aunt Rue. He planned on dividing his herd with Aden, his nephew. He also wanted to shear the sheep and sell the wool for a better price at his Uncle Eliab's market in Aenon. Many travelers passed through Aenon during this time of year.

"Son of Anak!" Malachi complained to Adva as he paced about the roof in the early afternoon. "Some days I can do nothing right for your father."

Adva sighed but really didn't know how to help the two men get along better. "You know, Moses lived with his father-in-law, Jethro. That puts you in good company. Perhaps Moses kept sheep to get some time away from Jethro," she replied while folding clothes from the wash and preparing for his trip with the sheep.

"Well, I am no Moses," he chortled.

She laughed, "Yes, I know." Quickly, he charged at her from his stool. She playfully tried to run away, but he pulled her close and kissed her.

"Your mouth needs something else to do besides making fun of your husband," he said, pulling her into their room for a moment in the heat of the day.

Eleazar watched them from the barn door and ached for his Tirzah. He could hear the giggles of Havilah, Abigail, and Miriam as they played with Goshen and Jaspar. Eleazar returned to the task of sharpening knives and sickles that would be needed for the next harvest. There was a rumble of thunder off in the distance.

"Ah yes, some rain would be nice *Adonai*," Eleazar whispered.

It was indeed raining by the time they had their evening meal. Adva cleared away the dishes as Eleazar invited Havilah, Abigail, and Miriam to read with him. "Tonight, we will read of the blessing that Jacob, now called Israel, gave to Joseph," stated Eleazar. Clearing his throat, he began:

> *Israel stretched out his right hand and placed it on Ephraim's head, although he was the younger. Crossing his hands, he put his left hand on Manasseh's head, for Manasseh was the first-born. Then he blessed Joseph and said, "May the God before whom my fathers Abraham and Isaac walked—the God who has been my shepherd all my life long to this day, the angel who has protected me from all harm—bless these boys. May my name be named in them, and the name of my fathers Abraham and Isaac. May they grow into a multitude on the earth."*[36]

Eleazar laid his hand on Havilah's forehead, then Abigail's, and finally Miriam's. "To all my daughters," he declared, "may you be fruitful and continue the line

[36] Genesis 48:14-16. NET.

of Joseph with *Elohim's* blessing. Blessed be *Adonai*, the Eternal One. Amen."

"Amen," mimicked Miriam.

"Amen," replied Eleazar with a smile. A clap of thunder punctuated the moment.

"Amen," echoed everyone in the room in reverence.

The four weeks during which Malachi was gone went by quickly as there was always much for Eleazar, Adva, and Havilah to do. Miriam was fussy because she was getting a new tooth. Abigail was right there with her, giving her grapes, carrots, and apple slices to soothe her gums. Miriam began to say new words, calling Malachi, "*Achi*," the Hebrew word for brother. Havilah was teaching her younger sisters some of the songs that Tirzah used to sing to her, and it made Eleazar happy to hear those songs again and remember his beloved wife.

On the night that Malachi returned, Eleazar again enjoyed having the young ones on his lap for the readings of Moses. It reminded him of a time not long ago when he had read with Adva. Adva put the little ones to bed and went up to the roof while Eleazar and Malachi caught up with all that had transpired while he was away. She was at the top of the stairs when Malachi bid Eleazar goodnight. With sweet anticipation, he raced up the stairs to meet her in their rooftop home.

"Hello wife," he said with a smile as he entered.

"Hello husband," Adva said as she undid her braided hair, knowing how Malachi loved watching her brush her hair. Malachi did not think he would ever grow tired of watching her brush her hair. Adva knew she had his attention. "I thought you were coming home last week?"

Malachi took another brush and carefully began to groom his own hair and beard. "I was, but I remembered that you would be on your womanly rest and it would have been torture for me to be here without you in my bed." At those words, she dropped her brush to the floor. She turned on her stool to look at his face.

"I did not have my womanly rest last week. How did I forget that? How did it not come? What is wrong with me?" asked Adva.

He smiled then knelt at her feet. He took her hands in his and kissed them. "Adva, you are with child!" Malachi stated jubilantly.

"What?" Adva replied shaking her head in disbelief. "Praise *Adonai*!" she declared with a wide smile.

Malachi stood then picked her up and swung her around, knocking over the stool. "Aunt Rue said you would be pregnant before the apple trees bloomed."

"May *Adonai* bless Aunt Rue!" exclaimed Adva, hugging him tightly.

"I will take you to see Ziva tomorrow and you can share the news with her," said Malachi, placing her gently back on the ground. "We will make plans to go see Tamar. Would you like that?"

"Yes, I would. I want to tell Father in the morning."

"I am certain he suspects something. He did not try to get me to talk longer," said Malachi as he disrobed and crawled into the bed.

"Yes, there are no secrets from Father Eleazar," replied Adva. "We should celebrate."

Malachi patted the linens beside him, "I know how I want to celebrate. Come here, my wife."

The two awoke very early the next morning and hitched the oxen to the cart to go fetch water from the well. Adva whispered to a sleepy Havilah that she would return soon. They arrived at Jacob's well as the sun was rising. They brought every jar from home they could find. Malachi hauled the water buckets and Adva brought the pottery vessels to fill. They had almost filled the cart with their jars of water when Ziva came from town with her own yoke and water jars.

"Malachi, do you have strength for two more buckets of water? Here comes Ziva."

They waited for her to arrive. She did not notice them for a while as she walked.

"Good morning, Ziva!" Adva called.

"Adva! Malachi! It is wonderful to see you both this morning!" Ziva exclaimed.

"If we fill your jars, we can give you a ride back to town," said Malachi.

"I would like that," replied Ziva with a bow to Malachi.

"You two talk while I fetch the water," Malachi stated as he lifted Ziva up on the cart beside Adva.

"Ziva, I have the best news. I am with child!"

"Praise *Elohim*! When will your little one be born?"

"In about nine months. I missed my time of rest last week."

Ziva sighed, "Alas, I am the last one of us to be with child."

"You are also the youngest of the three married sisters, perhaps your body is not yet ready for a baby. Be patient. *Adonai* has not forgotten you," said Adva, noticing that Ziva's breasts were still growing. She transformed into a woman more and more each day. Adva had noticed some of those changes for herself and it pleased Malachi greatly. The sisters rode back to town chattering all the way. Malachi came to a stop at the main gate of Sychar.

"We must hurry. I promised your father my help this morning," said Malachi.

"Do not tell anyone, Ziva. We have not told Father yet," said Adva. "I plan to make soap starting tomorrow. Father wants me to teach Havilah. Do you want to come help?"

"I would like to come tomorrow," replied Ziva.

"We will stop for you on our trip to the well for more water and supplies," stated Malachi. "*Shalom* to Benjamin."

"Thank you, Malachi. Until tomorrow," Ziva said as she waved goodbye.

When they came into the courtyard with their water, Eleazar was walking to the barn. "Father! I have wonderful news!" called Adva.

Eleazar smiled knowingly, "Adva, what is your news? Is all well with Ziva?"

She climbed down from the cart without waiting for Malachi's assistance and she ran to her father. "Ziva is fine, but I am going to have a baby!" she exclaimed.

"Oh, that," Eleazar teased. "I already figured that out. I was just waiting for *you* to realize your blessing."

"You tease me. Are you happy?" asked Adva.

"Yes, it was difficult for me to contain my joy this last week. I did not want to spoil your discovery," he said wisely. "Congratulations, Malachi. Now our children will grow up together just as you wished not so long ago."

"Aye, yes, I remember that wish," Malachi stated. "See, I told you he had figured it out before you."

"Yes, there are no secrets from Father Eleazar," repeated Adva. She hugged her father tenderly, then ran inside the house to tell Havilah while the two men walked to the barn together.

Since the flax was planted, Malachi began to get restless and Adva knew it was time for him to take his sheep to Mt. Ebal. Adva brushed her hair as she prepared for bed. "Father is going to take Havilah to Tamar's to have her help with the birth of his first grandchild. He is doing that so Havilah can help me with our little one," announced Adva.

"This is good," replied Malachi as he removed his tunic and quickly climbed into their bed. "She will be a great help to you when your time draws near."

"Yes. When you return, it will be time for apple picking. Father hopes that Tamar will have her baby before the rainy season begins." Adva stopped brushing and pivoted to get a view of Malachi. "Have you thought about what it will be like to have our own child?"

"My dear Adva, I have thought of having a child with you for the last four years. I have dreamt of showing my son the joys of raising sheep. I have imagined taking him with me to Mt. Ebal. I cannot wait to show him to Uncle Kenan and Aunt Rue. I look forward to telling him about our olive trees and how we cared for them in our first months of marriage."

"What if our child is a girl?" asked Adva, somewhat fearful that he would only want a son.

"Then I will delight in watching her help you. She will learn to weave and cook."

"Yes," she replied, her mind wandering to other things that needed to be done before the child arrived. "I will soon have new flax to spin. You will need another tunic and I need to make this child some clothes. Oh, there is so much to do," fretted Adva.

"Adva, come to bed," commanded Malachi. "Do not worry. You have time to get ready. Your sisters will help you. But for now, I have need of you." Malachi patted the linens and beckoned her to join him.

Adva put down the brush and walked to the bedside. "Have you truly imagined being married to me that long?"

"Yes, all the other girls in Damascus, Beth-shean, and Sychar did not compare to my Adva. They were silly and flirtatious. Every year I would ask Eleazar to allow our marriage and to claim you as my own. However, it was the fear I might lose you to Levi that made me realize that I had to change and become the man that you needed as your husband," confessed Malachi. "It was Aunt Rue who made me understand that as I complained of your father's reluctance to betroth you to me. She is a wise woman."

"May *Adonai* bless Aunt Rue!" exclaimed Adva.

"Did you imagine being married to me?" inquired Malachi.

Adva was quiet for a moment. "Husband, I was nine years old when you arrived at our farm and I did not think about such things yet. At that time, you frightened me and smelled of sheep." They laughed together, then Adva continued quietly, "when I became a woman and soon after my mother died, I knew in my heart that you were the man that *Adonai* had chosen for me."

"Adva," Malachi coaxed. "Come close, let me love you."

Adva pulled her tunic over her head, causing her hair to fan over her body and release a fragrance of sage and rosemary. Malachi sat up on his knees, kissing and sucking at her breast.

"Ouch!" Adva exclaimed. "Be gentle, my husband. This child is changing my body as he grows within me."

Malachi's hands cupped her face and he kissed her lips gently with a tenderness that the two had not yet experienced. Their passion for each other helped Adva to forget her doubts and worries; for this moment, she rested in her husband's embrace.

After their night's rest, it was easier for Adva to release her husband to roam with his sheep. With the knowledge that he would soon return to her, she seemed more at ease with the idea of his absence.

16
Jaspar Returns

It was the distant clang of Jaspar's bell that Adva heard first. She closed her eyes and took a deep breath, expecting to hear Malachi's voice. But when she turned around, there was only Jaspar. No sheep. No Malachi.

"Jaspar, where did you leave my husband?" she mused, placing her hands on her hips.

She walked Jaspar back to the barn. "Father, is Malachi with you? Jaspar wandered into the apple field by himself," she stated. Eleazar immediately came close and examined the goat carefully for any wounds or signs. He found nothing out of the ordinary. He knew that Jaspar would never leave the flock or his master and just wander away.

"Get my pack. I will go look for Malachi and be back before dark. Keep yourself and your sisters close to the house and barn. Do not wander out to the apples or to the fields," commanded Eleazar.

Her father's commands frightened Adva. She was now worried, rubbing her belly for comfort. Adva entered the house to get Eleazar a skin of water and a wineskin to wash any wounds. She added cloths to the pack and some yarrow leaves to stop any bleeding. She met Eleazar in the barn coming up from the root cellar. "Do not worry, Adva. We do not know that Malachi has been harmed, but

Adonai knows everything," comforted Eleazar. "I will be back soon."

Eleazar hitched the oxen to the cart and immediately left for Mt. Ebal. Jaspar's bell tinkled from the sheep's pen.

"Jaspar! My friend is home!" exclaimed Havilah with Miriam on her hip and Abigail skipping from the house. "Where are the sheep? Where is Malachi?"

"We do not know. Father has gone to look for him."

"Oh," replied Havilah, sensing the gravity of the moment. "Let's go up to the roof and keep watch. We can card wool if you need something to do?"

"Yes, of course," stated Adva quietly, taking Abigail by the hand. Havilah gathered some fruit for Miriam and Abigail from the kitchen then climbed the stairs to the roof. They watched Eleazar take the oxen to the edge of their farm and beyond. They could not see anyone or anything else from their vantage point, but they stayed on the roof until the heat was unbearable.

The sun moved slowly across the sky. As evening was approaching, Havilah took care of the goats and returned with some extra milk for the young ones and prepared a small evening meal. After they ate, Adva bathed the girls and rubbed mint-scented olive oil onto their skin. The room smelled sweet, and it reminded Adva of her wedding tent. The sun was setting when Eleazar returned alone.

"I made it to Askar and spoke to some herdsmen who were going on to the springs of Tirzah. They will ask of him for us and deliver a message on to Kenan in Beth-shean."

"Father, I am frightened," whispered Adva.

"I am too, Adva," replied Eleazar. "But *Adonai* knows where Malachi is and he shall protect him."

"I will sleep outside on the roof tonight so I can listen for him," said Adva.

Havilah brought some food for Eleazar and placed it before him. He took a bite before speaking again. "Thank you, Havilah. Adva, you must protect yourself and your baby. I plan to go to the well first thing in the morning and I will have Benjamin and Ziva come to stay with you. I will travel to Aenon and perhaps Beth-shean, and I will return as soon as I can. Try not to worry. *Elohim* will protect us all."

Adva began to cry because of the child within her. She felt helpless. Abigail came close and patted Adva's arm to comfort her. Adva picked Abigail up and hugged her tight. Putting her thoughts on Abigail, Adva stopped crying. Then Miriam began walking towards them; it was her first long walk across the room without falling.

"Well, look who's walking!" Eleazar exclaimed, clapping his hands. "*Adonai* be praised."

Miriam, enjoying her father's attention, tried to turn toward Eleazar but that caused her to fall. She quickly got up from the floor and toddled over to her father who swept her up into his arms. "Beautiful daughter of mine, Miriam. Havilah, what is that lullaby you sing?"

Havilah sang as Eleazar joined in. "*Numi, numi yaldati, Numi, numi, nim.*"[37] Abigail sang along.

Miriam sang "Nu, Nu, Nmm" as best she could.

"Well, I had best put the animals to bed," said Eleazar, setting Miriam on her feet.

"Father, did you tend to the oxen when you arrived home? I have fed the goats," said Havilah, grabbing Miriam's hand.

"Yes, I did. Very well, I will prepare for tomorrow. I shall return soon." Eleazar took a lamp and went to the barn to sharpen his knife and make sure everything was ready for an early departure in the morning. As he approached the house, he could see Adva's form on the roof, pacing.

---

[37] These are the lyrics of ancient Hebrew lullaby.

"Do you see anything, Adva?" Eleazar asked.

"No," she sighed. "With no moon tonight, it is too dark to see anything."

"Go to sleep. I will wake you in the morning before I leave for Sychar."

"Yes, Father."

It was still dark when Adva heard Eleazar in the barn hitching the oxen to the cart. She arose and joined him.

"Oh good, you are awake," said Eleazar. "I am going to Sychar to get your water. I will fetch Ziva and bring her back with me and ask Benjamin to come here tonight to stay with you. I will also tell Joseph and Deborah to look after you all. Be vigilant. Pray. Have Benjamin read to the girls each night. *Elohim* sees us and knows what we need to do. Listen to *Adonai*."

"Yes Father, just bring Malachi safely home," Adva said with a quiver in her voice.

When Eleazar got to the well, there were shepherds encamped around it. Eleazar began watering his oxen and then drew the water for the farm. Once the oxen had their fill, he continued to put water in the trough. As the sheep began to come near to drink, he recognized a few of them as part of Malachi's flock. One of the shepherds came over and thanked Eleazar for drawing water for the flock.

"*Shalom*," said Eleazar. "Sorry to disturb you so early, but I am looking for a shepherd by the name of Malachi ben Lamech. Have you seen him grazing near Mt. Ebal?"

"Yes, we shared camp for a night. He was going on to Aenon said the shepherd. "He told us about this well and that we could rest here on our way south."

"Did he have a pack goat with him when you saw him?" inquired Eleazar.

"Yes. He traded us some sheep for a trio of goats," said the shepherd.

"Did he say why he needed goats?"

"Yes, he was taking them to his uncle in Beth-shean to clear some of their land. It was to be a gift," said the shepherd.

"How long ago did you see him?" Eleazar asked.

"It was about two weeks ago. We went to Sebaste first before coming here," he replied. "Why do you ask?"

"He is my son-in-law and his pack goat came home without him yesterday."

Some other shepherds were gathering around the well to listen. Eleazar filled the trough with water one more time for the shepherds and the sheep.

"You have been very helpful. I must be off to search for him. *Shalom*," said Eleazar.

He jumped upon the cart and headed to town as the sun began to rise. Upon his arrival, he climbed the steep stairs of Benjamin and Ziva's home and knocked at the door. "Benjamin, Ziva, it is Eleazar!" When his daughter came to the door, Eleazar gave her a jar of water as she swept hair from her face. Inside, she placed the water on the small table that filled the near-empty room.

"*Shalom*," said Eleazar, smiling at his youngest married daughter.

"You are here early this morning, Eleazar," stated Benjamin, tightening the belt of his tunic.

"Yes, I have come to ask a favor. I must go to Beth-shean to look for Malachi. Jaspar came to the farm without him yesterday. Pack goats do not leave their masters and I fear that something has happened. I was just at the well and there were shepherds who had spent the night there. Some of Malachi's sheep were with them. One of the shepherds said that Malachi traded some sheep for a trio of goats as a gift for his uncle in Beth-shean. I believe their story, but I still think something has happened to him. I need you and Ziva to stay at the farm while I am gone. Can you do that?"

"Yes, of course," said Benjamin. "May I use your grinding stone to continue my work?"

"Yes, indeed."

"We can ride back to the farm with you as soon as I pick up my work from the shop. I will return quickly." Benjamin raced down the steps and made his way quickly to the blacksmith stable on the corner.

"I will pack a few things for us. There is no need to leave your water here," said Ziva.

"You are right. I will put it in the cart with the others. Please hurry with your packing. I will go tell Joseph what is going on."

"Yes, Father. I will be right down. We will have breakfast at the farm with my sisters," said Ziva as she grabbed some vegetables from the counter. "Do you think you will be gone a week?" she asked.

"I will return as soon as I can. But I may be away for two weeks," stated Eleazar.

"Yes, of course."

Eleazar made his way down the stairs to the cart with the water jar. "*Aye*! I am getting too old for these narrow steps," he mumbled to himself. He placed the jar in the back with the others, then stepped across the street to Joseph's shop just as he opened for the day. "*Shalom*, my friend," greeted Eleazar.

"*Shalom*, Eleazar. It is good to see you this morning," said Joseph. Eleazar explained his mission to Joseph and Deborah.

"How is Adva?" asked Deborah.

"She is worried, as am I," replied Eleazar.

"We will visit and share Sabbath with them," said Joseph.

"Thank you. I will return as soon as I can. I hope I will not have to go to Damascus," confessed Eleazar with concern.

"We will pray for you both to return safely," stated Joseph. "*Shalom.*"

Benjamin met Eleazar at the cart. "Jacob has offered you his finest horse team," said Benjamin, pointing to the blacksmith that stood in the doorway.

"Thank you, but I do not think I could withstand the speed of his horses," Eleazar replied, and waved to Jacob. Benjamin put the packed sacks into the cart. He helped Ziva onto the cart and climbed aboard.

As the cart traveled down the road at a steady pace, the oxen created thick clouds of dust, which forced everyone to keep their mouths shut and pull their tunics over their faces during the ride. Benjamin jumped down from the cart when they arrived at the farm. He brushed the dirt from his hair with his hand. "We left in such haste we were not prepared for such a dusty ride," he said.

"You better wear a *keffiyeh*[38] when you go to Aenon or the dust will make you unrecognizable by the time you arrive," said Benjamin.

When they approached the house, Havilah opened the door and welcomed her sister. Abigail came running out and hugged Eleazar, who kissed her on the forehead. Miriam toddled along behind Abigail for her hug and kiss.

"Oh, look who is walking!" exclaimed Ziva. "She is getting so big!" Eleazar hugged Miriam, gave her a kiss, and gave her to Ziva. But she squirmed until she could get down.

Benjamin and the girls got the rest of the water from the cart. As they entered the house, they eyed the large breakfast

[38] A *keffiyeh* is a Bedouin kerchief (cloth) worn as a headdress to protect the wearer from sand and sun.

that Adva had prepared for them. Ziva hugged Adva and gently patted her small baby belly. She saw Adva's eyes well up with tears. "Papa will find Malachi," she promised. "He has a good plan." Adva just nodded her head and then returned to the firepit for the family's bread.

"Now, where would you like us to sleep. Do we get the barn?" asked Ziva.

"No, I think you should have Papa's bed here on the first floor. The girls can sleep upstairs with me," Adva replied. "I need to be on the roof."

"Okay. I brought our bed linens. Next week is my womanly rest. We will have to figure out something else for all of us," stated Ziva.

"We have time to figure it out," said Havilah. "Perhaps this time I can join you."

"Well, I will move to the barn without hesitation," said Benjamin. "But perhaps you will drink the farm water and magically be with child."

"Oh Benjamin, that would be wonderful!" Ziva exclaimed, hugging his arm before giving him a kiss on the cheek.

Eleazar entered the house and spied the full breakfast. "Adva, you are in good hands. I am going to eat quickly."

"Papa, do you have everything you need?" Havilah asked. "Blanket, lantern, water, food, grain for the oxen?"

Eleazar took a bite of bread and shakshuka and considered what Havilah had asked. "I need to take some olive oil for the lantern. Do we have a container with a lid?"

"Here Father, take this jar. It has a cork," said Adva.

"Adva!" Ziva exclaimed as she recognized the wedding potion pot, "have you used all your potion from Zipporah?"

"No, I changed containers so that I could use this jar for something else," said Adva feeling a bit embarrassed.

When Eleazar finished his meal, Adva handed him the jar filled with olive oil. As he stepped out into the courtyard, the family joined him.

"You had best leave soon so that you can get to Aenon before sunset," said Adva. "Malachi's Uncle Eliab has a market there. You could stay with him, I am sure. Take Malachi's scarf to prove that you are who you say you are. Be careful, Father. Just bring Malachi home." Adva choked on the words.

"Take care of my girls, Benjamin," said Eleazar as he climbed onto the cart. He wrapped his *keffiyeh* around his mouth and beard, tucking it into the folds, and he signaled to the oxen to begin their trip.

Adva had gone to the roof to watch from above. "Adva sad," said Miriam as she pointed to the roof.

Havilah picked her up. "Yes, *Achi* will be home soon," she promised.

"Who does she call '*Achi*'?" asked Ziva.

"Mal-*achi*."

"Ah, of course," said Ziva. "Let's go filter the water we brought home from the well before I forget."

"Filter?" asked Havilah.

"Yes, the road was very dusty. We could use some rain," replied Ziva.

Benjamin leaned over to kiss his wife. "I am going to the barn to sharpen the tools I brought from the shop," he declared. "Jacob is taking orders for me today and I will pick them up tomorrow. It should keep us going for a few days. I think you should go up to the roof and make the best of the day."

"I will go put our bed linens on father's bed and go up to the roof," stated Ziva.

In the evening that first night, Benjamin read to the little ones. It was a lovely moment of tradition that would be upheld in Ziva's new family as well. Benjamin did not yet have a scroll to read in their home, but he was saving his money for one. He read one of his favorite stories to the girls, where Moses parted the Red Sea and the Egyptians followed the Israelites only to drown in the water.

After the reading, Havilah scooped Miriam into her arms and Adva took Abigail's hand. The four sisters went to the rooftop, leaving Ziva and Benjamin on the first floor. Havilah snuggled the youngest into their beds and joined Adva, who was pacing and praying on the roof.

"What does your heart tell you, Adva?" asked Havilah.

"I am so full of fear that I cannot feel *Adonai* near me. Will you sing the song that Mother used to sing to us?" Adva asked as she clutched her wedding kerchief. "Do you remember it? I need for Mother to be near me tonight."

Havilah began to sing the song their mother had sung many times. "Lai, Lai, Lai, La, Lai . . ." Adva and Havilah were comforted by the melody and went inside their room to sleep until the morning light.

17
Kinsman Redeemer

It had been ten days since Eleazar left to find Malachi. Tomorrow was the Sabbath, which would prevent him from traveling. But it was nice to have Ziva and Benjamin at the farm, and Ziva tried to keep things fun while they waited for Eleazar.

Benjamin, who had walked to town with Ziva and Havilah, had stayed in town to return with his father later. Deborah had joined the girls in the walk back from the well to help prepare for Sabbath.

The child that Adva carried was very active today. Miriam and Abigail giggled as they put their hands on her swollen tummy. Miriam put her ear to Adva's belly and said, "Shhh Baby, go seep!" It was strange how the child would in fact seem to quiet down for a brief time, which allowed Adva to rest too. The young ones and Adva napped on the blanket that Adva shared with Malachi.

An hour into their nap, Adva woke up screaming Malachi's name, which startled Miriam and Abigail awake. Havilah and Ziva ran up the stairs to see what was wrong. Deborah followed less quickly. Adva held tightly to the little ones and rocked them back and forth as she cried.

"What is wrong? Are you well?" asked Ziva and Havilah as they entered the room. Deborah took the young girls downstairs to play and allowed the sisters to comfort each other.

Adva pulled the blanket up around her. "Malachi is dead. I saw him in my dream."

"Adva, it was a dream," said Havilah, while coming to sit and hug her sister.

"Yes, Malachi may come home today," Ziva replied. "He is a strong man." Ziva tried to console her sister, but she struggled to find the right words.

They heard wagon wheels in the courtyard. "Benjamin!" squealed Ziva. "I'll be right back." She took off like a shooting star down the back stairs to see her beloved.

"Papa!" cried Miriam and Abigail running out to the barn.

"You do my heart good," Eleazar said, scooping them both up into his arms. "Where is Adva?" he asked Ziva.

"She is on the roof," replied Ziva. She spotted another cart coming from Sychar. "I will stay to welcome Benjamin and Joseph. Deborah is in the kitchen. Havilah is up with Adva, who just woke up from bad dream. It scared Miriam and Abigail."

"I will go talk to her. Caleb, Malachi's brother, is in the barn. Malachi has died," stated Eleazar bluntly. Ziva gasped and sat down on the bench outside the barn. "Can you get the things Caleb will need to make a bed in the barn?" Eleazar asked quietly. Ziva nodded. Eleazar went into the house and said a quick hello to Deborah. He grabbed a wineskin and wearily climbed the stairs to the roof.

"Adva, may I come in?" called Eleazar.

"Yes, Father," Adva replied.

He swallowed hard hearing the innocence in her voice. When he opened the door, he saw her wrapped in their blanket like a cocoon. She was pale and crying. Havilah sat

"Havilah, will you braid my hair and put a dark scarf around it? I will mourn in a plain tunic tonight but I will go to town for a black one after Sabbath."

"Maybe I can go with you," replied Havilah.

"That would be nice," Adva whispered with tears returning to her eyes.

All eyes were on Adva as she walked down the stairs from the roof. Eleazar rose from his seat at the table to come and offer his hand to her as she descended. Havilah scooped up Miriam, whispering something into her ear, and took the hand of Abigail. She led them both to their place at the table. Eleazar seated Adva at the table beside him with Joseph on her other side. To Adva, they were a wall of protection but also a stifling enclosure. She wanted to run away but had nowhere to go, so she went to a deep, dark place inside herself. She registered the sound of the voices around her but did not respond because she did not know how to answer. Occasionally, tears would fall down her cheeks, but she did not make a sound.

After the meal, Miriam went to Adva and stroked her hand. "Adva sad. *Achi* come soon." Havilah jumped up from her seat and took Miriam and Abigail by the hand to lead them outside to the barn.

Caleb and Benjamin went outside to discuss the sleeping arrangements for the night. Deborah leaned over to Joseph and stated, "We must leave soon if we are going home before Sabbath."

"I think we need to stay," Joseph replied quietly.

"I will prepare the food for tomorrow and set it aside," she said.

Eleazar leaned over to Adva and put his arm around her, "Let us take our walk before the sun sets." Adva rose from her seat at the table and walked to the door. She gathered her shawl from the peg by the door as Eleazar opened it and directed her outside.

It was Caleb who held out his hand for Adva as she exited the house. Adva took his hand and gazed into his eyes with great sorrow. Caleb wasn't sure if she saw his face or Malachi's. He knew for certain that she had loved Malachi with all her heart and it would be difficult to take his place. But it was this strong love for Malachi that made him begin to love her as his own.

Adva stared at his face a little longer than was proper. There were so many of the same features on Caleb's face despite their difference in age. Caleb's face was gentle and kind, not demanding or urgent. Even his eyes were a softer brown than Malachi's. His hair was short and his beard was cut close. He was well groomed and did not smell of sheep. Although he was about the same height, he was not clumsy in his walk or his touch. As a merchant of Damascus, he smelled of spice and his hands were not rough and calloused like Malachi's. Although he seemed quicker to respond to the needs of others, Adva wondered if he would like it here on the farm in the middle of Samaria, miles away from the city's charms.

Eleazar offered his arm to her, breaking her trance. She took his arm with her other hand. Caleb gave a slight bow and stepped away.

Caleb watched her as she walked towards the apple grove. *She is regal*, he thought. *Even with child, she walks with grace and certainty. She is beautiful*. He noticed how her rounded hips swayed very little. Caleb's hand was hot where she had touched him and he brought his fingertips to his lips as if in a kiss.

Benjamin waited patiently for Caleb's attention before continuing to talk to him about the sleeping arrangements. As Adva rounded the corner and went out of sight Caleb replied, "I think you and Ziva should sleep in the guest room in the barn. I will sleep in the loft. There is plenty of straw to make a nice bed for me. I just need a blanket."

"I will have Ziva get us a blanket or two from the house," Benjamin replied thoughtfully. "You already love Adva, don't you?"

"I think I loved her the first time I met her. I thought Malachi was the luckiest man alive," he revealed. "I just hope she will learn to love me as much as she loved him."

"Give her time. Adva is a very strong woman. She will reemerge from her grief," Benjamin declared.

Eleazar walked Adva around the corner, listening to the evening din of birds and frogs. "Let me know if I walk too fast. Your mother was always asking me to slow down for her."

"You still miss Mother, don't you?" asked Adva.

"Yes, I do. But every day gets better, with less pain and more fond memories. I miss her voice. Occasionally, you or Ziva sound just like her in the things you say. It makes me smile."

"I suppose it will be that way in time," she said as she patted his hand then adjusted her shawl. "Tell me how you found Malachi. In my dream he was bitten by a snake while watching the sheep."

Eleazar stopped still in his tracks and turned to his daughter in disbelief. "Adva, that is exactly what happened to your husband. *Elohim* has given you a vision. What else was in your dream?"

"Malachi was alone and afraid of something coming to harm the sheep. Jaspar stomped his feet and kept the sheep very close together. I did not know if the danger was a wolf or a bear. But Malachi found some sort of rock fence and laid down in the entrance to keep the sheep in the pen.

The snake had been sunning in the warmth of the day and lashed out at him for disturbing his resting spot. Malachi did not know that he had been bitten, but his leg began to swell and he tied a belt around his knee or thigh. But by that time the poison had begun to take his life. Before he died, he called out my name . . . and I awoke calling out his!" she sobbed.

Eleazar held her in his arms as she wept. Between gasps, he used her shawl to dry her face.

"My dear sweet Adva, I believe that *Adonai* has shown you what I could not have known. We found Malachi at the top of a hill in a beautiful green meadow. There was a small lake there, which many creatures relied upon for water. We saw tracks of a bear, a lion, and wolves. I am certain that Malachi was protecting his sheep. There was a pen of rocks just like in your dream. It was like a cave without a top," Eleazar explained. "Perhaps I should start from the beginning," he said as he began to recall more details of the trip. "When I arrived in Aenon, it was too close to sunset to go searching for Malachi, so I had to wait for daybreak. It was frustrating to wait another day, but if what *Adonai* showed you is true, Malachi was gone before I arrived." He paused to gather his thoughts before continuing.

"Father, can we go inside your workshop? The wind seems cold to me," asked Adva.

"Yes, of course, let me light the lamp before you enter. I do not want you to trip or fall over anything." Eleazar opened the door and went inside to strike the flint and light the lamp. When he returned, he took Adva's hands in his and led her inside to his workbench to show her his latest creations: two cribs ready to be sanded and oiled.

"Malachi helped saw the wood for the crib. What do you think?" he asked.

"Father, they are lovely, but you better make Ziva one too. She will have a little one of her own soon."

"Has she said anything to you?" asked Eleazar.

"No, but she is late for her womanly rest."

"This is good news for sure. I will start on another one right away. Which one do you like?"

"I think I like this one," said Adva. She ran her hand across the rail and got a splinter. "It looks like this one picks me too," she chuckled, picking the splinter from her hand. "Father, please finish telling me about your trip."

"Yes, of course," he said. "Aden and Kenan were there when I arrived at Aenon to visit with Eliab. I was glad they were there to help. Aden was able to take us straight to where they had rested the sheep last year. We walked to the top of the hill in Aenon. I am sure that Malachi had been to this spot many times," Eleazar said, pausing to take a big breath.

"Eliab had a donkey that we took with us to carry the things we needed. When we found the firepit of the camp that Malachi had used, we knew we were on the right track. We climbed a little further and saw vultures circling overhead, so we continued in the direction of the birds. We then heard sheep bleating and saw the large birds feasting on the carcass of a ram. Malachi was face down at the entrance of the cave. We knew his sheep had been trapped there for a few days because once we moved his body they ran for a drink at the lake." Eleazar paused again.

"It was Kenan who noticed that Malachi had tied a belt around his leg. At first, we thought perhaps the leg was broken but then we found the marks of the snake bite. Adva, please know that Malachi tried to save himself by tying the belt around his leg," he said coming close to her and putting his hand on her shoulder. "The birds had not yet harmed Malachi's body."

"Praise *Adonai*!" Adva said releasing her breath.

"We loaded his body onto the donkey and headed back to Aenon. Our Laws would not allow us to transport him back here for you. Being closer, we made plans to lay him to rest in Beth-shean with his mother and sister. The family burial cave is not far from Kenan's olive trees. We buried Malachi on the third day after Sabbath. I returned to Aenon and then came home from there. I am sorry it took me so long."

"Father, you did the right and honorable thing for Malachi," said Adva patting his hand.

"I brought back the tunic that your mother made and had given to Malachi. I thought you might want it. It must be washed because it is unclean. He was wearing it when he died. If you do not want it, I would like to have it. It was the last thing your mother made for me."

"Yes, I believe you should have it. I will wash it after Sabbath," she replied. "We had better get back to the house. It is getting dark and time for Sabbath to begin. Thank you, Father."

She walked to the door. The sky was filled with crimson and purple clouds and a breeze blew from the Great Sea. Eleazar blew out the lamp and joined Adva as she stood at the doorway admiring the sky. Jaspar's bell rang from the pasture.

"Father, where are Malachi's sheep?" asked Adva.

"I sold some in Aenon to buy what was needed for the burial. Kenan will take some to Beth-shean. Right now, they are in Aenon. Do you want some of his sheep?" Eleazar enquired.

"I would like more wool from his sheep. I would like to weave a blanket for his baby."

"I will get word to Kenan in Beth-shean. He will have some of the sheep. However, I think we may have some wool in the barn from our last shearing."

"Yes, I believe you are right," she replied in agreement. "That will be more than enough for the baby's blanket."

"Maybe you can make one for Tamar too."

"That is a good idea. I best make three," said Adva. "We sisters do everything together."

Adva went into the house, hung her shawl by the door, and washed her face. Eleazar entered right behind her and sat at the table. Deborah came beside Adva and handed her a cloth to dry her face. Then Deborah gave her a hug.

"Thank you, Deborah. Do you and Joseph have what you need for your rest tonight?"

"Yes, I think it has been decided that Joseph and I will have Eleazar's bed. Eleazar has chosen the table. You, Havilah, and the little ones will sleep upstairs if that is good with you? Ziva and Benjamin are sleeping in the guest room in the barn and Caleb has chosen to sleep in the loft in the barn."

"Caleb cannot sleep there. It is over the oxen and filled with mice. He deserves a better place than that." Adva stated.

"I think he has already set up his bed there. He found some wool and made a nice bed. He says he has the best place to sleep," Deborah answered with a calm voice.

"I will find a better place for him to sleep after our Sabbath," Adva said. "The poor man has done so much for so little reward."

"I do not think he feels that way, Adva. Even now his love light shines for you," Deborah whispered.

Adva looked toward the table and Caleb was watching her. Embarrassed, he looked away quickly and returned to the conversation with Eleazar, Joseph, and Benjamin.

Adva walked to the table. "Where are Abigail and Miriam?" she asked, about to sit.

"Havilah took them upstairs to lie down," replied Benjamin.

"I best go upstairs too," stated Adva.

"Please send Ziva down when you can. I would like to go to the barn to rest soon," replied Benjamin.

"I will tell her." As she turned to go, Caleb stood up to give her his hand to help her up the stairs. "Thank you, Caleb. We will talk more tomorrow. Sleep well." Caleb smiled at her. Adva noticed how easily he smiled. It was a kindness that she admired. Adva went up to the rooftop. Havilah had the little ones tucked in and fast asleep.

"Ziva, Benjamin says he is tired and wants to go rest for the night."

"Yes, of course. Adva, are you going to be able to sleep tonight?" asked Ziva.

"Yes, I think so. I am restless, but tired," she confessed.

"It looks like a good night to look at the stars," Havilah added. "All the clouds have left the sky. It is beautiful."

"I will be fine, Ziva. Go to your husband. Enjoy your night in the barn," said Adva. Ziva gave Adva a hug and left the roof to be with her husband. Adva and Havilah waved to them from the roof as they walked to the barn. Caleb also came out of the house.

Adva wasn't ready to sleep so she sat down with her back against the wall. "You may have to help me up from here but this feels good against my back right now," said Adva.

"I will gladly help you up when you are ready," said Havilah. "We have certainly had some good times on this roof."

"Yes, we have. Do you remember all the time we spent spying on the boys who came to visit our farm?" asked Adva. "Most of the time we were hiding from Malachi's temper tantrums."

"Yes, and spying on Benjamin and Levi," Havilah said with a smile.

Adva took a deep breath of night air. They heard a flute being played near the herb garden. It was clear that whoever was playing the instrument was a skilled musician. The sound was low and melancholy, almost holy. It was not one of Havilah's songs nor was it a tune she recognized. It sounded Egyptian or Turkish."

"Havilah, can you see who is playing?" Adva asked.

"I think it may be Caleb," she said. "You know, he enjoyed the music so much at your wedding. He danced with me, Abigail, and Miriam most of the night. He kept us entertained and away from the brides and their grooms. He is walking back."

"That was short. Ask him why he stopped."

"That was lovely Caleb. You play well," said Havilah. "Why did you stop?"

"I thought it was too loud. I do not want to disturb anyone, especially Adva."

"She is here listening too. She just cannot get up from her position," said Havilah.

"Here help me up, Havilah," stated Adva. With a firm tug, she righted Adva to her feet.

"See?" said Havilah.

"I hope I did not bother you with my playing. I find it relaxes me," said Caleb.

"It is lovely, Caleb. I thought it was helping me to relax too. Do you know another tune?" asked Adva.

He sat down on the bench by the barn door and played again, low and soft. From where he sat, the moon was rising directly behind the women on the roof. He played while Havilah helped take Adva's hair down. Adva turned to go inside her room and Havilah waved goodbye. He waved back and played one more tune to lull them to sleep. The song he played was Malachi's favorite. The music was a great way to honor his brother and it helped Caleb to say farewell.

The day after Sabbath, everyone piled into the two carts and headed to town. Ziva purchased a black tunic and scarf for Adva, who changed her tunic at Deborah's home and was now ready for a visit to Zipporah's. Eleazar and Caleb went to the elders and arranged for the wedding of Caleb and Adva at the third hour.

Adva had a good report from Zipporah. Everything with the baby was going well. Adva planned to have the baby at the farm but could stay in town if needed. Havilah would be attending the birth. They would talk about that more as the time got closer.

After meeting with Zipporah, Adva was escorted into the town's square where all the men stood to witness the oath of the kinsman redeemer. Caleb was nervous; he knew no one in this town and his family was not here to support his decision. Benjamin stood by his side, but he too was a stranger and not much of a comfort to him. Eleazar presented Adva to the crowd and told them of Malachi's death. Adva cried silent tears of sorrow and grief.

Adva and Caleb stood in front of the Priest of Sychar as he declared that Caleb ben Lamech was the rightful kinsman redeemer as the brother of the deceased. The priest asked Caleb if there were any other brothers or kinsmen of interest. "No, there are no other kinsmen closer in relation than me," Caleb replied.

"Are you choosing to marry Adva and redeem your brother's child?" asked the Priest.

Caleb swallowed and turned to face Adva. He took her hand and looked into her eyes, "I choose to marry Adva, daughter of Eleazar ben Joachim and the widow of my brother Malachi. I choose to be the father to my brother's unborn child." Adva was mesmerized by the tenderness in his voice and blinked in disbelief and wonder, allowing a single tear to run down her face.

"May *Elohim* bless this marriage with long life and abundance," blessed the Priest.

"Blessed be Caleb and Adva! May their children be many!" shouted the people in the square.

After signing the document with the priest, Caleb wrapped his arm around Adva and guided her through the crowd to the cart to go back to the farm. He placed her on the back of the cart on a blanket he had brought from home. Adva scooted herself to the wall opposite of all the water-filled pots and left a place for Caleb to join her. He helped to put Havilah, Abigail, and Miriam on the front of the cart with their father, Eleazar, as the driver. Caleb returned to the back of the cart. "May I join you?" Caleb asked politely.

"Yes, I saved you this spot. Is it enough room?" Adva replied.

"The best seat in the house is beside you."

Adva smiled at his kind words. "I may have to lean against you on the ride home. I fear it will be a bumpy ride."

"Do you want to sit up front? Havilah and the girls could sit back here."

"No, this gives us some space to ourselves."

"I agree," he said, settling in beside her. "I will have to put my arm behind you and hold on to keep from falling off at the first bump."

"Well, let me shift this way." Caleb put his arm behind her and she snuggled into his arm as if she belonged there.

"Here, you had better use my extra scarf to keep the dust out of your mouth and nose," Adva said, giving him her tan scarf.

Eleazar released the brake and nudged the oxen for home. He went slowly to keep the water from spilling and to keep the dust to a minimum.

They had not traveled very far before Adva surrendered to exhaustion and slept on Caleb's shoulder. He wrapped his protective arm around her and drew her towards him, causing her to sigh and snuggle closer. He did not take this personally, because he knew she was reacting as if it was Malachi and not him. Caleb leaned his head against hers and rested also.

The cart came to a stop in front of the barn and Caleb gently woke Adva from her sleep. She stared into his face as he pulled the scarf from his mouth and nose. "It is Caleb. We are home, Adva," he said gently.

"I am sorry, Caleb. I did not mean to fall asleep," Adva said quietly.

"I did not mind," Caleb replied. "I will help you down when you are ready."

"Thank you. My legs also went to sleep."

"Let me take some of the water inside, and I will come back for you." Caleb got down. He helped Havilah by taking the sleeping Miriam inside.

"*Achi*?" Miriam said quietly, waking up and patting his beard.

"No, my name is Caleb. Malachi was my brother."

"*Achi* not come home. Caleb stay?" she asked.

"Yes, Caleb will stay," he answered.

"Miriam happy."

"Caleb is happy too," smiled Caleb as he sat Miriam down on a stool at the table.

Adva sat on the edge of the cart and swung her legs back and forth trying to stop the tingling in her legs.

"Are you ready to get down? Will your legs hold you?" asked Caleb.

"Yes, I think so."

Caleb lifted her from the cart and sat her feet on the ground. She wobbled a bit. "Here take my arm and I will walk with you," Caleb urged.

"Put me on the bench by the barn," Adva replied.

After Adva was seated, Caleb took a few steps away and then returned to speak quietly, seeing that they were alone. "Adva, do you mind if we wait until this child is born before we share our marriage bed? We need time to get to know each other. I want you to see my face and not Malachi's. I think you will like me when you get to know me."

"Caleb, you are a delightful man. I already like you. But I, too, want to get to know you more while we wait for Malachi's child to be born," said Adva.

"Then it is settled," declared Caleb.

"What is settled?" asked Eleazar, who stopped at the bench to ask Caleb for his assistance.

"Nothing, Father. What do you need?" Adva asked.

"I would like to take Havilah to Sebaste to help with Tamar's birthing. I need to tell Levi the news and visit with them. Caleb, will you tend the farm?"

"Yes, Master Eleazar, I can do that for you," replied Caleb. "Who will be going with you?"

"We will go inside and ask the others. Let me unhitch the oxen then I will come inside. I will leave the cart here for now," stated Eleazar.

Eleazar entered and washed his hands. They all sat down to the table to eat a small meal and discuss the trip to Sebaste. Abigail and Miriam wanted to stay with Adva; they were tired of wagon rides today. Havilah quickly packed a bag. She missed Tamar and was looking forward to being with her for a few weeks.

"I am so excited. It has been over a year since I have seen Tamar!" exclaimed Havilah.

"I told Benjamin and Joseph to look after you while I am away. They will be here with you on alternating Sabbaths. I should return after the third Sabbath unless Tamar has her baby," replied Eleazar.

"Caleb can have Father's bed while the girls and I sleep on the roof," stated Adva, wanting to give her new husband a better place to sleep. "Miriam and Abigail, you had better give Papa a big hug and kiss. He will be away for a while."

Abigail got down from her seat and ran to her father, who lifted her up into his lap. She snuggled into Eleazar's beard and gave him a loud kiss on the cheek. Everyone laughed.

"I am a blessed man!" Eleazar exclaimed, squeezing his daughter tightly. "Blessed indeed."

Here's a sneak peek of Daughter of Samaria Book 2.

You have met Caleb, Adva's second husband,
the delight of her life.
You will also meet husbands three, four, and five.

Kinsman Redeemer

The familiar story of the woman at the well.

Turning quickly, Adva lost her footing and began to fall. Caleb caught her in his arms. "Be careful, dear one. We have another month before this child is born."

"Caleb, I am frightened," confessed Adva. "I am afraid to give birth."

He bent over and whispered in her ear, "*Il Raa'ee. The God of Abraham sees you*. He will care for you."

With this fleeting memory of Caleb, Adva crossed her arms across her chest trying to comfort herself and quell her fears. She remembered that conversation as if it were yesterday, even though ten years had passed. Reuben, her fourth husband, had taken her away from Sychar to Damascus. She was at his command now. As she carried his first child, she was again frightened. "Although Reuben swore a vow as my Kinsman Redeemer, what will become of me and my children if he loses everything in his favorite game of chance?" Adva lamented. "I must tell Lamech. These are his grandchildren. He will know what to do," she whispered to herself. "Il Raa'ee."

~※~

Adva had a lifetime of grief and disappointment when she met Jesus at the well.

Kinsman Redeemer is book two in the Daughter of Samaria Series and the continuation of Adva's story. Adva's prophecy is fulfilled and she finds her true redeemer.

Sources For Further Study

Brand Chad, Eric Alan Mitchell, Steve Bonds, E. Ray Clendenen, Trent C Butler, and Bill Latta. 2015. *Holman Illustrated Bible Dictionary* Revised and expanded ed. Nashville, TN: Holman Reference.

Farmer, Craig S. n.d. "Changing Images of the Samaritan Woman in Early Reformed Commentaries on John." *Church History* 365–65.

Glahn, Sandra. 2017. *Vindicating the Vixens: Revisiting Sexualized Vilified and Marginalized Women of the Bible*. Grand Rapids, Michigan: Kregel Academic.

Hunt, June. 2013. *Verbal & Emotional Abuse: Victory Over Verbal and Emotional Abuse*. Torrance, CA: Aspire Press.

Isbouts Jean-Pierre. 2018. *Atlas of the Bible: Exploring the Holy Lands*. Washington, D.C: National Geographic.

Keener, Craig S. and John H Walton. 2016. *NIV Cultural Backgrounds Study Bible. Bringing to Life the Ancient World of Scripture*. Grand Rapids, Michigan: Zondervan.

Keener, Craig S. 2019. *Zondervan Illustrated Bible Backgrounds Commentary: John. Volume 2a*. Grand Rapids, Michigan: Zondervan.

Speedie, Bronwen. "Samaritan Sinner, Celebrated Saint: The story of the first Christian missionary." CBE International, Minneapolis, MN Published December 5, 2016. https://www.cbeinternational.org/resource/samaritan-sinner-celebrated-saint-story-first-christianmissionary/

Tsedaka, Benyamim. 2013. *The Israelite Samaritan Version of the Torah: First English Translation Compared with the Masoretic Version*. Grand Rapids, Michigan: Eerdmans.

Tsedaka, Benyamim. 2017. *Understanding the Israelite-Samaritans from Ancient to Modern: An Introductory Atlas*. Jerusalem: Carta Jerusalem.

Vamosh, Miriam Feinberg, Yizhar Hirschfeld and Garo Nalbandian. 2001. *Daily Life at the Time of Jesus*. Herzlia Israel: Palphot Ltd.

Vamosh, Miriam Feinberg. 2008. *Women at the Time of the Bible*. Nashville, TN: Abingdon Press.

Acknowledgments

Many people have been instrumental in the writing of this book. I am deeply grateful for each of you and your many talents. You are a blessing to me. Special thanks to:

Kary Oberbrunner and the Author Academy Elite team who helped me transform this book from a wish into a reality.

Dr. Joseph Dongell, professor of Biblical Studies at Asbury Theological Seminary, who gave me help with the Samaritan Religion and Ancient Hebrew language at the very beginning of my writing adventure.

The Asbury Theological Seminary Library Staff who helped me study first-century Israel and the Samaritan religion in the middle of pandemic closures.

The Roanoke County Public Library staff who helped with Interlibrary Loans, suggestions, and encouragement.

My prayer partners—Barb Albert, Sandra Lewis, Terry Wood, Rochelle House, and friends at GCC—who held me up when I began to tire and gave clarity as needed.

My grammar police and pre-editing friends, Amy McGee and Laura Spafford, thank you for the hours that you gave to help me turn the rough draft into a manuscript worthy of sending to an editor.

My beta readers—Sandra Lewis, Chip Blankenship, and Ed Stanley—who helped me fill in some holes and reassured me that my characters produced the intended emotions in the reading process.

My cover designer, H-Izz design, who worked with me to make adjustments and to complete the final product.

My editor, Annah MacKenzie, you are a gift and a skillful word surgeon. Thank you for understanding my thoughts and my writing.

My writing coach and fellow author, Faye Bryant, thank you for guiding me through the confusion and helping me take my Next Best Step!

You need an accomplished speaker who can take your event to the next level.

Jeanette Brewer
Mended4More.com

"Jeanette uses her talents as a Distinguished Toastmaster and a John Maxwell-trained coach to help audiences understand that our brokenness is a part of our journey. Her relaxed, authentic style and valuable content set her apart as a top choice for your organization. Jeanette will bring a message of redeeming love and eternal hope to your next event."

-- Clint Atwater, Storyteller, Speaker, and Producer
Storytelling Connections
Storytellingconnections.com